For my husband and best friend, Philip Hahn

You're my favorite!

the Iron Butterfly

Chanda Hahn

ISBN: 1475070373
ISBN: 978-1475070378
THE IRON BUTTERFLY

~I~

When I first awoke in the darkness that was my prison cell, I was brave, fearless and I still had enough fight in me to question the rules. But after my third beating by Scar Lip, I learned to hold my tongue in his presence. After my first taste of torture on the machine, I learned obedience. Down in this hell, silence was more than golden; it was the difference between life and death.

And where we were, there was a whole lot of death.

The sound of a distant door slamming snapped my mind back to the present. Footsteps slowed and my cell door opened with an ominous creak. The light from the hall fell across my bruised face, making my eyes flinch in pain. A small whimper and the rustle of straw drew my attention to the other forgotten occupant of my cell, a small girl named Cammie. She pathetically tried to scoot away and put as much distance between her and the man about to enter our cell.

My mouth formed the word NO, as an ugly bulldog of a man ducked under the too short door frame. I knew without looking it was Scar Lip. He had a crooked nose, dark unwashed hair and cruel black eyes that hid beneath a furrowed brow. He smiled in delight at Cammie's attempt to evade him, which made the pale scar that transected his top lip stand out.

The smell that accompanied him was a mixture of sweat and rot, which permeated from the layers of dried and crusted blood that coated his blacksmith's apron. He had come to take one of us to Raven.

Drips of sweat beaded across my forehead as the footsteps drew closer. It was too soon. I wasn't strong enough for another session on the machine. I groaned when I saw the smear of blood coating the back of my hand, leftover from last night's experiment. I knew that if he chose me again, I wouldn't survive. I tried to raise my head from the cold stone floor as he came closer to stand over my prone form. But a sudden wave of fear made me vomit what little was left in my stomach.

Scar Lip paused over my dry heaving body and backed away in disgust. When the convulsions stopped, I heard him move toward Cammie and the sounds of scuffling as she crawled farther into the darkness of the cell, hoping its shadows would hide her from his gaze. It was no use; all she did was back herself into a corner.

Cammie whimpered. "Please!...don't," and was smacked in the face by Scar Lip.

"No talking! You know the rules," he sneered.

Her lip quivered and a small amount of blood appeared at the side of her mouth. She tried to wipe at it with the back of her hand, but only smeared it across her chin. She bit her bottom lip between her teeth to keep any more sound from coming forth.

"That's better," he growled. "The Raven has a new experiment to try and needs another volunteer." Scar Lip grabbed Cammie by the arms and dragged her out into the hall, her feet twisting and fighting behind her, trying to slow his efforts. She hadn't lost her fight, but if she survived the week in this pit, she would.

I raised my hand toward them as if by that one action alone I could protect her and stop what was about to happen. The large cell door shut with a thud, and I waited to hear whether the lock turned. It did. I counted the steps as Scar lip dragged Cammie up the stairs through another door, mentally tracing the intricate path they would take until they reached a huge iron door that once opened, would let out a smell of iron, sulfur and death. I knew from experience that a table waited behind that door with cold iron shackles and as well as...I shivered at the mental picture that formed of the nameless machine they used to experiment on us.

When the sound of the door at the top of the stairs closed, the pain in my chest exploded because I was holding my breath. I cried in relief that I wasn't going to be tortured and experimented on again, that I survived one more day. I dropped my head to the floor and let the grief pour out of my body in loud aching sobs, as I realized in shame that I was happy he chose Cammie.

I woke to the familiar sound of a tin plate being shoved through the food slot in the bottom of the door and bolted upright in fear and anticipation. Hungrily, I snatched the small lifesaving plate of food and dragged it far from the door to where Cammie slept. But where Cammie usually laid curled up in slumber, there only remained a tattered blanket and straw.

I hung my head in shame. She wasn't strong enough to survive the experiments. Few were. I was one of the lucky ones. If you considered being tortured and beaten on a regular basis and survive being lucky.

With an air of renewed determination, I peeked through the slot in the door and saw boots covered by the blood-red robes of one of the Septori. He slowly made his way past the cells delivering the morning offerings of food to the other prisoners. I hunched by the slot waiting for him to pass my way. When he came within reach, I snaked my hand out and grabbed the hem of his robe. He stumbled to a halt.

Gathering my voice, I croaked out "Cammie? What did you do with Cammie?" He sneered at me and tried to dislodge my hand from his robe. My increasing courage only added volume to my voice. "What did you do with her? If you hurt her, I'll—"

"You'll what?" he interrupted. "You haven't succeeded so far in protecting any of the others, so why now?" He kicked my hand away from his ankle and stepped on my wrist, pinning it to the floor before I could yank it under the flap. He leaned down, putting pressure on my injured wrist as I gritted my teeth and sucked in my breath against the pain.

He peered at me under the flap and I could see the bottom half of his face and the crooked teeth that lined his sneering mouth. This one was known as Crow. Knowing his name somehow made him seem less terrifying.

"Don't worry about your friend," Crow spoke slowly, cruelly. "She has outlived her usefulness to the Raven. He was extremely disappointed in her results. She lacked, what did he say? Oh yes, the determination to live—unlike you. The Raven was displeased that you weren't able to help him last night."

Cocking his head to the side like a bird, he went on. "He was quite angry and unnecessarily took it out on the girl. So in fact, what happened to her is your fault." His eyes lit up with joy in sharing the news. He used his dirty fingernail to dig at one of my barely healed wounds until blood began to pool. I could see the red-raised skin of the brand that marked him for a member of the Septori: two slash marks within a circle.

"Such a pity that she doesn't have your strength. But few do." He slowly raised his hand covered in my blood to his mouth. "What a waste." He moved away, releasing the pressure on my pinned wrist. I yanked it back into the darkness of my cell. Away from the taint of having been touched by one of the hated and vile Septori. I was horrified and disgusted at what he had done.

"You lie!" I yelled uselessly at the locked cell door.

"Do I?" Crow's voiced crept through. "You will learn soon enough. You may even see firsthand what's left of her when the Raven sends for you tonight. And make no mistake, he will send for you tonight." His evil laughed echoed behind him as he walked up the stairs.

Normally those words would turn me into a terrified bundle of nerves. But I was too shocked by what had just happened and the news of Cammie's death. I knew better than to get emotionally attached to the other prisoners. I had learned my lesson after my first cellmate. I closed myself off after that as numerous girls came and went. None of them were as strong as me.

But this one was different.

She was different.

A loud droning noise filled my ears and I placed my hands over them to make it stop. Then I realized, I was making the noise and it was only getting louder with my pain.

"Control yourself!" a deep male voice barked from down the hall. "You can't fall all to pieces down here if you want to live."

The noise just became higher pitched with hiccups as I tried to control the sound. "C-Cammm ...Cammie's dead," I stuttered out. "It's my fault. If I were stronger, I could have...I should have."

"Hush," Tym whispered from across the hall. "There's nothing you could have done. You should be happy it wasn't you. If you don't quiet down and stop talking, they'll hear you, and then they will come back." A week ago his brother had never returned to his cell after a night with the machine. I hadn't heard him utter a word since. He had withdrawn into his own pain.

"It doesn't matter," spoke the first voice. "Let them come."

It was a voice I didn't recognize, so I assumed this must be the new prisoner they'd brought in a few days ago and it was the first time he's been coherent enough to speak.

"Who are you?" I asked.

"No one," he muttered.

"If we are going to die down here, I would at least like to know your name," I pleaded into the echoing halls.

"Kael."

"I'm Thalia," I said with a small smile. "Why are you here? Why were you drugged for so long? Are you someone important?" The questions came sputtering out.

"Someone important?" he made a snort. "No. They've kept me drugged because they know that I will eventually kill them all."

"Can you do it? Can you break out and take us with you?" The desperation rang in my voice.

A long silence followed and I prayed that Kael was planning an escape. "No." I didn't expect his painful answer.

I felt tears of disappointment burn at my eyes, but I wiped them away with the back of my dirty hand. My world crumbled around me once again, as my hopes of ever leaving were dashed.

"I could if I were stronger. I'm a Denai, or was." Tym interrupted sadly. "I can barely shift anything since they brought me here. Wherever we are."

"Hell!" Kael spoke gruffly.

"It's the drugs," I whispered. "It blocks all of your power and gifts like it did to Cammie."

"If only Sal were still here," Tym whined. "He would know what to do." A moment of silence followed before Tym became talkative again. "Why are we here?"

"I don't know." We could only speculate at what the Septori's motives were behind these painful experiments. I had never seen Raven's true face, for he hid behind a silver, hook-nosed mask and a robe. The sound of his raspy breath and his hollow-eyed mask haunted my dreams each night.

"What did I ever do to deserve this? I shouldn't be here!" Tym argued. I knew he was confused and rambling, but it was becoming annoying.

"I don't know? Why are any of us here?" I muttered. I started to wind my dark hair around my finger...a nervous habit.

Just then a loud pounding sound came from the cell down the hall. *Thud. Clang. Thud. Thud. Clang.* It sounded like Kael was throwing himself against the door and pounding his plate against the lock.

"You aren't going to open the lock with that plate," I remarked dryly.

"Don't need too. Just need to get their attention," Kael grunted between throws.

"What!" Tym hissed. "You can't be serious. You want them to come?" His voice changed to a higher pitch as his nervous laughter got the better of him. "He wants them to come down here? Th-they are gonna be mad. They're gonna b-b-beat us."

"Please don't!" My body started to shake at the thought of the beatings we would receive for breaking the rules. I could handle the pain, I couldn't handle the machine. "I don't want to go back into that room." Now my voice was quavering. "I can't take it anymore." Hoping my pleas didn't fall on deaf ears, I pressed my body against the cold door and prayed.

The noise stopped for an instant as if he heard me, and then picked up again with a desperate fervor. He interspersed the banging of the plate with kicking, pounding and yelling. I pressed my back to the cell door, slid down to the floor and resigned myself to the painful punishment that would be doled out to all of us equally.

"What's going on?" Scar Lip yelled as he opened the door followed by three sets of loud footsteps. He brought the guards.

I ducked to the floor and lifted the metal flap to try and see where he was heading. None of the Septori in their robes appeared. I wondered briefly where they were.

"Over here, you moron! I have information that your master wants!" Kael had immediately directed Scar Lip's attention onto himself, instead of Tym and me. The armed men rushed to the cell and gathered around Kael's door.

Scar Lip halted suspiciously outside Kael's cell door. "What is the information that you have for him? Is it valuable?" he asked.

"Oh, it's life changing all right."

Scar Lip licked his lips in anticipation. "What is it that you want me to know?"

"I thought it imperative that your master knows," Kael paused for effect, "That you are a slimy, no-good, rotten toad. A bastard son of a flea-ridden donkey."

"Quiet!" Scar Lip hissed.

"You can't even think for yourself. You grovel so much to the Raven, I think you must like the taste of dirt."

"Shut up!" Scar Lip pounded on the door. "Or you'll be sorry! I'll make you wish you'd never been born!"

"I'm already sorry. I'm sorry that I'm subjected to seeing your ugly face every day. You know only a dog or a mother could love that face. No, I'm wrong. Your mother must be a dog to love the likes of you," Kael taunted.

That did it. Scar Lip grabbed the keys from his belt with his thick fingers and shoved one into the lock. The other guards grabbed their clubs and entered one by one into the cell.

But all I saw was the dust cloud made from the scuffling of their feet. I heard fighting and grunting, and I hoped Kael was the one dealing the punches.

Finally, the fighting stopped, the dust settled, and I saw Scar Lip emerge from the cell with a victorious smirk on his face. Following behind him were two of the guards dragging Kael between them by his forearms. The third guard trailed behind.

Kael was either dead or unconscious. Long, dark hair covered most of his face, but a blue headband around his forehead was visible. His body was long, lean and well muscled, if a bit thin. In his current weakened condition, it had been suicide to try and take on all of the men at once. Based on his dirty and torn clothes, he was either a hired sword or a mercenary.

"Let's give him a session on the machine," Scar Lip roared angrily.

"But we're not supposed to enter Raven's workshop when the he's not there," a nervous guard spoke up.

"Shut up, you idiot," a second guard intervened. "No one will know but us, and believe me, this one needs another lesson in obedience."

9

As they drew closer to my cell, I started to feel an intense pressure in my mind; a headache that pulsed at my temples. I closed my eyes to stop the pressure, and I almost missed Kael spring to life.

Kael, who I thought was unconscious, moved in a flash and grabbed the knife from the guard's belt. He thrust the blade upward into the guard's throat, sinking the blade in to the hilt. As Kael pulled it out, the guard released him arm and fell to the ground choking, his life ebbing away.

Before the guard even hit the ground, Kael had gained his footing and slashed at the man holding his other arm. The downward arc forced the other guard to release him.

The rear guard rushed him, swinging his short sword. Kael's smaller blade made it look like he was playing with a toy.

Kael jumped back, missing the blow of the short sword, as he adjusted the weight of the confiscated knife in his hand. When the sword swung at him again, Kael ducked and rushed forward to take the brunt force of the sword handle on his shoulder. Wrapping his hand around the rear guard's arm, he rammed the handle of the knife into the man's temple, knocking him unconscious.

Scar Lip screamed obscenities at the last guard, "Grab him, you fool! What are you doing? Hit him! Don't let him up!" all the while keeping a safe distance.

But Kael was bleeding from his shoulder wound, and he was still outnumbered two to one and tiring quickly. The second guard, also bleeding from a slash on his arm, carefully stalked Kael, trying to push him back toward his opened cell. He pulled out a dagger from his boot and picked up the dead guard's knife. There was no way Kael could take out the guard with a knife and short sword unless he threw his dagger, giving up his only weapon.

The pain in my head became unbearable. "Do something!" I yelled at Tym.

"I'll try," Tym answered.

Tym reached his hand under the grate and grabbed at the uniform of the guard. A flash of light appeared, and the guard's clothes caught on fire. He screamed in panic and dropped both weapons to bat at his burning uniform.

Kael rushed the burning guard and elbowed him in the throat. The guard sputtered and dropped to his knees. Kael punched him in the face, knocking him out cold. As soon as the guard lost consciousness, the flames about him disappeared.

A small squeal escaped Scar Lip's mouth and he turned white with fright, as he realized he was the only one left to face the deadly Kael. Scar Lip turned to run up the stairs as Kael threw the dagger. The silver blade sunk into Scar Lip's back, and he fell over with a grunt, sliding down the stairs and coming to a halt on the bottom step.

Kael ran over and retrieved the keys from Scar Lip's still body and ran to Tym's cell. He quickly unlocked the door, and a wide-eyed Tym emerged, shaking. "Did you see that? I did it. I helped," he sputtered.

"Thanks!" Kael quickly shouted. "But you have to get out of here and quick."

Tym wasted no time and shot up the stairs and down the corridor toward freedom.

Kael unlocked my cell. As the door swung open I could see his face close up for the first time, and my heart fluttered with apprehension. Here was someone who wasn't afraid to die. A fierce look came from stormy blue eyes that were partially obscured by long dark hair. Kael's hard mouth was set in a firm line as he studied me. He looked beyond me into the darkness of my cell searching for an ambush or possibly another prisoner. Kael appeared older than me by a few years but was striking and fierce at the same time. Here was a man bred to be a warrior.

I knew what he would find in me, a short little thing, more like a child than an adult. My height stopped a few inches over five feet, and I was small compared to his towering frame. My hair hung dark and limp down my back, and my blues eyes must look sickly surrounded by my swollen face and bruises.

His expression was grim and determined as he reached for my arm, and then stopped, his hand inches away. "Come on," he growled, curling his fingers into a fist at his side.

I ignored his gruff demeanor. After all, I didn't know him and he did rescue me. I tried to stand, but all I was able to do was take a few steps and then stumble into the door. I was weak from malnourishment, and the intense pounding in my head made me feel awkward and unbalanced.

Kael inhaled his breath as if he were holding it and stepped back, not bothering to assist me. "Get going," he snapped.

The tone of his voice made me stiffen in resistance. I squared my shoulders and ordered him about. "Well, then move out of the doorway."

Kael moved to the side, letting me pass before he reached for a torch from a wall. He entered each of the opened cells and gathered all of the blankets, clothes and straw into a corner to make kindling. Once done, he set them ablaze. He deftly stepped over the dead and unconscious guards and moved to the hall. The hungry, crackling fire would soon spread to the wooden door and along the support beams in the wall. I hoped it would bring the whole thing down.

I stood watching him work, until I had a prickling sensation on the back of my neck. Then, I moved as fast as my feet would take me up the stairs and out the first door. Not bothering to notice that the stairs were empty of a body that was previously there, I hurried down the corridor to where the passageway split. To my left, I could smell the air of freedom, but to my right—down the other dark corridor—stood the huge metal door of the laboratory and possibly Cammie. I started to take steps away from potential freedom when Kael loomed up behind me.

"No, leave it well alone. GET OUT of here!" he yelled, as he dragged the still form of an unconscious guard after him. The other guard must not have survived.

"But Cammie could be down there!"

"You get outside. I'll go look for her." He propped the guard against the wall and ran toward the laboratory.

Nodding my head in assent, I silently made my way down the opposite passageway, realizing that I 'hadn't been eager in the least to travel the other one.

I followed the passageway by feeling the wall with my hand, wishing I had thought to grab a torch. The wood beams became sparse, and the ceiling slanted lower and lower until I was feeling the cross beams skim the top of my head. Anyone taller would have to duck to traverse the same path. My hands started to get entangled in roots that protruded from the wall. The gloom of the passageway seemed to go on forever until I encountered a wall of dirt.

Feeling a moment of panic, I felt around in the darkness, for a door or handle—anything to help me escape. Something rough brushed against my face and I squeaked in surprise. Touching the object, I found it to be a rope that dangled from the ceiling. Following the rope up with my hands I found that it was attached to a trapdoor in the ceiling.

By now the darkness was being lightened by the glow of red flames behind me. I pushed the wooden door and it barely moved an inch. I was so weak, it took me three tries to push it open. But I still had to pull myself out of the tunnel. Smoke began to fill the air and it stung my watering eyes. My bodyweight felt impossible to lift.

"Come on!" I cried aloud. I scratched the ground for purchase trying to find any handhold to assist me. I finally dragged my chest up onto the dirt floor bruising my ribs in the process.

I wasn't sure what I was expecting when I emerged, but it wasn't a stable. The trapdoor was carefully hidden in the back stall under straw. The whole prison and experimental lab was housed and camouflaged by a stable. The smell of the horses would definitely cover the smell of the prison, experiments and death.

Standing to my feet, I brushed my dirt-caked hands on my shirt and looked around for a means of faster escape. I glanced back down into the trapdoor, looking for signs of Kael or Cammie. But the passageway was empty, except for the faint glow of fire and a trail of smoke pouring out of it.

There were eight wooden stalls in the stable. Six were empty. I knew the Raven wasn't here because Scar Lip had said so, and I hadn't seen any of the cursed Septori. Where were they? Somewhere close? Or did they build a stable out in the middle of nowhere for this purpose? No, there had to be another building close by. I wasn't sure, but I didn't think the prison seemed big enough to house all of the Septori and guards. If they were in a nearby shelter, they would see the smoke and soon be upon us.

Two horses were still stabled and were starting to panic as more smoke poured in through the trapdoor. There were signs that a third had been here not too long ago. Tym had been smart enough to grab a mount.

Running to the wall, I grabbed the bridle from a hook and tried to put the bay's tack on. My hands shook so much that I kept fumbling with the cinch. Once finished, I reached for the roan's bridle. I 'wouldn't have time for saddles. I was tiring quickly, and I didn't have the strength to hoist the saddles onto the horse's backs.

My foot slipped in something warm and wet.

Looking down, I saw that I had stepped in a small pool of blood. Horror and shock froze me, momentarily, but the jerking of the horses pulled my attention back to the dire situation. Ignore the blood, get out of here. NOW!

I struggled to keep both horses under control as I led them out of the stable into the darkening night. The crackling fire and the pungent smell of smoke were getting closer, making the horses panic. The sound of a rushing river caught my ear and I half pulled, half sweet-talked the horses toward the water, away from fire. But once they caught sight of the water, they dragged me the rest of the way. Looking over my shoulder toward the stable, I prayed that Kael would hurry up and get out of there.

I reached the river bed, dropped to my knees and leaned down to wash the dirt from my hands. Cupping my hands, I drank the water down in huge gulps, the cold making my empty stomach cramp. But my stomach pain was soon an afterthought as I felt the cool prick of a knife at my throat.

I froze, hands to my side, still kneeling by the riverbed, the rocks digging into my knees painfully. Too scared to turn my head, my eyes followed the blade of a knife to Scar Lip's shaking body. He was angry, bloody and sputtering in rage.

"You little brat! He's going to hold me responsible!" Scar Lip grabbed me around the throat with his free hand and began to squeeze. "But you…" his voice became cold, hard. "…are the one who's going to pay, just like the boy!"

My mind flashed to the drops of blood I saw in the stable. Scar Lip had killed Tym!

Wildly, I clawed at Scar Lip's huge hands and tried to pry them from around my neck, to no avail. Dropping one hand, I dug frantic fingers into the dirt, looking for anything that could be used as a weapon. My fingers wrapped around a small rock.

White specks danced before my eyes. I was running out of time. And how strange! My constant headache had finally disappeared. In a final act of desperation, I swung the rock at his head.

Scar Lip yelled, dropping the knife into the river.

Gasping for breath, I scrambled to my feet. My hands reached for my bruising throat. It ached and I had trouble swallowing and catching my breath.

I turned to look for Scar Lip, when a large branch came out of the darkness toward my head. White blinding pain filled my conscience. Spinning with the force of the blow I fell backwards into the fast moving river. The coldness made me gasp for breath and water filled my mouth, making me choke.

I glimpsed the starry night turning bright with orange fire just before my world turned pitch black.

~2~

The smell of cooking meat and the sound of a crackling campfire brought me slowly to awareness—that and the small stone that was stabbing my lower back with a vengeance. Being very careful not to change the rhythm of my breathing, I listened and tried to take stock of my surroundings through lowered lashes.

I was laid out on a bedroll underneath the open sky with a cloak rolled up under my head. The scent of sweat, spice and horse mingled together and assailed my nose. The sound of numerous horses nickering warned me of the possibility of multiple people in the camp. I looked for any signs of the Septori or Scar Lip.

A brown haired, middle aged man wearing the most flamboyant outfit I had ever seen was tending a small fire. He was arrayed in patchwork blues, yellow and white. The clothing was wrapped so intricately I couldn't tell where one swatch began and another stopped. Light tan leather boots went up his calves and ended with ornately decorated designs of swirls and flourishes. I was staring so hard that I missed someone leaning over me until a shadow covered my face.

"Well, Darren, it looks like our little fish is awake," the shadow spoke.

All pretense of feigning sleep vanished as I found myself confronted with the most handsome young man I'd ever seen. I took in the wind-blown, sandy blond hair and dimpled smile. His deep green eyes were pools of emotions. Worry, kindness, hope were so evident in them that I soon lost all thought of being afraid. He was beautiful, too beautiful to be human. His attractiveness left me stunned and gaping wide mouthed like the fish he had moments before called me.

"How are you doing?"

His strong fingers went to my brow to adjust the bandage that was wrapped around my head. I flinched with the contact. He made shushing noises as I tried to protest the cup of water he was putting to my lips. But once the cool water touched my dry throat, I grasped his hand and drank greedily, moaning in protest when he pulled it away.

"No, that's enough. I'm sure you have plenty of questions, and we have some for you, but let me assure you first and foremost that you are safe. And we won't harm you. What's your name?"

"Thalia." I paused as I racked my brain helplessly for more. But that's all I was able to give him.

"Well, Thalia, you can call me Joss. The funny looking man burning the soup is Darren Hamden." He gestured to the brightly decorated man I was staring at earlier. My eyes skimmed Joss's outfit and saw that he too, was dressed in finely tailored clothes, although not as exuberant as Darren's clothes.

"Where are we?" I implored.

"Well, we are currently in Calandry," he said as he pointed across the river. "Right over there is Sinnendor, if that is where you would like to be?"

I stared blankly at Joss, waiting for him to elaborate.

He bobbed his head as he hurriedly tried to explain. "We stopped to water the horses and found you, injured and burning with fever on the riverbank." Joss nodded in Darren's direction. "Darren thought maybe you had a run in with some of Sinnendor's Elite."

I knew very little of Sinnendor. It was a country run by a king that hated all Denai. So the Denai stayed clear of their borders and the bloodthirsty king. But accidents happen, and sometimes Sinnendor's bloodline wasn't always as pure as the king hoped. Those with mixed blood tried to escape at night to Calandry, where all races were welcome. Most never made it past the border guards, or "The Elite." Sinnendor's fiercest warriors patrolled and killed anyone trying to enter or leave the country on sight. Their sole purpose was to keep the scourge of the impure out of the country and kill those with it, trying to leave.

Joss interrupted my thoughts, "We don't care much for the King of Sinnendor or how they run things, but that wouldn't stop us from offering help." The look he gave me was a questioning one, as if he himself was still trying to figure out where I fit in. "You were unconscious, so I took the liberty of healing your wounds."

"So you are a Denai?" I looked at him surprised.

Joss nodded yes. In embarrassment he looked down at the ground before looking back up at me, and it made me realize he was probably only a year older than me.

Taking a quick breath he went on. "You had intensive internal injuries and I wasn't able to heal everything. So there will be scarring...." he looked solemn and nodded to my arms.

I glanced at my arms and saw that the cuts, burns, and scars had faded to faint silvery lines; before they had been a deep, infected red. The bruises were gone. I hadn't felt so good in a long time, but I felt a cold sweat start to break out at the thought of Joss using power on me, while I was unconscious. It was too similar to what the Septori had done. I quelled the fear in the pit of my stomach and swallowed my pride.

I nodded to Joss in answer. "Let 'em be, scars can heal in their own time." I was about to say more when Darren brought over a bowl of broth with small chopped up vegetables in it. My stomach growled over the broth, and I immediately started drinking it right out of the bowl. I finished with only letting a little dribble down my chin, my gaze drawn to the meat roasting over the fire. When was the last time I had tasted meat?

"Well, well, well," Darren laughed. "Hungry little thing, isn't she? Don't worry; you can have more broth in a little bit. It needs to settle to see if it's going to stay down before you can have more." He caught my gaze drifting to the meat again. His demeanor became more serious as he politely explained. "Your body isn't ready for meat yet, little one; it will just come back up."

I took in his appearance now that he was closer, and I saw the neatly trimmed triangle of hair under his bottom lip. He sported one gold hoop earring with a single blue bead that added to the carefree rover look of him.

"Why don't you explain how you ended up in the river, and then we will give you some more broth, eh?" Darren interrupted. My thoughts immediately flashed back to my time as a prisoner and I began to shake uncontrollably.

"Now, now," Darren said. "It's okay, but I think it will get easier if you face your fears and talk about it."

Glancing at Joss, I saw that he had become quiet and sat back, as if steeling himself for the news. I shrugged my shoulders in indifference. "I'll talk as long as Darren keeps my bowl filled."

Darren's bold laughter eased the tension as he shook my hand to seal the deal.

Even though their friendly manners made me want to trust them, I wasn't ready to give them the whole truth. I was still a lone woman amongst two strangers and who knew? They might have lied about who they were. Maybe they were even part of Sinnendor's Elite.

I decided to play it safe.

"I was running away…and I slipped and fell in the river." I couldn't look either of them in the eye as I said it.

Darren's brows drew together and he frowned. It was as if he could sense my lie, and he pulled the bowl of broth back toward him, away from my grasp. "Sorry, girlie, I wasn't born yesterday. That's not the whole truth."

"Yes, it is," I countered. "I fell in."

"I'd wager there's more to it than that. So tell me what were you running away from?"

I couldn't help it. My gaze darted over their shoulder to check for signs of hooded robes.

Darren took a deep breath, kneeled in front of me and very gently put his rough hand on my shoulder. "Thalia, it is obvious that you are scared of something or someone. The state that we found you in spoke of more than just falling in a river. You show the signs of long-term abuse. And even though you just met us, I assure you that we will do everything in our power to keep you safe." Darren's voice spoke truth, and I felt the protective wall I had built start to crumble.

"The Septori. I was taken by the Septori," I choked out in a barely audible voice. This time it was Darren and Joss's turn to look at me in confusion.

"They are a cult led by a horrible leader we only knew as the Raven." My hands began to shake, and I dug my fingernails painfully into my palms in an attempt to quell the hatred that rushed me. "They kidnapped, tortured, and performed brutal experiments on us. I was lucky to escape with my life. Most didn't. They are a heartless group of red robed monsters," I spat out.

My palms stung, so I looked down. Fresh blood coated my fingernails. Feeling slightly ashamed that I had reinjured myself, I tucked my hands under my arms and looked at the ground. I hoped Joss wouldn't notice my self-inflicted injury and want to heal me. He didn't.

He sat back in shock. I don't think he was prepared for what I had said. "What were they trying to accomplish?" he asked.

"I really don't know and don't care. And I would prefer not to wait around until they find me." I glanced around the camp in urgency to see what I could find that could be used as weapons. Joss and Darren were hardly prepared for an attack. "But I can tell you this. There were others with me, even Denai. If they could be captured, there is no doubt that the Septori could take on you two as well." I tried to make my voice as steady and determined as possible, so that they would understand the seriousness of what I was saying.

"How did you come to be with them?" Darren asked, as he filled my bowl with more soup. I watched as he only filled it a quarter of the way full. I gave him a pointed stare, but he refused to add anymore to my bowl.

"I can't remember. I only remember waking up bound and gagged in a dark, dank windowless cell with two other girls. I was the only one who couldn't remember anything about my previous life." I held out my bowl to Darren.

He stared at me before shaking himself and refilling my bowl. This time it was almost full. He kept reassuring me that I would be safe.

"I don't know if we were purposely chosen or kidnapped or if we were bartered away, but all of us down there were experiments. The two girls I originally shared the cell with disappeared within a week. Others came and went. I was the only one they couldn't kill or break."

"What did they do to you, with these experiments?" Joss asked.

I dug my fingernails into my wet palms and my chest felt like it would explode. My breaths came in shallow gasps. All of the control that I had carefully gathered waned as fear took over.

Darren saw my panicked face and intervened.

"Joss," he spoke quietly. "Maybe you don't want to know. Some things are best left unspoken."

Refusing to make eye contact, I turned my head and decided that I wasn't going to say anymore, no matter how many times they filled my bowl up.

Joss jumped up in anger, throwing his tin cup into the fire. The splash of liquid on the flames made it sputter, and I jumped in surprise. "I wish that you were making it up," he fumed.

I stiffened at the comment and looked at him in confusion. "I'm not. I could never make up something as awful as that."

"No, I believe you, I just don't want to admit there are people as cruel and evil as that in our country. I know that you are indeed speaking the truth because I have seen the evidence. Maybe you really were in Sinnendor and didn't know it!" He began to pace back and forth, his anger evident in his posture and the clenching of his fists. But the way he did everything bespoke a natural grace.

I watched him pace as I asked myself the question I'd plagued myself with for weeks. Why I was there in the first place? I didn't understand why the Septori 'hadn't let me go. Of course, deep down, I knew the reason. The Raven would never let me go, because I had seen too much. The only way I would leaving that prison would if I were in a wooden box.

And then I started to dwell on Cammie, and how I sent Kael back for her. He was probably dead because of me. The guilt overwhelmed me, and I buried my head in my knees, wrapping my arms around them for comfort.

Even rocking back and forth didn't help. It was too much. The shock was finally wearing off and I could feel again. But the feelings and emotions were too much—they were consuming me. A few choked sobs escaped my lips as I rocked faster.

Joss and Darren glanced at each other in total helplessness.

"Don't look at me," Darren said to Joss. "Melani said I'm useless when it comes to understanding or comforting the female kind."

Joss kneeled next to me and tried to put his hand on my back. I stiffened in fright and spat out, "Don't! Don't touch me!"

He dropped his hand dejectedly to his side and reached for an extra blanket to wrap around my shoulders instead. I could tell by the look in his eyes I had hurt his feelings. But after months of being tortured by cruel people, it hurt too much to have anyone touch me without the memories of the tortures coming back.

Darren stoked the fire and spoke with a quick look over his shoulder. "Get some sleep. We have an early morning ahead of us. We are putting as much distance at dawn between the

Septori and us as we can. I want to get farther away from Sinnendor's lands. You are right, I have a feeling that whoever captured you will be looking for you. At first light we will head to Haven, the capital of Calandry."

Darren must have seen me flinch at the news of them postponing leaving until tomorrow, because he went on to quickly explain.

"Our horses are too tired to travel any farther tonight. We've been pressing them hard the last few days heading to the Citadel, so Joss can finish his training. There ain't anywhere in the world safer than the Citadel in Haven. It's the Denai training ground."

Goose bumps traveled up my arm at the thought of being surrounded by a whole army of Denai. There was something deeply ingrained in me that made me wary of them. I wasn't even sure why or where these feelings of mistrust originated from. But I was forced to share a cell with other Denai, like Cammie, and we were all subjected to the same punishment. And over time, because of an inherent need for survival, I learned to ignore most of my misgivings. The Raven was particularly obsessed with the Denai race.

Darren and Joss were whispering to each other and kept casting me furtive looks, before Joss went and sat by the fire. "I will take the first watch," he said to me. "So you should get some sleep."

They may have set up a watch to guard against the Septori, but deep down I had a feeling it was to make sure I didn't run away in the night. They were right to consider me a risk. I probably would have run. I had little desire to go to the Citadel, but I also had nowhere else to go.

I closed my eyes and tried to piece together what Cammie had said about her kind. She said the city of Haven was populated with both human and Denai. But the Denai race was slowly becoming extinct. Fewer were born each year. Whole clans tried to intermarry with them in hopes of breeding young and powerful Denai. It didn't work.

I forced my mind to think of the morrow and resigned myself to go into the Citadel in Haven with Joss and Darren. Maybe they were right, and leaving this all far behind would be for the best. Maybe in this city a young girl with no past could possibly forge a future.

"Haven," I whispered before I let sleep take hold of me.

~B~

We were on the road riding before the rays of the morning sun made an appearance. I could tell Darren was anxious to move in case the Septori were searching for us. His eyes kept scanning the woods as he hastily tossed me one of Joss' shirts and a pair of his own soft brown pants.

I was swimming in both. Joss's shirt felt soft against my skin, and I couldn't help but hold the fabric to my nose and breathe in the masculine scent. A rush of heat filled my cheeks from embarrassment at what I was doing, hoping neither one caught me in the act.

Darren's pants wouldn't stay up around my hips and kept falling down. I did the best I could with a spare piece of twine to keep them up. I didn't have boots, but I was fine since we would be riding. My feet were so calloused from not wearing shoes that I didn't even notice the cold anymore.

My own tattered garments, which barely resembled clothes anymore from all of the dirt and blood, lay burning in the fire. I stared, emotionless, as the cloth burned. The edges turned black, going up in flames, the fire hungry for fuel. I stared until the smoke made my eyes water and sting, but I refused to turn away until nothing remained but the gray ash. Feeling a sense of freedom, I turned my back on the remains of my past.

Breakfast consisted of day old bread and cheese, things that did not require a fire to warm. I bit into the bread and longed for the day when I could eat something else. The cheese had a nice smoky flavor to it, so I savored it, taking small bites. The camp was already broken down and packed away with last night's ashes spread into the trees, dirt and leaves covering where our campfire was previously. All signs of a camp were erased.

Riding behind Darren on his beautiful white mare Gypsy, I was able to rest my cheek against his back and doze a bit while we rode. Joss and Darren had a total of three horses. I was all for riding solo, but I didn't have the physical strength to keep the pace that Darren had set.

The tension in the air was suffocating and no one spoke for most of the morning. We stopped to rest the horses and give ourselves a break. Then we were on the road again. The farther we got from Sinnendor's border, the more relaxed Darren became. Soon he was jovial again, even ribbing Joss by telling childhood stories.

"And then there was the time Joss decided he was dead set on courting a girl in town so he cut all of the rare Zythan flowers out of his grandmother's herb garden. He gave them to the girl and they both had a bad case of hives for the next two weeks. Little did he know that they were a medicinal flower that if prepared right can be a great salve, but when cut fresh and handled with bare hands causes an unbearable rash. She never would talk to him again after that, and to this day she turns white at the sight of Joss and avoids him to all heaven!"

Joss's ears turned bright red. "I was eight years old and how was I supposed to know? They were a light blue. I thought that anything medicinal or dangerous would look like a weed!"

Darren's loud guffaws made Joss kick his horse to trot ahead of us, so he wouldn't be privy to any more embarrassing childhood stories.

"So have you known Joss long?" I asked.

"Only forever and a day," Darren sighed and his eyes took on a faraway look as he began to recall his days of youth. "His father and I were the best of friends. You should have seen us. We used to get into all kinds of trouble growing up. I try to visit every year during the warm seasons and in the fall, and I never miss the Wind Festival."

Darren's smile faltered a bit. "Joss's father decided to give up on the life of adventure and settle down to have a family. I've tried to settle down and stay in one place, I really have. But I can't. The open skies and the road calls to me like a beautiful woman. I never know what's around the next bend, and life on the road is like a story that never ends. Despite my roving lifestyle, I've been named Joss's godfather, and I take it pretty seriously."

Joss turned around in his saddle and rolled his eyes at his godfather.

I smirked at the friendly banter between the two. "So there isn't anyone that you've loved enough to settle down and marry?" I felt ashamed as soon as the question left my mouth.

"Ah, Melani," Darren sighed. "I hold her heart, but the road holds mine. I've tried to stay and do right, but the longer I stay in one place. The moodier I become and the harder I am to live with. Or so I've been told. Every time I try, it's fine for a while. Then Melani gets fed up and starts throwing dishes at me. She's a passionate one and a beauty when she's angry, which is why I love her. She'll be hollerin' for me to get out of the house, demandin' me not to come back until I have ridden off my restlessness." He shrugged good-naturedly. "So I try and find jobs along the way, errands to run, messages that need delivered. And I will usually go visit my godson—until a warm hearth, good food, and my woman call me home. I've tried to tell her that I'm no good for her, but she believes that one day I will tame my ways and stay for good. I tell you it's in my blood. My ancestors were rovers, scoundrels and thieves."

"Really?" I was shocked.

"Why of course," Darren went on. "But Melani always takes me back. I mean, why wouldn't she? I've got great taste in clothing, I buy extravagant gifts, and I know how to grovel when the rare need arises." He looked over his shoulder and raised his eyebrows at me comically.

It felt good to laugh. I felt as if a chunk of the imaginary shield I put around me had fallen off. The thought of continually being courted by someone like Darren had a warming feeling and made me laugh. Joss rode up alongside us with a questioning look on his face.

"Don't worry, Joss, I didn't tell her about the time you got into your mother's powders." Joss turned bright pink again and started to sputter. I laughed even louder at his expression. And then I caught Joss sharing a look with Darren. His face became calmer and turned understanding—as if Darren shared these for my benefit only.

After I had settled down, I gave voice to the questions that have been plaguing me. "Darren, tell me about the Citadel."

Darren paused a moment, deep in thought, before answering. "The Citadel is the heart of the city, not only by its location but because of its purpose. It was established as a facility to train and protect the few remaining Denai."

"Sounds like a prison," I quipped lightly, but my stomach actually knotted up at the thought of going there.

"Oh, no. The Denai's gifts are slowly disappearing, so the late Queen Portia II established the Citadel to help them try and strengthen their gifts. The queens have always been partial to the Denai."

"But why are you taking me there? I'm not a Denai."

"No, but Joss is. And other than the Palace, the Citadel is the safest place in Calandry. Even the Queen thinks it's almost impenetrable. And after all, this is a Denai matter. You said yourself there were Denai imprisoned as well. So I will take you there and let the Adept Council choose what to do next. Besides, if there is any news which might affect Calandry and not the Denai only, they will make Queen Lilyana aware.

I let Darren's words sink in, and before I could even begin to feel scared at facing a whole council of Denai, Joss rode up.

"There's an inn up ahead and it would be good to stop for the night." Joss actually looked eager.

"I don't know, Joss," Darren said, "I would feel more comfortable once we are inside Haven's city limits."

"It's better than being outside. Besides, I know the inn owners and can guarantee their silence," Joss argued.

The thought of a warm bed and fire made me ache for the ability to make the horses magically appear at the inn.

"Oh please, may we stay?" I asked longingly, touching Darren lightly on the shoulder. "I know I don't have any money for a room, but I could write you a lender's note and pay you back as soon as I'm able."

Joss looked horrified at the thought. "Thalia, please don't even think of paying us back. After what you've been through, you deserve a night of comfort. I'm only sorry we don't know who hurt you." I could tell by the look in his eyes that he meant it.

We may have only been a few miles from the inn, but it felt like a hundred. I practically danced in the saddle in anticipation of a real bed. Even Gypsy began to trot.

The two-story Ginger Dragon Inn was well kept with large stables in the back.

The stable boy eagerly took our horses and began unsaddling and wiping them down. After Darren made sure the boy knew his way around a horse, he gave him a silver piece. The boy's mouth dropped open when Darren promised the same if he would give them each one treat out of his bag. He handed the boy his own leather bag.

The boy's eyes grew wide at the silver piece, and nodded his head. "Yes sir, I'll take care of them, sir. One apiece."

"What's in the bag?" I asked Joss.

"Carromint cookies," he said, grinning. "Darren makes them especially for his horse. I've never seen a man so peculiar about his horse's treats, but he makes them from a secret recipe. The cookies guarantee the horses' loyalty, so they are less likely eat anyone else's treats."

The boy offered Gypsy a cookie, and the horse nickered.

"They don't taste bad either. I snitched one once and Darren caught me, and he about had my head. They taste like carrots and peppermints." Joss chuckled. "But human food is not for horses. Gypsy is spoiled and will throw a veritable fit if he doesn't get one."

I glanced at Darren's strong back and pictured him in a kitchen with an apron on making cookies for his horse and it made me chuckle. This information, though bizarre, only made me like him more.

Joss pulled his saddle pack from Anthem before handing his reins to the boy. "Anthem likes them as well."

Joss, on the other hand, wasn't forthcoming about information about himself or his family.

My stomach growled.

"Let's get inside. Mara will get us situated." Joss led the way while Darren gave final instructions to the stable boy and gathered our things.

Inside, the warmth enveloped us immediately. A stout man with moppy brown hair greeted us. I discovered he was Bran, the innkeeper. I watched him give Joss a few slaps on the back as they exchanged pleasantries. Bran offered a toothy smile to Darren and nodded his head politely to me in greeting. The innkeeper's features were bland and almost instantly forgettable, but his alert expression and hazel eyes belied a gracious wisdom.

Bran led us upstairs to two connected rooms at the end of the hall. The adjoining door could be unlocked from each side if we needed it opened. The room was clean, with a fire already burning in the fireplace, warming the small room. Someone must have watched us arrive to have been able to get the fire going already.

A blue, hand-woven rug covered the wooden floor and light white curtains over the shuttered windows added a touch of femininity to the room. A single wooden chair stood next to a table with a washstand and a pitcher of water. A towel and soap lay beside them.

My gaze drifted to the bed pushed against the wall. The soft, clean mattress with a blue flowered quilt beckoned to me. A knock at the hallway door kept me from diving toward the bed.

It was Joss. "Bran's wife Mara will have food ready for us as soon as you're settled in."

I looked at the bed longingly and then back to Joss. My growling stomach interrupted my sigh of remorse. "Okay, I'm so hungry I could eat a horse. They don't serve horse here, do they?" I joked.

Joss grinned out of the side of his mouth, his dimple showing.

We went downstairs to a simple spread of more bread, this time homemade with honey drizzled on top, beef stew with vegetables, and shepherd's pie. I dove into the pie and tried to eat the equivalent of a horse, I think. Darren kept giving me worried glances, but I ignored them and reached for more food. I ate a full loaf of the honey bread and finished with a pint of spiced cider, before Darren's jovial mood turned somber.

"Thalia, I've been meaning to ask you. How did you escape?"

Before I could answer Darren, a loud crash erupted from the kitchen, followed by a squeal of delight. "Joss! *Joss* is here? Why didn't someone tell me sooner?" Out ran a very beautiful girl with a sea of golden blonde tresses. She ran right to Joss and almost knocked him over out of his chair with her exuberant hug. Her green-gold eyes sparkled with happiness, and she had the comeliest spattering of freckles across her nose. She was curvy in all of the places I wasn't, and it made me all the more aware of my thin, half-starved state.

"I didn't know you were coming this way. I would have been here earlier, diligently awaiting your arrival. Why didn't you tell me?" she pouted. "I wouldn't have been out running errands for Mama."

"Hush, Vienna," Bran berated his daughter. "Don't bother them while they're eating. Let them finish. In fact…" He glared at her. "Go get them more spiced cider."

She flew from the table in excitement and returned shortly with more cider. She fluttered around Joss like a bee searching for nectar.

I couldn't blame her. From what I've been told, most humans react this way around the Denai. They are subconsciously drawn to the beautiful race and tend to fawn over them.

"The Dancing Swine has a fantastic singer performing tonight. I hear that one song will bring you to tears with joy. Will you escort me? Father won't let me go hear him unless someone comes with me. And he trusts you." She looked at him with such a pleading, angelic face that it actually made my stomach drop with displeasure; no one could resist someone so beautiful.

Was I jealous? I didn't have time to analyze. I glanced at Joss and paled, threw my hand up to my mouth, and dashed for the door.

I barely made it to the side of the inn before losing all of my dinner. Tears slid down my face in embarrassment. I started to hiccup and cry at the same time, so I pressed my forehead against the cool wood of the inn. I didn't want to go back inside. I didn't want Joss or the beautiful Vienna to see me like this. They would pity me, I knew it.

Darren came out to get me a few minutes later. He handed me a tankard filled with liquid. I sniffed at it warily, not wanting to have any more spiced cider.

"It's just water," he reassured me.

I rinsed out my mouth and spat while Darren disappeared around the side of the inn. He came back shortly with a bag of wood chips. He spread it over my embarrassing display of overeating and then returned the sack.

"Come on. Let's go in."

"I don't want to." I sounded childish even to my own ears.

"Don't worry, they're gone."

I wasn't sure whether he was referring to Joss and Vienna or Bran and his wife, but I didn't want to face anyone. I scurried in and raced up the stairs to my room at the end of the hall. I looked at the clean bed in despair, not wanting to crawl into it wearing my dirty clothes. But I was too embarrassed to ask for a tub or borrow clothes from Joss.

I was debating what to wash first with my small bowl of water when a knock came at my door. I opened it to see a small boy about ten or twelve who resembled Bran, rolling a small wooden tub into my room. He left only to return a few minutes later with buckets of water from the well. Bran's wife Mara, a plump blonde woman with a kind smile, followed with kettles of hot water to add to the cold water to make it warm. She seemed quiet and reserved, unlike her daughter. She brought with her a clean pair of boy's slightly worn brown pants, socks, black boots and a white top. They must have belonged to the boy who brought the tub.

"Darren said not to give you skirts, because you had more riding to do." Mara spoke before handing me a folded handkerchief. I unwrapped the handkerchief to find a wood comb, a simple blue ribbon, and a bar of sweet smelling soap.

I started to cry at the simple gesture, and I grabbed Mara in a desperate hug and released all of the hurt and anguish that I held deep inside. Her yellow shift turned a deeper amber color as my tears soaked her shoulder. She gave me a strong, reassuring hug that only a mother knows how to give.

"There, there, dearie," she rubbed my back. "Having to travel with men all the time must be hard. Now, I know that Joss and Darren are good wholesome people, but if they mistreat you or hurt your feelings, you come and get Mara now, you hear? I'll knock some sense into them." She gazed at me with determination, and I saw some youthful spitfire flow into her face. She was definitely Vienna's mother.

I wouldn't count my time floating unconscious in the river as a real bath, because I was still filthy. Mara stayed and waged a personal war against the layers of dirt caked on me. She scrubbed me raw, and every red spot on my skin was a promise that I would soon be clean from the taint of the prison.

She left and came back shortly with a jar of foul smelling liquid. Working it through my hair, Mara casually commented that it would kill any bugs living in it. Lice! I had lice! The itchiness that plagued us in the cells had become nothing more than a slight annoyance compared to the beatings and torture we received regularly.

The burning sensation on my scalp gave me hope. There was no way anything could still be alive. My nose and eyes started to burn, and I began to question Mara's wisdom in using it on a person's body. And I told her so.

She called her son, Danny, and they carted water up and started the bath process all over again. But this time she let me soak the soreness out of my muscles.

Mara hummed while she lathered my hair up with the sweet smelling soap and I almost fell asleep while she massaged my scalp. Soon I was clean again, wearing a patched up oversized work shirt that Mara said belong to her husband. The top reached comfortably past my knees and would serve as a nightshirt.

Mara didn't stop there; she brushed my black hair until it shone in the firelight and then braided it in a single plait down my back. Danny knocked again a few minutes later and came to remove the tub. Mara excused herself as well and left me alone in the room.

I hadn't been alone in…I didn't know how long. As I listened to the crackling of the fire, the darkness of the room became suffocating. I jumped up and ran to the shutters to throw them open. The fresh night air pour in, and I inhaled it deeply. The panic that had almost assailed me from being shut in dissipated.

Turning back to the room, I crawled into the bed—so much softer than I was used to. I rolled over, closed my eyes, and soon fell into a fitful sleep.

"Hook her up!" a voice snarled. Struggling against the cold hands that gripped me, I arched my body in defiance. The freezing points of metal stabbed me in the spine, and I tried one last kick of freedom before I was bound in the machine. The deadly looking bands were locked into place around my body. Waves of hooded red robes floated around me.

"She hasn't shown any signs yet. Give her another injection."

I heard chanting as the Septori in red robes gathered around the machine, preparing to send an electric current into large bands that looked like eerie wings. The inevitable pain would course through my body.

I searched for the faces of the Septori, but only saw was evil, yellow eyes that glowed from the darkness of their hoods. Sharp, pointy, metal teeth glinted menacingly in the candlelight. They lunged toward my body as ominous laughter egged them on. They flowed toward me as ghostly phantasms. And then they moved through me.

Gasping, I began to fall. The earth opened up, and a gaping hole formed in the ground around my bare feet.

My head pounded as I was falling, falling.

Then pain. "Ouch! Blistering son of a scorpion!" I cussed. I lay tangled in my blanket on the hard wooden floor of the inn.

I had fallen off of the bed.

"A dream!" I breathed in relief. "Oh, thank the heavens." Grabbing the pillow from the bed, I curled up on the hard floor and tried to fall back asleep. The pounding headache of my dream persisted, and my heart raced at what I secretly feared the headaches might mean.

I was normal, I desperately told myself, I was still human. Closing my eyes, I missed the shadow outside of my window move away.

The pounding in my head continued through most of the night, followed by stomach cramps before which faded away near dawn.

At first light, the pounding started again and got louder and louder.

"Oh, *stop!*" I said, grabbing my head, before I realized the pounding was coming from the door.

"Thalia? Are you all right? Answer me! Thalia!" The voice began to get frantic.

"I'm coming!" I yelled as I wrapped the quilt around my body before limping toward the door. My muscles screamed in protest at the use. It had been moons since I'd ridden a horse. I took a second to steady myself before unlocking it. I opened the door to a worried Joss.

"Oh, it's you!" I stated grumpily. After last night, I was in no mood to talk.

"What...what happened to you?" He began to step into the room, but I pushed the door back into him.

"I was sleeping."

"Yeah, but I've been knocking for at least five minutes. I was about to break down the door."

"Uh, I was asleep!" I replied sarcastically. "I guess I'm a sound sleeper." I was not about to tell him about my nightmares.

He peered over my shoulder and glanced at the pillow and the extra blanket on the floor. When he looked back at me, the tension left his perfect brows only to be replaced by a slight worried look.

I stuck my chin up at him in defiance, and I tried to move and cover the view of my room. In the processes I stumbled on the edge of the blanket and bashed my forehead into the doorframe with a thud. Joss grabbed my arm to steady me, and then he studied me a little closer before releasing me.

"So there *is* a girl underneath all of that dirt," Joss spoke with a twinkle in his eye.

My eyes went wide at the comment, and I tried to step on his foot in revenge.

But Joss dodged it merrily.

"We are having breakfast in a quarter hour, and then we shall reach Haven by late this afternoon. Can you be ready?" He grinned at me, one corner of his mouth going up in a laughing manner.

I ran my hand through my sleep-muffled hair and felt in horror that Mara's beautiful braid had come undone. It must have happened because of my tossing and turning.

"Yes!" I squeaked, realizing the state of disarray I appeared in. I pushed the door frantically against him, and he stepped back into the hall laughing.

Turning back toward the room to change, I felt my legs turn to pudding and I stumbled toward the bed. It seemed that no matter what, I didn't have a graceful bone in my body.

I was ready in ten minutes and took the stairs slowly, dreading the thought of getting back on a horse. Mara took one look at my unsteady stance and went into the kitchen. She came back out with a salve.

"Here Thalia, it's my mother's own special recipe, for your muscles." I opened the container and got a faint peppermint smell. I took it back up to my room and applied it to my aching legs, feeling immediate relief. Before I could hand it back to Mara, she clasped her hands around mine and told me to keep it.

Breakfast would have been perfect except for the fact that Vienna served it. The way she fussed over Joss made me feel sick to my stomach. I shouldn't be feeling these pangs of jealousy over Joss. He wasn't mine by any means, and I had just met him. It was the fact that he paid equal attention back that hurt. I was still underweight and pale looking, but at least I was clean. And I hadn't been just a girl under the dirt. I wanted to be considered a woman, not necessarily by Joss, but by anyone.

What I went through at the prison made me feel old in comparison to my years. I wanted someone to look at me the way Vienna looked at Joss.

When we saddled the horses to leave, Joss offered for me to ride double with him. His earlier comment still rankled, so I ignored Joss and walked over to Darren's mount. Grabbing the reins, I tried to swing myself onto Gypsy and immediately slid back down, not having the muscle strength it took to lift my own body weight.

Ashamed and red faced, I kept my face to the horse. Joss looked a little hurt, but then assisted me onto Gypsy and saddled Anthem without giving me another look. Darren missed the whole exchange since he was attending to the stable boy with the silver piece.

I didn't know why I was acting this way. I kept imagining him and Vienna holding hands and laughing at the Singing Swine or Happy Hippo Pub, or whatever that place they probably went to was called.

I definitely didn't want to be leaning against his solid back while picturing it. I wanted to be a strong independent woman. Not a sick child that need saving from her shadow.

~4~

My first distant view of the city of Haven took my breath away. The Ginger Dragon was on the outskirts of the province, and the scenery slowly changed from forests to rolling hills the farther in we traveled. In the distance, what I took for clouds turned out to be large, snowcapped mountains. The closer we came to Haven the more travelers and merchants we met, each giving us a friendly wave as we passed.

We crested the last hill and the valley lay open below us, offering a view as far as the eye could see of the city. It was blindingly beautiful. The city was a mass of shops and tall towers with brilliantly decorated flags. Even from a distance, we could see a castle set apart from the city, high on a hill looking untouchable and alone. To the right, in a valley, sat the Citadel.

I had to squint as the glint of blue reflected from the training arena's glass-dome and stabbed my eyes. Off in the distance at the bottom of the mountains lay what appeared to be ruins.

The city itself looked like a rainbow had come to rest upon it, for each building was painted in a vibrant color. I asked Darren and he said that the city was split into color districts—something that began with one thrifty merchant many years ago.

It began when a hopeful, young merchant moved to Calandry in hopes of making his fortune. But without a clientele base built up, he soon struggled to make ends meet like everyone else. So he did something to make his small business stand out from the rest. He painted his shop a very bright green. It was the best bit of advertising he could do, because people came from far and wide to see his bright green shop. It began a trend and soon others started to paint their shops brilliant colors to compete. Soon it became hard to navigate the city.

The Merchant Guild finally got together and formed the color districts. They assigned colors to each vendor based on goods they sold and were allowed to paint their stores any shade of that particular color. If you needed exotic fabrics, you went to the yellow district; if you needed jewelry and accessories, you went to the red; if you were looking for bakers, look no further than any orange stall. And so Haven was nicknamed the city of light.

"Who was the merchant that started it all?" I asked, intrigued by the story.

"No one really knows. If you ask any one person they will swear on their mother's grave, and boast that it was their own great-great-grandfather," Darren said.

I laughed. I enjoyed the trip through the bustling city of Haven, smelling the fresh baked goods, the sounds of children playing and vendors hawking their wares. There was a general happiness and contentment in the air, free from fear and oppression.

I was left speechless once I saw the Citadel up close. Nothing Darren described had prepared me for the intricate beauty hidden within every structure. Human hands did not construct the Citadel or arena—even the roads were extravagant. The streets turned from simple, cobbled brick into a mosaic of colored stones, which changed in tone as the horses' hooves walked over them. These singing tiles led up to white stone guard towers on either side of Citadel's gleaming silver gate. The architectural design in the columns, archways, and stonework could have only been made by those with the gifts of the Denai.

Today, the gate was open, manned by four guards with swords and crossbows.

After Darren stated our business, they gave directions for us to take our horses to the stable.

Darren glanced around the Citadel's grounds. "Ah, good. It looks like Adept Lorna Windmere is in."

I looked around the almost empty courtyard and asked Darren how he knew. Darren pointed out that three of the large white towers surrounding the grounds were flying colorful banners. He went on to explain that if one of the Adept Council members was in residence, their flag was flown. Often times one or more was on errands for the queen.

"The white banner with a falling star is Adept Lorna Windmere's. It gives the students an added sense of security to see that there is always an adept in residence, in case of an emergency." He also pointed to a blue banner with a gold helios flower as Adept Breah Avenlea's and the black banner with three silver slashes as Pax Baton's. The empty towers would normally fly a green banner with three intricately looped gold circles for Cirrus Thornwood and a red banner with a sun and moon for Kambel Silverbane.

A loud barking announced the arrival of a short elderly man and a large bundle of fur that turned out to be Stable Master Grese and his blue-eyed sheepdog, aptly named Dog. After quick introductions, we were escorted into the large main hall of the Citadel, which also flew the banners for each member of the Adept Council. Along the walls were colorful tapestries inlaid with gold and silver depicting Calandry's history.

The marble floors continued through the main halls into each of the wings. I learned there was a wing for classrooms, the training arenas, and student dorms, while the servant's quarters were off the kitchen that surrounded the dining hall. The grounds of the Citadel led into a huge outdoor courtyard which contained the greenhouse, stable, training paddock, guard's quarters and the infirmary—each through a different archway.

A servant led us to Adept Lorna's office and I waited in the outer room while Joss and Darren went into the inner office with the adept. Half a candle mark later, the door opened and a young woman wearing a rich, velvety cloak stepped from her office, escorted down the hallway by no fewer than five guards. I couldn't help but stare after her wondering who she was and why she needed so many guards.

Someone cleared their throat and I got my first view of Adept Lorna. She was a tall woman in her mid-forties with glowing tan skin that spoke of a life used to the outdoors. Cropped white hair and ethereal blue eyes surrounded her pointed face. Her stern gaze held mine as I heard Darren and Joss discuss me.

"I really think I should be in there for this," Joss argued.

"Joss, we discussed this before, we brought her here and agreed that we would let Adept Lorna handle this situation. You agreed to come here to finish training, and that's what you are here to do. What happens to Thalia now is out of our hands. I'm leaving for home, and you need to concentrate on your training. You promised your father." Darren gave Joss a stern look.

Joss's jaw clenched and he looked at the Adept Lorna. "Will she be allowed to stay?"

The adept pursed her lips and then spoke up for the first time. "That is for the Adept Council to decide. I need to hear what she has to say, and then I will speak with the other adepts and Queen Lilyana. She's a stranger, and the farther she is from the queen the better. We will do the best we can to find her family, but Darren is right. She is out of your hands. We need to discuss this, and you need not worry anymore." Her matter of fact tone didn't leave room for argument.

My pulse jumped at the implication that I may not stay. I had nowhere else to go, and this could be the last time I would ever see Joss or Darren. I started to feel dizzy and I sucked in my breath and held it, looking between the two people that had been my lifelines since my escape. I had a feeling that Joss would soon insult Adept Lorna by insisting he stay for the meeting, which would ruin his chances for a good start at the Citadel.

I wanted what was best for him, so I decided right then and there that the best did not include me. Otherwise he would spend more time worrying about me rather than his own studies. What I was about to do to him was cruel, but it needed to be done.

"I don't need a mother, Joss, so stop acting like one!" I said in the most offhanded, snotty voice I could. I stood and walked over to the silver-paned window. "Thank you for bringing me to the Citadel and to Adept Lorna."

He made a motion as if to interrupt me, but I went on. "Your services and friendship are no longer needed or desired." I turned my back on him and gazed out into the courtyard, willing myself to not flinch or turn around. The sound of loud footsteps, followed by a heavy door slamming was indication enough that Joss had left. What surprised me more was to see that Darren had slipped out as well. I about crumpled to the ground in despair.

"Well done, girl. It seems you do have a bit of a backbone after all." Adept Lorna walked to her inner office door, opening it for me. "That one has the chance to become great and the potential to become a High Adept if he works hard. You were right to discourage him."

She closed the door behind me and I took in the utilitarian gray features of her office with its high, vaulted ceiling surrounded by wide windows and simple white curtains. The floor was a simple tile in muted grays, black, tan, and ivory. A black desk sat in the middle of her office surrounded by a no-nonsense tan rug. There were no personal touches evident in the room, but it was grand in its simplicity. The walls were bare except for the sconces to which held torches for more light when needed. A set of stairs at the back of the room led up to another level to what Darren had explained would be Lorna's private apartment. Each adept lived above their offices so they would always be close by in case of emergencies.

I sat in one of the two uncomfortable, high-backed chairs that faced her desk. She went over to a table and poured me a drink from a decanter before coming and sitting on the edge of her desk and handing the drink to me. She wore gray clothes, clearly made for a man, but tailored for a woman to show off her best features. Comfy and practical, I thought. I could definitely see her riding a horse and not being encumbered with skirts, and I was slightly envious.

I took a sip and swirled the drink on my tongue, tasting sweet cinnamon and honey, which covered an earthier ingredient I couldn't identify. Taking another sip, I tried with great difficulty to adjust myself in the uncomfortable chair. And then I realized, she probably bought these chairs for the sole purpose of intimidating students by making them uncomfortable. I wanted to dislike her just for her choice in furniture.

Leaning forward, Lorna watched me before placing her hand on her knee and addressing me. "I've heard quite the story from Darren Hamden and the ever-exuberant Joss. What I would like to hear now is the story from your own mouth."

I started to speak but felt a fuzzy feeling in my head. She listened quietly while I told her everything, even the bits I had refused to tell Joss and Darren, only pausing to collect my thoughts and feelings when it became painful to tell. Partway through, I felt a faint prickling at the back of my mind. When the question and answer session was over, Lorna remained silent for a moment, appearing thoughtful.

"And you have no clue to the real identity of the leader of the Septori, this Raven?" She sounded frustrated.

I shook my head.

"What about the Septori, do you know what country they were from? How many there are in total? Were there any signs that they were allied with the King of Sinnendor?"

I shrugged.

She stood up and began to pace in front of her desk, a slight wear pattern in the tan rug evidence that this was a regular occurrence. Stopping abruptly mid stride she turned and began a new set of questions.

"How many in the cells were Denai, how many human?" She got a quill and began to write.

I recounted how many I knew of, including the ones that had passed away or disappeared. "What do you think the Septori were doing?" I asked.

"We need to discuss this with the other adepts, especially Kambel Silverbane, our resident historian, who arrived shortly before you." She pulled on a small pull cord, and a page quickly appeared. Lorna scribbled a message on a slip of ivory parchment before handing it to the boy. "Come."

Following Lorna down a series of back stairways and hallways, I soon lost all sense of direction. Our destination was a large meeting room with heavy drapes covering the windows and obscuring all outside light. Candles, which lit up a large, framed map on the wall, were the only light within the room. Closer examination of the table showed a duplicate map of the lands of Calandry, Sinnendor, and the other surrounding provinces burned into the wood by an artistic hand. This must be the Adept Council's meeting room. Adept Lorna nodded for me to take my seat. A lone chair sat in the middle of the room, and it looked suspiciously like the ones she kept in her office— hard and uncomfortable.

We didn't have to wait long before the main door burst open to a whirlwind of yellow robes and fluttering hands. It was Adept Breah Avenlea with her shoulder-length, brown hair. She was dressed in a soft yellow dress and was talking animatedly to Adept Kambel Silverbane, who looked every inch the part of a historian.

Adept Kambel was short and slim with wavy, unkempt gray hair that blended into his long, gray beard. His intuitive brown eyes peeked out of small silver spectacles. Ink spots littered his somber green robe and the tips of his beard, as if he would accidentally dip his beard in the ink instead of a quill. They were quite the comedic pair, tall, slender Breah talking with her hands in a frenzy and short Kambel bobbing his head in agreement to what she was saying. It looked as if Adept

Breah were conducting a symphony and Kambel's head were the orchestra.

The mood abruptly changed when the door opened again and the largest man I had ever seen entered the room. He was dark as night with a bold demeanor and muscular stature, dressed all in shades of black. Three silver slashes marked the collar of his shirt. I remembered the same slashes on a banner and identified him as Adept Pax Baton. His shaved head reflected the candlelight and the small gold earring he wore looked too delicate for the warrior's frame. He strode into the room and took a seat at the table, which looked like a child's tea table in comparison. Surprisingly he expertly maneuvered his frame into the seat and spread his long legs out before him.

"I'm glad you got my missive," Lorna stood and waited while Adepts Breah and Kambel took their seats. "It's unfortunate that I had to send Cirrus away this morning, but this can't wait for him." She quickly relayed both my story and Darren and Joss's tale of finding me floating in the river.

"How do we know she is telling the truth?" came Adept Pax's deep timbre of voice.

"Because I put Alethiem in her tea earlier and tested her mind for shadows and hints of deceitfulness."

This took me by surprise and I stared at Lorna feeling betrayed by her dishonesty and low handed tactics. It was as if any trust she had previously built up was destroyed with a few words. I could feel the resentment start to rise to the surface and I had to bite back an angry retort that I was ready to spout out.

Adept Lorna turned to me with a solemn face that spoke sincerity. "I'm so sorry Thalia, please forgive me. Alethiem is an herb that when ingested makes it impossible for the speaker to lie."

"I didn't lie! I told you the truth," I snapped out.

"I know, I know," she said guiltily. "But I also was in your mind reading for any half-truths and implanted memories, which could have been a possibility since you couldn't remember your time before imprisonment. Your memories could have been tampered with and we had to be sure. You will be happy to know that I didn't find any evidence of that." A small smile crept up Lorna's face in an attempt to reassure me.

"If you would have asked, I would have agreed to it without you having to do it covertly. I'm telling the truth, and I'm sorry if what happened to me and the others is an inconvenience to you!" I was starting to get worked up, losing the little control I had on my emotions.

"We know," said Adept Lorna. "You see, this is not the first time rumors of a rogue group have surfaced. We have not located them, because they seem to be constantly on the move. They have hidden their identities from us and even though we have searched, we've only found this." She stepped forth with a piece of cloth.

Unfurling the material she showed me a design embroidered into the scrap. It was the familiar design, the Septori's design: two slashes in a circle. "This was found in the mouth of a dog belonging to a shepherd. It seemed one of them tried to steal his sheep."

"That's them. That's the mark of the Septori. Each one of them have that permanently branded somewhere on their body. If this isn't the first you've heard of them, then why haven't they been caught?" I was astounded and angry. Maybe if this Council had done their job, I could have been saved, Cammie would never have died.

"Because we don't know where they are!" Pax Baton interrupted. "A few stolen items, wagons missing, and a lot of speculation was not proof enough to start a war on a hidden enemy. The Queen ordered them watched, but no one could ever find them. It's like they disappeared into thin air." His large hands flew as he spoke enunciating each syllable.

"Or across the border," Breah added.

"You could have prevented this! If you had looked into the missing items, lives could have been saved!" I yelled.

"Calm down, child," Kambel spoke up. "We will find them. But we also have another concern."

"What could that possibly be? What could be more important than catching them?" I asked indignantly.

"What they obviously were trying to do to you?" Kambel intoned.

"You see, what was done is against the law. More than that, what was attempted is the stuff of legends and myth. Theories that have never been fully documented or proven, only speculated. And most of the High Council have always been against this kind of experimentation. This is very troublesome to us."

"But I don't understand. What didn't work? What happened to me?" I felt tears of frustration start to sting the back of my eyes as I held them in.

Kambel actually seemed to get excited and sprang from his chair, walking quickly around the room speaking as if to himself. "It's just a guess, but it sounds as if Raven, the, uh, leader of the Septori, has gotten hold of one or more of the Horden journals that we believed were lost for all eternity." He stroked his beard in thought.

"The Horden Journals?" Adept Pax asked.

"They are the mad rantings and experiments of a half-crazed human." Kambel looked around at the confused expression on Adept Pax's and Adept Breah's face. Rolling his eyes at the ceiling, he quickly filled us in. "A human known as Lord Horden had lost his only son in a terrible accident and went crazy with grief. He tried to force a young Denai to bring him back to life, but the Denai couldn't. Infuriated, Lord Horden began conducting secret experiments, trying to bring the dead to life. He documented everything until he ranted that he had found ways to become more powerful than the strongest Denai. Of course, his lab was investigated and they found the remains of his first attempts. Lord Horden was immediately imprisoned for his heinous crimes against humanity, but the notes on his experiments and findings were never discovered. Even after many trials, and bribes, he refused to tell anyone where they were hidden, and he was eventually executed." Kambel slowed down to catch his breath before intoning slowly, "There wasn't any proof that he succeeded, but there wasn't any proof he didn't."

Silence filled the room. No one stirred or moved. My mouth dropped open as I sat frozen in my chair, afraid to move lest I bring myself to their attention. I wanted someone to speak and break the awkward silence. "So," Kambel spoke again. "They forbade any further testing and experiments. They burned down his lab in hopes of destroying his hidden journals."

I tried to swallow, but my mouth went dry, as I watched closely the reactions of the Adept Council members.

"It sounds like someone found the Horden Journals, and is trying to duplicate Lord Horden's experiments. I'm just not sure to what end though," he continued.

"But that's against the law!" Adept Pax shouted, his heavy hand pounding the table with a closed fist. "To do any kind of experiments is inhumane, especially to a child."

There it was again, the statement that I was a child.

"The people of Calandry wouldn't stand for it," Adept Pax growled.

A nervous swallow escaped Kambel. "Yes, it is against the law here, but she was found in the river which borders Sinnendor and Calandry." His mind was spinning with excitement. "What if she was over the border of Sinnendor?"

"But the people of Sinnedor hate Denai since the war. The country is anti-Denai," Adept Breah spoke, the worry in her voice making her sound younger than her years.

"Exactly, so it would be the perfect place to do these kinds of tests. Sinnendor might even be in league with them," Kambel stated.

Adept Lorna stood. "But that would implicate King Tieren, Can we presume that he has known this was going on?" She leaned into the table. "It could cause a war. No! We have to keep that idea to ourselves. We must look at all aspects and directions before we accuse a neighboring country. Especially when we have a strenuous treaty as it is. But at least we know that it was unsuccessful? Right, Thalia?"

It took me a moment to register that I was being addressed. "Believe me. I'm still the same person," I answered with hesitancy. Was I sure that was true? I looked around the room at the worried faces of the adepts and suddenly felt tired and old.

"But why can't I remember anything from before?" I asked. I was getting answers but so far none of them were encouraging. Slumping down in the chair I started to pick at the table.

"I tried to look farther back into your memories when I was testing for the truth," Lorna answered. "I really did, but there is nothing there. You have no emotional memories before your capture. They are gone."

"But how can that be, Lorna?" Breah pondered aloud. "You're the strongest when it comes to reading minds."

"I can't read what isn't there. There is the space where they existed but nothing more. Her mind is like an attic that once was full of dusty boxes. Once the boxes are gone, only their outlines are still there, marked in the dust. It's as if they've been erased," Lorna mused.

"Erased! How can someone just erase away my memories, and why would they need to? We obviously weren't supposed to make it out of there alive." I clenched my fingers in anger and felt my knuckles pop.

"Obviously, it was to hide the identity of your abductors, which leads us to believe it may very well be someone you knew."

This new information froze me to the bone. I had never considered the possibility that someone I knew helped kidnap me, but the longer I pondered it the more sense it made. I looked up to catch the last half of what Lorna was saying.

"There are numerous plants and herbs that, when ingested, can remove memories, but unfortunately there are no known cures. Maybe over time they will return," Lorna said solemnly. She walked over to a side wall and pulled a golden cord. This time a different servant came in response to the summons.

"Thalia, you must be tired, and we have much to discuss. Forrest will take you to the kitchens and show you to a guest room. Tomorrow morning, we will meet again to decide what we will do with you." Lorna spoke softly and then turned her back to me.

That's it. I was dismissed. But she was right, my stomach was growling and I suddenly felt very exhausted. I let Forrest lead me down the halls as I stared at his back. Forrest was an elderly servant with a noble demeanor. He never spoke as he led me to the kitchen and patiently waited while I grabbed a handful of stuffed pastries, fruit and bread—items that would keep and be easy to eat later. Taking a bite out of an apple, I followed Forrest to a small guest room. I didn't feel like eating in the kitchen or dining room and have to answer any more questions. The guest room would do.

It was small and cozy, with a single window that overlooked the garden in the back of the keep. The bed was very soft, too soft, and once again I found myself unable to sleep. Grabbing a blanket I curled up on the hard floor and prayed I wouldn't dream.

~5~

"**I**t's been decided," Lorna spoke on behalf of all of the Adept Council members except for Cirrus, who was still absent. "Until we have more information about the Septori and their leader, it would be best if you stayed here within the Citadel."

I let out a puff of air I hadn't known I was holding. We were meeting in the same room as yesterday and from the looks of it, it seems that the adepts got as much sleep as I did, which was slim to none.

Lorna studied me thoughtfully before continuing. "Since you are not Denai it would be useless to enroll you in our program. Also, it is too dangerous to send you out into the city without protection and no way to make a living, so we agreed that it is in your best interest if you become our ward. Queen Lilyana has agreed as well and is personally looking into this herself."

I could see out of the corner of my eyes a few members of the Adept Council nodding their head in agreement with Lorna.

My heart fluttered apprehensively in my chest. It sounded too good to be true, and I found myself second guessing their decisions and looking for an ulterior motive. No one was this kind without wanting something in return. There were no such things as handouts. Maybe I was just blinded by the cruelty of the Septori and expecting an ambush in the darkness that would never come.

The only reason I could see for letting me stay in the Citadel was that they wanted to keep me close, and rightfully so. They didn't trust me and I didn't trust them. When I thought about their request, I realized I was exchanging one prison for another. Although this cell was much bigger, with a ready supply of food and a softer bed, it was still a prison.

And yet, I had been up most of the night dreading the possibility of being turned loose on the street with no way to support myself. Since I couldn't remember whether I had family, I wouldn't know where to turn. I had pondered different methods of survival. Just the thought of living on the streets made me shiver.

And I did.

"For how long," I asked, hesitating, "would I be allowed to stay? How long would I be a ward of the Citadel?" Becoming a ward could have any number of implications. It could mean the adepts would have total control over what I did until I reached adulthood, or until they decided the Septori was no longer a threat to me. I needed to hear that there was a way out, a backdoor to this prison that I could escape without fear of being tracked down by their guards.

It was Adept Kambel who leaned forward and spoke quietly and reassuringly. "For as long as you want or until your family is found." A small smile escaped the corner of his mouth and I could see that he at least was pleased with the announcement. My eyes darted and I could see Adept Breah staring daggers at the tapestry behind me, refusing to speak or make eye contact with anyone, her anger evident in her flushed cheeks.

I looked at the tapestry and couldn't see anything out of the ordinary—just a depiction of a hunter on a horse bringing down an elk.

"The Queen is concerned and is sending a detail of men to search for the Septori. She is also to try and locate your family. We will do the best we can to find them," Lorna finished, interrupting my thoughts.

Breah snorted, either in anger or disgust. She looked tired, her hair was slightly unkempt, and she wore the same dress as yesterday, evidence that they talked through the night.

"What would I do here at the Citadel?" I asked, feeling a sense of unease. I wasn't used to being idle. I couldn't stand to be cooped up any longer without anything to do. I had also learned that nothing in life was free and to never trust the gift horse, period.

"Do you have any particular talents or skill set?" Pax asked.

"I...uh. I'm not sure?" I was becoming flustered and angry at the same time. "I would like to stay active though."

Lorna pondered a moment and then clapped her hand against her thigh in decision. "Well then, we shall give you to Tearsa as a helper. She is in charge of the running of household duties at the Citadel and will find work for you to keep you busy. She will also figure out a wage for you and get you situated in a room. If there are no further objections, you can begin today. Forrest will take you to get your things."

I bobbed my head. Of course I didn't have any objections—a roof over my head, a bed to sleep in, meals, and a wage. It was more than I could possibly ever hope for. But the most important part was that I would be safe within the Citadel's walls. I knew better than to expect a cushy lifestyle here at the Citadel. Just because they were taking me under wing and I wasn't taking classes, didn't mean I would have it easy and get to lounge around all day. I would still be expected to pitch in.

Forrest waited outside the meeting room for me. Without speaking a word, he led me back to the guest room to get my belongings. I fumbled nervously with the door knob, because other than the clothes I was wearing and Mara's container of balm in my pocket, I had no other belongings. I turned around toward him and said, "I'm ready."

A slight blush ran up the back of his neck as he realized his mistake, and he dropped his eyes to the floor as if in apology. He quickly led me down several back hallways and into the main dining room where a stout lady in a muted topaz dress with a white apron was meeting with the Citadel's staff. I presumed that this must be Tearsa. Her hair, a dull red fading toward gray, was pulled into a severe knot at the base of her neck. I waited patiently with Forrest until she was done.

"I will not tolerate laziness again or your day pass privileges will be revoked. We have a lot to do before training resumes tomorrow. The whole place must be thoroughly cleaned and aired, linens washed, silverware polished." She slowly turned her hard gaze over everyone, making a few of the younger staff squirm in their seats. When they had enough she dismissed them, tucking her list into her pocket.

Turning to Forrest and addressing him, she asked, "So this is the one?"

He nodded.

"What am I supposed to do with her?" she appealed in exasperation.

He shrugged his shoulders and walked off, truly a tribute to his name, silent like the forest.

Tearsa let out a frustrated sigh and looked me over head to toe. Her sharp eyes were a little too close together and sat above a small pug nose. "You won't last a week here, in your condition. You hardly look strong enough to haul a bucket of water. Oh well, I have my orders and you better not embarrass me. Do you understand?"

"Yes, I understand."

"What's your name?"

"Thalia."

"Well, Thalia, go get your things. I will show you to your new quarters."

Heat rose to my cheeks in embarrassment as once again, within the span of a few minutes, I was reminded of how destitute I was. Following behind Tearsa, I quickly spoke up, "I have everything I need."

She stopped walking and gave me a searching look as if trying to discern my true reasons for being dumped on her. Her gaze seemed to measure me, and for a split second her eyes softened before disappearing behind a sterner work face. "Doesn't matter. Come along then."

She followed her down another hallway until we came down to a corridor of rooms behind the kitchen. I could feel the heat from the ovens and smell the fresh baked bread.

"In here."

An opened door revealed a small room a little bigger than my previous cell. It contained two simple trundle beds, one with bedding and the other an empty mattress, a closet, and nightstand. Glory be! There were two windows. The thought of being in this small room would terrify me if it weren't for the windows. The room was bare compared to the guest room I stayed in the night before.

But I was happy that I would earn a wage. I could add personal touches to the room later.

"You will share this room with Avina. There may be times when we will hire on extra help and use the spare trundle beds, so your room occupancy will double over night. But that won't be for a few weeks. Go find Berry now. She's our head seamstress and will set you up with a set of clothes and bedding. And then meet me in the kitchen for your first shift."

I turned around to ask Tearsa where I could find the head seamstress, but she was gone as quickly as she had come, off to her next task.

Biting my lip, I began to walk up and down every corridor looking for the head seamstress. I tried to peek into open rooms and take into account my surroundings. I did notice that servants' uniforms consisted of muted blues, gray, and white. Simple styles, with little decoration and very gender neutral in appearance. This was my first time being able to look around the Citadel unescorted, so I kept stopping whenever an interesting painting or sculpture caught my eye. Totally enraptured with my surroundings, I turned a corner and walked right into an argument between two women.

"You can't possibly consider this to be my dress. I It's awful. You must do my dress over." This was said by a tall blonde girl, with dark brown eyes and soft feminine features, which made her nasty tone seem out of place.

I could only assume the recipient of her tongue-lashing was Berry. The Citadel's head seamstress was a petite woman with uncontrollable brown curls, which were held at bay by a single red ribbon. A smattering of dark freckles framed her pert nose and slim mouth.

Hands on her hips, she didn't back down from the blonde. "Syrani, we are on a strict budget and time table. If you want a dress made with different fabric than what the Citadel keeps in stock, then you must bring us the bolts of fabrics yourself," she replied.

"That's preposterous. You are the Citadel's seamstresses. What else are you here for if not to create dresses for me?

Besides my father has strict orders that I must be kept happy, which I'm not."

"Syrani, we are employed by the Citadel and therefore have hundreds of people to clothe and thousands of garments to mend and alter. You should be grateful that they found time to finish your dress. If you are unhappy with it, then I will have them alter the dress again as soon as you pay for the first one."

"Don't speak another word. There is no way in heaven that I will be subjected to pay for that piece of trash. It feels like burlap, and they were sloppy in their work. What can you expect from lowly peasants? They messed up, plain and simple."

Now I could see that Berry was getting angry at the insult to her helpers. "All of our clothes are made from the same material. Those women you are insulting are very talented ladies, and I know for a fact that their work is impeccable." Berry challenged. "Their station in life does not by any means make them less important than you."

"Not one of them has my bloodline, and they will never be equal to me." Syrani yelled. Her nostrils expanded in anger and her eyes darkened.

My mind scrambled for a solution to resolve the problem, but before I could intervene Syrani stormed away and ran right into me.

"Watch where you're going!" Syrani snarled at me.

"No! *You* watch where you're going!" I caught her off guard and she stepped back in confusion. I couldn't help it. After hearing her berate the seamstress, I took it one step further. "Really? A bad dress, maybe you should have had your father's household seamstress outfit you before coming here instead of taking advantage of good people. Or does he not know of your extra orders?" I let the smugness show on my face, which made her fume.

"What do you know? You're so skinny you look like a drowned rat and the only things that a rat attracts are dogs and disease." And with that she smiled triumphantly and left.

"Ugh, what a horrible girl," Berry spoke as she came to stand next to me, eyeing Syrani's retreating figure warily.

"Please tell me that not all of the Denai students here are like that?" I sighed, motioning with my head down the hall toward Syrani.

"Oh no, they are great for the most part. You will find that most of the Denai are easy to get along with. There are only a handful that are as difficult as Syrani. She thinks she's superior because her family has a long line of powerful Denai. She is actually Adept Cirrus's niece so she tends to try and throw her weight around before she is even an adept herself. Who knows? She may well one day become one, and then we are all in trouble." She paused and seemed to really notice me for the first time.

"Oh, I'm sorry. I'm Berry, I'm the head seamstress." She held out her hand to me.

"Thalia," I shook her hand, liking her immediately.

"What can I do for you, Thalia? I think I owe you one for insulting Syrani. You did what I would never dare for fear of being fired on the spot," Berry grinned.

The euphoric feeling of telling off an obvious bully disappeared with her statement. I hadn't realized that my intervention may have consequences of their own. What if the adepts heard and chose to release me from their protection or to throw me out into the streets? Suddenly I felt a little sick and flustered. "Uh, I actually need a few items. I'm to start work here. Tearsa sent me for bedding and a uniform." I felt as if my face was turning green.

"Oh!" Berry's smile dropped slightly when she realized the same thing I did, but she recovered faster than me and her smile widened again. "You are going to work with us here? How very lucky you are. I know families that have been trying for years to get a job here. Tearsa is very particular about who gets hired on. You must know someone important or have great references." Knowing the circumstances under which I was given the job, I made only a noncommittal noise.

Berry opened the door behind her and entered. A wooden sign depicting a needle and thread hung above the door to her workrooms.

The room consisted of table upon table of workspace. At each table sat two or three young ladies in different stages of sewing projects. Along the wall were shelves with a wide selection of bolts of fabrics, from colored silks from far countries, to homespun fabrics, linens and furs. Various baskets held buttons, ribbons, and lace. The room was well lit from various skylights in the ceiling. Numerous sconces lined the walls to keep it well lit into the night.

Berry entered a back room and came back with a basket full of various cloth items. "Here you go. You have bedding, sleep clothes, underclothes, and uniforms, but we will have to get those adjusted after you put on some weight." A slight blush rose to her cheeks. "I can tell you haven't had it the easiest, but believe me, after a couple of weeks of the Citadel's food, you will fill out all right." She began to giggle and covered her mouth with her hand.

Berry pointed me toward my room and made me promise to come back and visit her. But even with directions, I was still lost until I spotted Forrest and asked him if he knew were Avina's room was. He nodded his head and took me there without a word.

"Thank you so much, Forrest!" I squeezed his arm in thanks, and I saw a blush come to his weathered cheeks reminding myself to not overlook the silent servant.

Taking the bedding and setting it on the bed, I went to the closet and started to hang up the night clothes, when I noticed the other items that Berry had slipped into my basket. There were some ribbons, a small hair comb, and a bar of sweet smelling soap. Bless her! I made a promise to myself to buy her a present in town when I got my first wages, but first I had to get to the kitchen.

I quickly changed into my uniform. It was a sturdy, simple blue skirt, white chemise, and gray bodice. She had included an apron as well. I donned the uniform with the same boy boots I had before and hoped my skirts would cover the fact that they were still a little big.

Fully dressed, I hurried in the direction of the kitchen. After a few wrong turns, I found the back entry and was immediately put to work doing dishes. I was awkward at first and didn't work fast enough. When it came time to serve the students, I spent the whole time hiding in the kitchen. I ate lunch with the rest of the servants at a long worn wooden table.

One of the cooks, a man named Donn, introduced me to the rest of the kitchen staff, and I got to meet Avina. She was a short girl who looked about fourteen with red braids and freckles. I smiled at her and watched her grin back at me in delight. After how bad my luck had been lately, I figured it was a godsend that I got someone young who was happy to have a roommate instead of someone like Syrani.

Dinner followed the same routine, working in the kitchen preparing food, or stoking the ovens. Tearsa handed me a peeling knife and I started peeling potatoes for the soup. The assignment was my punishment, I believe, for being so slow on the dishes. Before long the heat of the kitchen got to me and I was covered in sweat, soap, and soup, when I heard the students begin to enter the dining hall for dinner. I ached to catch a glimpse of Joss, but at the same time I was embarrassed.

Joss was the one constant in my vastly changing world, but the way I had treated him the other day had guaranteed a change in our friendship, if we even had one anymore. Still the thought that we were both still at the Citadel gave me the hope to go on and try and make a new future here for myself.

When dinner began to die down, I took a peek into the hall to see if I could spot him. I froze in shock at seeing a room full of Denai. I had never seen so many beautiful people in one place and it took Avina giving me a nudge to bring me back down from the visual high.

I searched for Joss, and sure enough, his tall frame was surrounded by a bunch of girls vying for his attention. As a new Denai, he couldn't help but draw a crowd. Among the flock of skirts, a familiar blonde held his attention the most.

I couldn't help but roll my eyes and duck into the kitchen before he saw me spying. What could I say? She was gorgeous, even if she was mean-spirited, and it sure looked like Syrani was laying on the charm.

After dinner, the kitchen staff again ate together, and I deftly avoided too many personal questions with quick, one-word answers. Before long, they got the hint to not pry—everyone except for Avina, who in her childish exuberance didn't know when to stop with the chatter. Her questions followed me back to our room where I crashed in exhaustion onto my bed after I changed into my nightclothes. I didn't even bother to make the bed with the clean linens Berry had given me earlier in the day.

Avina changed and crawled into her bed explaining that because she was a baker's assistant, she worked very early and would try and not disturb me.

Yawning, I assured her she was fine, and I rolled over and looked out the window at the moon.

My thoughts drifted toward Cammie. Avina reminded me so much of her! And the brooding Kael. Even if he was rude, I still prayed that he was safe. Then I thought of Darren, hoping he would be home to see Melani soon and that he could forgive me for treating Joss and him cruelly.

Had it only been a day since I had come here? It seemed like it had been weeks since I left Joss and Darren's care. So much had changed in a day.

~6~

The following weeks became a routine of working in the kitchen or running errands. Even though I would have preferred to work outdoors, I didn't dare ask. The Adepts had done so much for me. Each week they would meet with me in their office, and I would hear what they had to say about their search so far.

At the first weekly meeting I met Adept Cirrus. He was an even-tempered man with blonde hair that he wore long in a ponytail, and I would him to be in his late forties. He was seriously concerned with what had happened, and wanted to hear the story again from me personally, not just repeated from the other adepts. He said he would make arrangements to meet with me.

I received his summons in the form of a sealed note delivered by Forrest a few days later. Entering his round office, I was surprised at the difference between his opulent rooms and Lorna's simple aesthetic design. Adept Cirrus's office had heavy gold drapes hanging from the four windows overlooking the grounds. His walls were a deep green, covered with paintings from every era, while a crystal chandelier hung in the center, mysteriously illuminating the room without help from candles. His walls were lined with tall bookshelves, on which sat rows of heavy, neatly organized books and manuscripts. The smell of books and rosewood assailed my nose. His desk was clean except for an open and a quill ready in his hand. I felt a moment of hesitation. He gestured to a plush maroon chair that I sank into with weariness. I almost disappeared deep into the cushions. Adept Cirrus and I studied one another—he intently, I warily.

"I really don't want dig up all of this again," I told him. "The memories are painful."

"I completely understand, Thalia. And we can stop whenever you want to. But I was really hoping to record everything that happened so I can personally look into it further."

I raised my eyebrows in question. He recovered quickly. "So that we can catch this person and make him pay for what he did to you. This should have never happened to begin with, and I want to make sure it never happens again. And to do that, I need accurate notes of everything you can remember." His voice became slow, fatherly-like.

The strong scent of incense perforating the room began to make my eyes water, so I made the quick decision to tell him and get it over with so I could leave. I told him everything, everything I could remember about my imprisonment and escape—even Kael's involvement. He took notes diligently and rarely interrupted me, except when it came to the actual experiments. He wanted specific details concerning the experiments and their results.

"Well, they failed," I stated.

"How so?" Cirrus asked.

"I'm not different. I can't do anything special."

"Ah," he remarked thoughtfully, "but have you tried to summon it, since your escape?"

"No, I wouldn't even know how."

Cirrus got up from his desk and went over to a bookshelf and pulled down a palm-sized black orb. He brought it over to me and set it on the desk in front of me with a challenging look in his eyes.

"Lesson number one: There is always a cost for power. We don't poof, wave our hands, and make things appear without there being a price to pay for it. Lesson number two: The world is made up of energy and elements—the chair you're sitting on, the stone floor itself, and even the air you breathe. If I concentrate hard enough, I can see the flow and lines of the energy in the world around me."

I stared blankly at Adept Cirrus. Unperturbed by my reaction he went on with his lesson as if I were his student. "If I think it's a little hot in here, I could push the wind toward the window to open it." As he said this, the window opened up and let in a cool breeze. "If I thought it was too cold, I move the wind toward the fire to get it to blaze a little higher. Do you get it?" This time the fire burned higher in the grate.

I began to understand the concept of what it actually took to do what the Adepts did, but I still couldn't comprehend how this lesson was going to help me.

He held his hands out, palms up, like a scale in front of me. "It is a delicate system of checks and balances. One can't control matter without exhausting their own energy supply. The stronger one is, the more they are able to control and do. With many of the Denai gifts having been lost over the centuries, who's to say what you can and cannot do?"

His words began to sink in, and I felt a chill race over me at the possibility of never being able to put the past behind me. Maybe I needed to try once and for all to see if I had any abilities.

"Now back to this orb. Concentrate on it. Can you see any colors around it?" Not wanting to appear as if I didn't care or wasn't trying, I stared hard at the black orb and furrowed my brows in concentration

"This orb is Denai-sensitive. It responds almost willingly to a Denai. All it would take is a little nudge, and because it's round, it will move very easily." He waited patiently, encouraging me silently with his own will.

I kept staring at the black orb so hard I began to see double. I willed the stupid orb to move across the table. Nothing. Moving my hands in front of me, I flicked them at the orb as if swatting a fly. Nothing.

I looked at him, afraid I would see disappointment in his eyes. Instead, something else flickered across his face before disappearing behind a smile.

"Don't feel bad, Thalia. We had to be sure after all." He came around the desk and I stood up. Politely, he put his hand on my shoulder and led me out the door. "Thank you for your help. Rest assured, I will find the people who did this to you. Go my child, and get some rest."

I stood outside his closed office door feeling somewhat miffed. But in a way, I understood. I would have been a novelty, if I had been gifted with powers. Something he could study and write books about. Instead, fame would await whoever uncovered the leader of the Septori. His time would be better spent on finding them. That encounter had been four weeks ago.

That night, I was bringing up apples from the cellar, when Tearsa told me that they were short servers in the hall. "You'll need to help bring out the food."

My face paled and I swore I felt my heart stutter. There was no way I could avoid running into Joss if I went out there into the dining hall. I missed him and Darren something awful, but I felt as if they were stations above me now. So much for believing that equality speech Berry had given.

Gathering my courage, I grabbed the large tray of cranberry stuffed goose and used it as a barrier between my head and the students. I skimmed the outer wall and looked for the table that was missing a goose. Quickly depositing it without incident, I escaped back into the kitchen and searched for a quick exit. Maybe I could feign illness?

As soon as I stepped inside, Donn the cook handed me another tray filled with bite-sized ham and spiced cheese. I looked at the petite food in dismay. There was no way I could hide behind this, so I decided try for speed instead of stealth. I rushed out aiming for the closest table to find they already had a spiced ham and cheese tray. Backing up, I moved to drop it off at the next empty table. Another servant with a tray almost took my head off, but I ducked quickly to avoid a collision. Too late. Something caused me to stumble.

I fell forward into a young page carrying pitchers of cider.

The world slowed as the pitchers flew up, up and then down all over me and a few students that were unlucky enough to be close by. The young page, whose name I was unable to recall, looked horrified. I could hear murmurs followed by laughter as students began to gather and applaud at the mess I had made.

A piercing laugh rang out louder than the rest, and I looked up through my now sodden tresses to see the sneering face of Syrani. She was sitting precariously close to me and, oddly, was the only one who was not covered in cider. Her friends and colleagues didn't look amused as they glared at me.

Tears stung my eyes as I tried to stand up, the laughter continuing as puddles of cider pooled around my feet. Keeping my head low in embarrassment, I bee-lined a hasty retreat, only to slip again and stumble into a broad chest. Hands grabbed my arms to steady me. I would have recognized his scent if I didn't recognize his voice. Joss.

"Thalia? Is that you?" The shock in his voice made me panic. How awful I must look at that moment, with wet hair hanging down my face! And my uniform stained from the cider. I looked pathetic and needed to escape his piercing eyes and forthcoming pity. I tried to move away, but he still held me by my upper arms, trying to get me to look him in the face.

I kept my head turned away.

"You…You're…you're all wet!" he stuttered, looking somewhat confused as if he just noticed the cider seeping through my shirt onto his hand. Or maybe he was used to seeing me like a wet mess. "You look awful!" he muttered.

Those words pierced my soul like a fiery dart. That was it? That was all he had to say after weeks of not seeing me? "You look awful"? I had gained back a lot of the weight I had lost, my face had filled out—but not too much—and I had regained soft color to my cheeks. My eyes didn't have dark circles under them, and my dark hair shone in the firelight. I knew I wasn't a beauty, but I had been hoping for a better impression than awful.

"Look what Joss caught…a rat," Syrani laughed the joke that only she and I would get, but her clique joined, in laughing anyway.

Joss's hands tightened on my arms angrily. Whether it was in response to me or Syrani's barb I didn't know.

"Joss, why don't you let the kitchen rat scurry along back into the kitchen? You did promise you would help me with my history lessons after dinner," she pouted beautifully.

I looked up at Joss for the first time in weeks and studied his outline up close. His jaw showed the shadow of stubble, he was tanner and a little broader in the shoulders, but other than that, he was the same. Except now his dimple was hidden by the clenching of his jaw. His fingers were like a vise on my arms, he still hadn't released me, and he showed no signs that he planned to.

"I'll be right there," he said as he let go of one arm and pulled me away from the curious onlookers and Syrani. I glanced over my shoulder at Syrani's enraged face and knew that I would pay for it later. Joss pulled me toward a hallway.

"Joss, you have to let me go. I'm going to get in trouble." Ignoring me, Joss tugged me down another hallway. As soon as we rounded the corner, he stopped suddenly. I ran into him. Joss turned on me, a heated look in his eyes.

"Have you been here the whole time?" he spat out. I could tell Joss was furious, which surprised me.

I hung my head in shame, refusing to look at him. "Yes, I've been living and working here at the Citadel for the past six weeks." I kept my gaze on a spot over his shoulder so I wouldn't have to look him in the eye. He couldn't see how guilty I felt.

"And you didn't think to come see me? To tell me that you are all right? I had no clue what happened to you after you told me off. I've regretted every day walking out on you." He ran his hand through his blonde hair, messing it up. I sighed inwardly at how becoming it him appear.

"I wanted to be there for you when you spoke with the Adept Council, but after what Darren said and then the way you acted, I lost my temper and left. I was angry with you. I told myself you were out of my hands and I wouldn't give you another thought. But that was a lie." He turned to me, his green eyes softening. "Two days later I stormed into Adept Lorna's office and demanded to know what happened to you. That infuriating woman only smirked and told me that you were in good hands."

Speechless, I looked at him, wondering what I meant to him. A guilty thrill raced through my body. But then I remembered what Lorna said about what he could one day become.

I remembered my station and dared to not even hope.

He slammed his fist into the wall. "But, darn it. Don't you understand? I...I, when I pulled you out of the river you were almost dead and I kept you alive. I feel responsible for you."

My back stiffened. "So that's all I am to you? A responsibility?"

"No, that's not it."

He started to lean forward, and I was pinned between Joss and the wall.

"Then what is it?" I prompted, almost dreading the answer.

"I don't know, but I..."

He didn't get to say anymore before Avina rounded the corner obviously searching for someone, but stopped when she saw the way Joss was leaning over me.

Joss looked up.

"Thalia, you have to get in here now! Donn is turning all shades of red because you haven't come back." Avina ducked back into the kitchen.

I turned to go, but stopped as Joss's hand touched my shoulder. "Promise me we will talk later?"

All I said was, "Syrani's waiting for you." And I walked into the kitchen. I was a glutton for self-punishment. By pushing Joss away, I was protecting myself. He was a student at the Citadel and would one day be a great Adept. I was a drowned river rat, a nobody that had no real future and no family that had stepped forward to claim me. I had been scared that all Joss really felt was a protectiveness over me, and I had been right.

He felt responsible for me, and I didn't want him to.

I could take care of myself. Joss deserved someone that wasn't as messed up in the head as me, someone beautiful, but not like Syrani. I thought of all the girls that threw themselves in his way and became more determined to build a wall up between myself and the very handsome Joss. I wouldn't hope or dream because I didn't think my heart was strong enough. And in the end, I was afraid that—after everything that had happened to me—if my heart shattered, I wouldn't know how to put it back together again.

Slipping into the kitchen, I resumed filling trays of food and carrying them out into the hall, no longer worried about confronting Joss. I had already embarrassed myself. Depositing the tray on a table, I scanned the room to see if I could spot him. He was gone, and so was Syrani. I was glad that he was gone, but depressed at the same time because he was with her.

I decided to take Avina up on her offer to go into the city and spend some of our hard earned silver tomorrow, since it was our day off. And I had promised myself I would buy Berry something. I definitely wanted to spruce up our room and get some clothes that looked nothing like my blue and gray uniform. Because I felt a little lighter on my feet at the prospect of getting out of the kitchens, the rest of the night flew by.

~ 7 ~

reedom! The colors of all the districts, smells, sounds and the fact that Avina and I were running around laughing was the best healing therapy that I could ask for. The smells of the baker's district made my mouth water and the chocolate pastries made my mouth melt with delight. We had decided to pool our money and share everything we bought so we could try a wider variety of food. It was the absolute best idea, for I couldn't remember having a more relaxing day. I was laughing so hard my cheeks hurt.

After purchasing a book for myself, I was drawn to a colorful stall with small jars of scented perfume. The elderly woman was busy with another customer, so I took the chance to study the perfumes further. There were various herbs and flowers in beautiful bottles of blown glass with rubber stoppers for decoration. I picked up a beautiful, light blue orb that felt warm to the touch from being in the sun. Unstopping the bottle, I was overcome with the faint hint of vanilla and cinnamon and a wonderful feeling of absolute contentment.

Once I plugged the bottle of perfume, the feeling faded. Now interested more than ever, I grabbed an amber colored bottle that, once uncorked, unleashed a feeling of bubbling happiness with the scent of sunflowers on fresh wind. The perfumist was obviously a Denai who was able to capture feelings within her perfumes. This amazed me about Haven the freedom in which Denai practiced their art and sold their handiworks. My fingers drifted over the tops of the other bottles in wonder.

"Now that bottle right there will make you feel like you're in love," spoke a gravelly voice over my shoulder. I jumped and almost knocked over a few bottles that I quickly steadied.

A cackle erupted from an elderly, gray haired lady whose face was covered in laugh wrinkles. Her sun-lined face showed that she probably spent most of her times outdoors, and her skin had a hint of sparkles. "Don't worry; it doesn't make anyone fall in love with you. It just gives you a feeling as though you are in love. You wouldn't believe how many married women wish for the feeling of being young and in love again," she winked at me.

I looked more closely at the bottle.

"It's my best seller. I'm a Weaver. I weave feelings into my perfumes so that women can feel confident or beautiful while they wear them."

It took a moment for her words to sink in. Weavers were able to make a pot that would never boil over or silverware that would never tarnish by weaving power into their items during construction. I had seen some of the items first hand in the Citadel's kitchen.

It made me wonder if it were possible to weave in hurtful feelings as well. "Do you ever weave hate or fear into them?" I asked cautiously.

Her eyes darkened. "That would be abusing the gifts that God gave me, and I would never do that." Her voice became louder, almost a shout as she ranted. "I only weave light, not darkness! Never darkness! The dark does not like to be ignored, and its call is sweet like honey, but it will devour you whole and spit you out." Her anger rose and then quickly dissipated when she saw my obvious distress at her tone. Her voice lowered and she seemed to regain clarity and looked around warily. "Not saying someone else couldn't do it, but I won't do it. And no one can make me."

"Please don't take offense." I held my hands out to her, palms out as if I were soothing a frightened animal. "I should have known better than to question your methods. Your work is beautiful and I would never wish to insult you, but my curiosity at the wonder of what you can do made me speak without thinking." I put every ounce of comfort into my voice, trying to soothe the woman who seemed so close to the edge of reason.

The woman visibly softened.

"Ah child, don't let old Ruzaa's bark worry you. I do get a little irrational about my gift sometimes. Once, long ago, a terrible man thought I could weave a potion to force people do his bidding." She looked tired and worn out as she went on, "I was even been beaten as he tried to force my hands to work dark and evil things into potion form." She held them up and I could see the white mangled tissue of faded burn marks around her knuckles. "I wouldn't do it. To give in, to take something that was meant for good and use it to do evil is a sin. And I refused. They could've killed me for all I cared." Her gaze turned steely in determination before flicking to a movement over my shoulder. She dropped her hands and hid them behind her apron.

I turned but saw nothing.

My heart lurched with empathy. Here was a survivor, a kindred heart, someone who had lived through unbearable circumstances and arose to live on. I had more in common with this unstable female than anyone I had met in Calandry.

"Ruzaa, stay strong. Never change who you are for anyone." I reached for her hand under her apron and held it in such a way as to expose my own scars. Ruzaa's eyes widened with understanding, and she looked up at me as tears rimmed both of our eyes. A bond between two survivors formed—one old, one young.

Avina, not understanding the exchange, finally spoke up with her childish exuberance. "What about getting a boy to kiss you? I could really use something like that!" Ruzaa laughed out loud and I smiled at the excited look on Avina's freckled face, when my gaze was drawn to the flowers that were drying and hung around posts from the booth. An idea struck me.

"Ruzaa. What about dyes? Can any of your flowers be used for dyes? I'm looking for a gift for the Citadel's head seamstress. I would love to give her something to experiment with and get a color that no one else has?"

Her aged eyes grew thoughtful as she pulled a plant resembling holly but a rich, deep blue. She put it in a small cinch sack. "Try this. I would say she could get a wonderful deep blue and some indigo. But here is a secret." She leaned forward and whispered, "Whatever garment she makes with this dye, the wearer will always have feelings of hope." She winked at me. I couldn't help myself. I hugged her with delight, almost knocking her over. Ruzaa's surprised laughter stayed with me as I carried my small prize with me down the street. She had even given me a wonderful deal on my present. Avina, who was very patient during this exchange, was now buzzing with excitement.

"You know she's crazy right?" Avina whispered in a hushed voice, hoping that Ruzaa wouldn't overhear.

"Aren't we all?" I answered back.

"Come on." Avina pulled me toward the mercantile district and their brightly painted yellow shops. "We have to get you some material for a new outfit for the Founding Celebration. Oh, and a mask!"

"Founding Celebration?"

Avina rolled her eyes at me. "You know, the Founding Celebration, the midwinter celebration in honor of the founding of Calandry. Are you going with anyone?"

My mind immediately went to Joss but then a picture of him and Syrani flashed in my mind. "Um no, I didn't know that you had to go with someone, I thought you could go as a group?"

"Of course you can go as a group. But on the final night of the celebration, the palace holds a masked event. It's the one night of the year when everyone in the Citadel is equal, and of course there is dancing and contests. But the best part is when the Faeries pass out matching dance tokens to the male and female guests; you are supposed to find your match to redeem your dance," she rushed out almost in one breath. Her eyes got a dreamy look before finishing. "And then at midnight, when the bell tolls, whoever kisses you is meant to be your true love." I was getting lost in her babble of love, fairies and tokens.

"That seems unlikely. It sounds like the drivel a bunch of desperate girls would make up," I chuckled.

"But, Thalia!" Avina whined, eyes opening wide, "I am a desperate girl. And it's not drivel. I didn't make it up. It's tradition."

"It's a stupid tradition." I could see that my comment hurt her as her shoulders slumped dejectedly. Leaning over I nudged her. "So are you going with anyone?"

"No, I wish though."

"Well I'm not going with anyone either, so I don't see the point of getting all dressed up, especially when no one knows who you are."

"I see your point Thalia, but still…" Avina's words drifted off as she pretended to dance with an invisible dance partner. Doing a curtsy in acceptance, she spun around and around until she accidentally bumped into a man. That caused her to trip and go flying into a crate full of passionfruit.

"Now look here!" A stern vendor with a full beard yelled at us while his upset wife came rushing out into the street to try and save the fruit. She grabbed the closest crate and attempted to put the passionfruit in it while Avina followed the fruit rolling into the street, nabbing them and putting them in her apron.

"Sorry! I'm so, so, sorry," Avina cried. A wagon drawn by two horses came rushing down the street, and the driver didn't slow down as the bounty of fruit was crushed beneath the hooves and wagon wheels.

"Nooooo! Oh, this is terrible. What am I to do?" she cried.

By this time the merchant was furious and the wife was crying into her apron. He wagged his finger at Avina, demanding payment for their very expensive fruit, imported from a southern province. A baby began to wail in the back of the store and the wife rushed in to calm the crying baby. She returned red-faced and teary-eyed, the same emotions mirrored on her baby's face.

"Oh, please, how much was that crate of fruit?" Avina asked, opening up her small coin purse, getting ready to dump it all into the merchant's hands if need be. When he stated the cost of the fruit, she paled and her hands began to shake. "I don't have that much." She looked at me in despair. I looked at my coins, and even if I gave her all of my money, we wouldn't come up with a quarter of the cost that the merchant was demanding.

"Oh, come now," a cultured voice interjected. Looking up, I was surprised to see Adept Cirrus, his white blonde hair no longer pulled back in a ponytail. He was dressed in non-formal attire, but the attention to detailing on his clothes still proclaimed his prestige and obvious wealth. His grace and demeanor called for respect. "Even if you got them fresh off of a caravan yesterday, I know for a fact they wouldn't be worth that much. And I can tell by the slightly acidic smell, thanks to the horses no doubt for smashing them, that they have gone a bit too ripe."

"Adept Cirrus!" The man balked, and his wife hastily took the baby into the house. Regaining his composure, the merchant put on his best smile and jumped head first into the negotiations of the price of his fruit, knowing that this is what he did best.

"They were not going bad, I assure you. You must be smelling something else." His voice had an unmistakable accent now that he was no longer yelling at us.

"Are you calling me a liar, Jeron? I just happened to purchase this fruit yesterday from a vendor across the district and his fruit was beautiful and sweet and cost four coppers less per piece than what you are obviously charging these ladies for your spoiled fruit." He waved his hand dramatically across the way, drawing attention to his lambskin gloves. He pulled them closer in front of the merchant and looked him in the eye.

"I'm right, aren't I, Jeron? Because I know you're lying. Are you forgetting that I'm a Denai and I can tell when you lie?" The vendor's eyes looked at the ground in shame.

"Now I think you must be mistaken in your calculation of how much your fruit is worth, or how many fruit you had spoiled in total." Glancing around at the damage and what was salvaged he turned back to the vendor. "I will pay you four silver pieces for the whole lot and we will call it done."

"I can't take less than seven, Sir." He began to draw his eyes to the floor and the tone of his voice turned pleading. "You see, your Honor; I've got a family to feed and a young one on the way." I started at how easily the man could change his approach from raging bull to poor, meek vendor.

"Five silvers and I forget you lied to me and I do not report you to the merchant's guild."

"Done!" the vendor's eyes gleamed greedily. Avina and I started to count out our money when Adept Cirrus held up his hand to stop us. "Don't waste your valuable, hard-earned money greasing this one's pocket on what was obviously an accident." He pulled out his money pouch and withdrew five silver pieces and laid them in the palm of the vendor who quickly took the money and ducked into a back room.

"So young one," he placed his hand on Avina's braided head and smiled. "I take it we have learned our lesson and will hold off on dancing in the streets for a while?"

"Yes, Adept Cirrus!" she squeaked. "I mean, no, Adept Cirrus, Sir." She looked upon Cirrus in awe and followed behind him like a puppy who had found a good and kind master. I could understand her eagerness to please, because despite his age he was still pleasing to the eye and generous. He walked with us a ways.

"I'm sorry, Thalia, that we have not gotten anywhere with finding out more about what happened to you." Cirrus slowed his pace and let Avina walk ahead of him until she stopped at a vendor that was selling pretty glass trinkets. "The queen has sent guards looking for signs of the Septori but without more information, we don't know where to start looking. They haven't made themselves known before now."

He seemed generally frustrated at their lack of ability to find the Septori.

"Adept Cirrus, you have been so kind and understanding, and if I remember anything else of importance you will be the first to know." I stopped walking completely and faced him.

Cirrus let out a sigh and looked over my shoulder in defeat. "That's all I ask, Thalia. All I ask is that I be the first to know." Looking back at me, he forced a smile onto his face and waved Avina over to us. "Well, don't let this old man keep you from your shopping; I'm sure you have much more to buy today! And for being good sports and letting an old man enjoy the company of two beautiful women, I feel I must bestow a gift upon you." He pulled two gold coins out of his pouch and handed one to each of us.

Avina's green eyes lit up in excitement as she argued Cirrus's statement. "You're not that old."

Cirrus laughed in merriment. "My young lady, I am old enough to be your father."

"No! She balked. "My father is really *old*. He is thirty five winters!"

"Well, I am thirty eight winters. Therefore I am older than your father and must be considered ancient. By that note, I am halfway to the grave already," he chuckled.

"Avina! Let it go." I smiled as I saw her brain working on a comeback to bring her out of the hole she kept digging herself into.

"Adept Cirrus, thank you for handling the vendor and paying for the fruit, but I really don't think we can accept this."

I offered the gold coin back to him, feeling the weight of it in my hand along with a feeling of guilt.

"Nonsense, Thalia," he interjected. "I'm sorry I wasn't there when the Adept Council first met with you. This is my own way of apologizing that you must work as a servant at the Citadel. It's not the future I would have chosen for you."

He curled my fingers around the gold piece in my hand, the coin's edges burning in implications. "It's guilt money, plain and simple. Mostly because of our lack of results in resolving this horrible conflict with the Septori. We are trying, believe me. We just aren't getting very far."

"You know that isn't necessary." I held the coin back up to him. If I took it, I would somehow be indebted to him. And I did not want that helplessness. I already owed Joss and Darren for saving my life. Cirrus stepped away from my hand, tipped his head in farewell, and disappeared into the crowd of people.

"I didn't thank Cirrus for his gift," Avina said, sticking her small bottom lip out and pretending to look hurt. But recovering in record time, she grabbed my arm and pulled me down the street toward more shops. "Come on, I want you to meet Pim." Racing down the street, she dragged me through numerous twists and turns until we ended up in a dead end alley where we found a young boy of about eight or nine years playing a game with wooden sticks and stones.

Pim wore brown britches that were too big for him with rolled up hems. His blue shirt and yellow vest were speckled with colorful patches, and his bare feet were covered in calluses and dirt.

Despite his appearance and obvious lack of wealth, this young boy's smile was contagious. Avina handed him a pastry that she had saved for him from earlier and promptly plopped herself down on a wooden crate.

"Sorry it's all squished," she grimaced. "I had an incident earlier today."

"Mmfffittsss fokay," he said through a mouth full of food. When he had swallowed his mouthful, he carefully split his pastry in two and set half aside to save it. Looking at me warily he asked, "So, who's your friend?"

"Pim, this is Thalia. Thalia, Pim." She made the introductions perched on her crate, legs swinging in contentment. Looking around she asked, "Where's Jury?"

"Right heeeeeeeeeeeere!" someone shouted, and I heard a small giggle as a little tow-headed girl dropped down from what appeared to be an attic door in a side building of the alley. She landed in a wheelbarrow of straw. The crates we were sitting on were stacked so they could easily access the door and pull it closed behind them.

Rolling out of the straw, Jury was a little thing wearing a dress in about the same shape as Pim's clothes. With pieces of straw sticking out of her hair and clothes every which way, she resembled a moving scarecrow as she ran over and grabbed the other half of Pim's pastry; eating it in two bites.

"Do you live here?" I asked in the kindest way I could.

"Yeah," Pim stated nonchalantly. "It beats being put in a workhouse or orphanage. There would be a good chance Jury and I would be split up if we went there." So that explained it; they were orphans.

Avina leaned over to me and whispered, "Jury is a Denai and neither one wants to be separated from the other yet. So no matter what I do, I can't convince either one to come back with me to the Citadel."

I didn't want to ask them how they survived, because it would seem like I didn't think they could, so I asked something less intrusive. "So how do you get along out here?"

"Oh, Pim works odd jobs doing deliveries," Jury piped up.

I was just about to ask more questions when I heard a low growl from behind us. Looking over my shoulder, I froze in mid-sentence. Five of the largest dogs I have ever seen approached us, baring their teeth. Each dog easily outweighed me by at least 50 pounds and blocked the exit from the alley.

Never in my life had I seen a mixed breed like these—the size of a Dane, the build of a Doberman, and the jaw of a bulldog. I moved across the alley to stand in front of Pim and Jury. The dogs growled threateningly at my movement. The biggest one moved away from the pack and shadowed my movements.

"Avina! I whispered urgently. "Get them up the crates and into the attic, *now!*"

As soon as she moved to help Jury climb, the dogs charged. I grabbed a broken piece of crate, the splinters digging in my palms, and I aimed at the lead dog as it leaped for Jury's leg. I hit him squarely on the nose.

Yelping, the dog backed off and pawed his nose before turning on me again, an angry red gleam in its eye. The other dogs tried to climb the crates after Avina and Jury.

One lunged forward and latched onto my leg. I could feel teeth tear through muscle, and I heard a sickening crunch. Screaming, I tried to kick the dog in the face with my other leg.

Pim raced to my rescue with a large stick and swung it madly at the dog's face. The dog didn't release until Pim used the end to gouge the dog's eye, and it spurted blood. Scrambling up from the ground and leaning most of my weight on my good leg, I tried to block the other dogs from approaching the crates.

Distracted, Pim didn't see the larger dog coming. It pounced on him from behind, knocking him to the ground. I screamed at the dog, swinging my stick wildly in an arc and forcing him to back away from the boy. I had to widen the space. "Get up there!" I ordered.

Pim scampered up the crates as Avina leaned out of the attic, her arms reaching out to grab him. One of the pack dogs, alerted by the movement of fleeing prey, lunged after him snapping and snarling. The dog scrambled up the first crate and then the second as he tried to reach the top and Pim.

"*Jump now!*" I warned as I knocked the crates down onto the dogs. Yelping in pain, they scrambled out of the mess of crates.

Glancing up, I saw that Pim had jumped and Avina had caught his arm. She was even now with Jury's help pulling him into the safety of the attic. I had succeeded at knocking the crates down and saving the kids, but I had inadvertently blocked my only chance for escape. Now between the exit and me were the pile of crates and a pack of dogs that were now mad with blood lust.

They circled me, snarling, with drool dripping from their canines. Strange. There were only four dogs, not five.

Avina screamed my name as a huge weight on my back knocking me to the ground. My head smacked into the street hard enough that I saw stars. Instinctively, I curled into a fetal position to try and protect the exposed nape of my neck as I waited for the sting of five pairs of raging teeth on my flesh.

The snarling continued. I waited for the end, but nothing touched me. A hurt yelp reached my ears, and I opened my eyes to a knife inches away from my face dripping with blood. I gasped, but then realized it wasn't coming closer. The knife was held by a black clad man, hunched down in a fighting stance, protecting me from the pack of dogs. Two feet away, a dog lay prone, blood pooling around him, eyes glazing over in death. Another dog charged, leaping in the air and aiming for the man's throat. The man brought his arm down, knocking the dog to the ground and simultaneously bringing his knife down into the back of the neck.

As he pulled the blade out of the dog, the man spared me a glance. Kael. I recognized those intense blue eyes. My heart sang in joy that he was alive, and it cried in sorrow as the remaining three dogs leaped toward him as one.

With a flick of his wrist Kael flung a throwing knife from his arm sheath. The brown dog stopped midair and fell to the ground, the handle protruding from its chest.

The other two dogs landed on Kael, pulling him to the ground. Using the knife in his left hand, he slashed the smaller dog in the face while the bloodied-eyed leader locked his jaws around his right arm, shaking his head back and forth.

Kael grunted in pain, keeping the leader away from his throat with his arm and devoting his attention to the smaller dog also aiming for his jugular. Kael wasn't giving in. He slashed at both dogs until the smaller one felt the sting of the blade one too many times and finally backed away, running down the alley, tailed tucked between his legs.

He had only one opponent left now, and his arm was being jerked and his torso shredded by the enraged dog's paws. I cried out Kael's name in worry. In one fluid motion, Kael flipped the handle of the knife in his hand and stabbed the dog in his already gouged and bloody eye, forcing the tip into his brain. The dog twitched once, twice, and then quit moving all together.

The blood rushed back into my body, and I breathed a sigh of relief and watched Kael sit up and push the dog's lifeless corpse off of his body.

Kael had put on muscle in the last month. Even covered in blood, he still looked handsome—not to mention dangerous. The difference this time was that Kael was armed to the teeth with knives, blades, and arm sheaths. I wondered briefly where he had gotten them; they looked like they belonged on him. His black vest survived, but the dogs had shredded the under shirt. From the amount of blood seeping out no doubt that his torso was equally shredded.

Kael came over, kneeled by me, and inspected the damage to my leg without touching me. My leg was a bloody mess, but I would survive. I was more concerned with the blood I saw oozing out of his stomach and disappearing into the folds of his dark black pants. The blackness of his clothes disguised the blood and other injuries I knew he must have been hiding. I reached for his stomach and opened my mouth to ask about his own injuries, when he flinched from my touch and interrupted me.

"So, you're still getting into dangerous situations that you can't get yourself out of." His brows furrowed and he wouldn't look me in the eye. My arm dropped limply to my side.

"*What?*" I was dumbfounded. It was the absolute last thing I expected to hear. This was all wrong; this is not how I pictured a reunion with Kael to be. If I pictured a reunion at all, considering I didn't even know if he was alive. I looked at his face more closely and noticed he had a cut along his cheek. His square jaw had drops of blood on it, but obviously no damage to his head to blame the sudden moodiness on.

"Here, put this on the bites. It will keep it from getting infected until you get back to the Citadel." He handed me a small leather pouch, which I unfolded to find a salve that smelled like cat urine. The smell distracted me from even asking how he knew where I was staying.

"Ugh, no thank you. I would rather wait until I can see a healer," I pushed the pouch back at him.

He grabbed the pouch and ordered, "You *will* put this on. I won't argue with you." He flung it at me instead of handing it to me, which only made me grit my teeth in stubborn refusal. My head pounded and I started to feel a throbbing ache in my leg.

"I will not! Even if it smelled of roses, I wouldn't put it on because of how callous you are being toward me. What have I done to you?" I tried to stand and collapsed, crying out in pain, realizing that my leg was hurt worse than I thought.

Once again he reached out as if to help me but stopped before he made contact with my skin, his blue eyes changing from anger, to worry and then back to stubbornness. "You need to learn to be more careful. I won't always be here to watch out for you when you decide to get cozy with a pack of dogs." Before I could even think up a mean retort, Kael held out his hand to silence me.

Curiously, I watched as he cocked his head, listening to something in the distance. He burst into action. He ran, pulled his knives out of the dead dogs, jumped onto two of the crates, and leapt onto the roof of a building. He was gone.

"Thalia! Are you okay?" I looked away from where Kael had disappeared over the roof and saw that Avina, Pim and Jury were running down the alley with what I assumed was a group of city guards. Dressed in dark uniforms, they rode closely on the children's heels. Dismounting at the entrance to the alley, they started on foot toward us.

"I'll live," I smiled sheepishly at her. "How did you guys get down from the attic?"

"We crawled out through another door that let us drop down onto a roof the next building over, but we had to hurry across a couple of rooftops until we could find another way down. We were running for help, and we ran into the commander."

The commander was bald with a gray beard, and before I was finished studying him, he'd taken charge, giving orders to some of his men to remove and burn the dead dog's carcasses. His eyes were quick and calculating, his face and hands showed faded scars of previous battles, and his towering frame left little doubt as to who was in charge.

Commander Meryl leaned down and looked at my leg. "Are you all right?"

I nodded, still confused over what had happened and the reason Kael disappeared. Rising, the commander called over another of his men and gave orders for a splint. He picked up the leather pouch that Kael had thrown to the ground by my feet and opened it, giving it a quick sniff before declaring it an ointment.

"It's a good thing you had this on you. Those dogs may have had rabies, and this will kill any foreign bacteria." He immediately started to apply the salve to my leg and all I could do was mentally grumble and complain that even though he wasn't here, Kael had won this round.

"It's called Hartswood, and it's great for horses and cattle when they get any serious cuts or scrapes."

"I'm not cattle!" I interjected.

The commander threw his head back and laughed. His deep laugh was reassuring even if it was at my expense. "Relax, it's also good for human wounds; it keeps away infection." He looked at me, his face going serious and still. "I'm not sure why those dogs attacked you. But my guess is that they were sick or diseased. In any case, this attack was highly unusual. But how did you kill them?"

A soldier with red blonde hair brought over strips of bandages and large pieces of the splintered crate. He expertly wrapped my leg to keep it still.

"I didn't," I said through clenched teeth, trying not to cry out from the pain. My tears betrayed me as they leaked out the side of my eyes. Seeing my discomfort, the commander let the question drop and opted to get me back to the citadel.

"Let's load up!" the commander yelled.

I looked around to see that Pim and Jury had made themselves scarce; Avina fluttered around trying to help an attractive young soldier, bringing him wood and tinder. The alley was lit up with a bonfire made from the broken crates and the burning canines. The smell of the burning flesh and hair made me sick to my stomach. A few soldiers stayed behind to control the fire as the rest made ready for departure.

When we were ready to leave, the commander handed me up into the arms of a mounted soldier. I noticed immediately that it was the one with the reddish blonde hair who had bandaged my leg. He carefully adjusted me so I sat sidesaddle and didn't put any weight on my injured leg. Grabbing the reins, he followed the commander out of the alley.

Avina, I noticed, sat in front of the same soldier she had been fawning over earlier. She caught my eye and gave me a huge smirk. Looking back at the soldier who skillfully maneuvered the horse through the maze of people, I noticed he had a slight scar on his chin.

"So what did you do to attract the attention of a pack of dogs?" His question was sincere and without accusation, but it brought to mind a different conversation altogether.

"I'm a rat, and that's what rats do—attract the attention of dogs." I spoke without thinking, letting Syrani's earlier comment rankle. Partially because of the pain, partially because I was now somber and morose from Kael's unreasonable cruelty.

He chuckled. "Well then, that must make you the prettiest, not to mention the luckiest, rat I've ever seen. Though I would have to say, not the best smelling. You smell like cat urine. No wonder you attracted the dogs."

"That is because of the smelly salve Commander Meryl applied," I said defensively. "Not because of my lack of hygiene!"

"Don't worry, I won't tell," he snickered good-naturedly. Then when he regained his composure he introduced himself. "I'm Garit…or Garit the Great would suffice as well, considering I'm the best to have around in case of major injury and a healer isn't near," he boasted. "And whom do I have the privilege of escorting to the healing ward?"

I told him my name and what happened in the alley but left out Kael's name. I'm not sure why I was protecting moody Kael, but I figured if he didn't want to stay around and meet the soldiers he must have a good reason. Keeping his name to myself was the least I could do, considering he had saved my life twice now.

Garit chatted amicably the whole way back, making comments about Avina and her very evident crush on the young guard Niklas. The shock of the whole attack wore off, and I began to feel the pain in my leg and torn muscles. The headache persisted the whole way back to the keep until I fell

Chanda Hahn

asleep against Garit's chest to the motion of the horse's gait and the sound of his lighthearted voice.

~8~

Voices arguing, while trying to maintain a whisper, woke me from a deep sleep. I could see it was Healer Prentiss from the night before, wearing her white smock over her simple pale skirt and top. She was the shortest woman I had ever met, with kind hazel eyes and chestnut hair pulled into a twist at the nape of her neck. Laugh wrinkles around her eyes and mouth betrayed her age. I barely remembered the actual trip to the healing wing because I was so weary from all of the excitement.

But I remember seeing Healer Prentiss in all her healer's glory the night before, as she directed the soldier carrying me to a small bed and gathered the students that were on duty in the healing wing. Even though I was a servant, I learned the schedule and workings of the training grounds and council rooms. The best way to learn about healing was for the students to practice it as much as they could and so they were put on an on-call rotation to work in the healing wing. So whenever a non-emergency occurred, the students were notified and present to help heal and learn. I guess a broken leg constituted a non-emergency.

Ever the efficient teacher, Healer Prentiss explained to the students as she drew energy and touched my leg around the gash marks. "First you must use your gift to look for infection and foreign objects and pull those from the wound. And now if you look closely, you can see the patient's body already trying to heal itself."

I quickly learned that once I was in the healing ward, I was no longer Thalia but a nameless patient. It was easier for the students to concentrate and learn if they weren't distracted by the emotional stories and names tied to the subject they were healing.

"First, we have to set the bone, which is always a painful process. Only then can we help the muscles knit together and speed along the healing process." Healer Prentiss spoke in a matter of fact tone of voice. "All right, we have enough student healers here that we can conserve energy and split you up. Some of you siphon off her pain; others work on the healing process."

A nervous student spoke up, "But Healer Prentiss, wouldn't we normally need to do this by ourselves? I mean, what if someone was hurt and there wasn't anyone else to rely on?"

Healer Prentiss looked displeased and harried by the question. Obviously, she wanted to hurry and start the healing process, her healing instincts making her short tempered with the interruptions. "If the injury weren't really bad one person could do it, but healing is very hard work and takes more energy than anything else. A Master adept would have no problem healing numerous people, but that cannot be said of a student. The pain could be too much for one student to bear alone; by spreading it out, it lessens the pain. Also, more healers working together can prevent one Denai from burning out." Her pointed glare made the nervous girl step back behind the other students. "Now if there are no more interruptions, we will begin."

No one spoke or even breathed.

Prentiss put a long cylinder of cork between my teeth, and I stared at the wooden ceiling as two grim-faced students stood on each side of me and grasped my hands. I could see them mentally preparing themselves to siphon the pain from me and into them. Knowing that this was going to be a painful process no matter how much power they used, I felt sick to my stomach.

I spit out the cork, shook my head, and yelled "No! Back away. I don't want you to go through this. I can take the pain." I closed my eyes to stop the tears from escaping my eyes. "Healer Prentiss please don't make them. They shouldn't have to go through this." I was overreacting; I knew that if both students pulled the pain away, it wouldn't be as intense. But after being the recipient of numerous tortures all against my will, I didn't ever want to inflict pain on anyone again. Not if I had a choice.

Healer Prentiss gave me a long, calculating look as if she were trying to read my thoughts. She must have understood my desire, because she signaled to the students, and both of my hands were dropped onto the bed. I lay back down and faced the wooden ceiling. Taking a deep breath and closing my eyes, I mentally prepared myself for what was coming. Again I felt someone pick up my hand, and even though I tried to pull it away, they wouldn't release it.

"Please, let go!" I pleaded. Wearily I turned my head toward the student and opened my eyes. I met the determined gaze of Joss.

"Hey, little fish," he said. "You may not want me to take the pain away and I'm not sure why, but I can guess." He leaned forward and whispered, "But there's no way in Heaven I'm letting go of you. So don't even ask." He brought up his other hand and enclosed my cold shaking hand between his large warm ones. How had I missed his handsome face among the students? I must be in more pain than I had realized. Of course, Joss didn't really need these classes, I could give first hand testimony to the strength of his healing abilities, but rules were rules.

"We're ready, Healer Prentiss," he nodded to her, and she aligned herself by my leg. I stared up at the now familiar ceiling and almost fainted from the pain of the bone being set.

Crying out, I immediately went into shock which sent my mind right back into the memories of the torture chamber. I began to relive all of it while I was wide awake and the pain wouldn't stop. All of the students gathered around me, their healing robes blurring to take on the form of the Septori.

A second adjustment on my leg, and the headache that had been plaguing me for weeks pounded mercilessly against my skull. Agony ripped through my head and body, and the precarious dam that I had built to hold back the floodgate of memories and pain…broke.

I screamed. I grasped Joss's hand hard as I tried to escape the terror and agony. I heard Joss call my name, but my world was consumed by pain as memory after vivid memory assaulted me. I tried to reach for Joss to help me, but I couldn't feel his hand in mine anymore. I searched and pulled until I connected with him again. But it wouldn't stop the memories of prison, the beatings, Raven, the cold hard table, the machine that was always thirsty for my blood, all of them.

I felt again the agony as the machine came to life with the current of energy pulsing through it. My body started to spontaneously convulse on the healer's table as if I were still in the machine.

For a split second, I saw Joss white-faced and in shock in the torture room with me, and then it was gone. I was falling into a black abyss of nothingness, and I wanted to let it consume me. To close my eyes forever and let the darkness take me, because then—and only then—would the pain end.

Slowly, my body quit falling. Warmth engulfed me, and the pain ebbed away. I felt myself floating in a warm pool of colorful energy, surrounded by the purest light.

The images of torture and pain faded away and then disappeared altogether. I saw colors floating above me and around me, and then they passed through me. My body began to feel tingly all over as if I was just waking up from a deep sleep.

"Thalia!" I heard Joss calling my name but I felt so comfortable in the pool of light, I didn't want to wake up.

"Little Fish!" he called again.

That's it. Now I was irritated. I was going to wake up and give him a piece of my mind, for giving me that ridicules nickname. I urged my body to follow the flow of lights out of the pool. Somewhat lost, I walked along a rainbow of energy until I felt my body finally begin to respond.

I opened my eyes. Joss was still holding my hand. He brushed my hair away from my forehead.

"I hate that," I mumbled.

"Hate what?" Joss questioned.

"Little fish!" I said. I could barely keep my eyes open. It was as if I weren't fully awake, just barely treading on consciousness. "It's stupid and childish, you should know." After I felt I made my point, I let my body and mind go into a deep, dark sleep.

Well, until a few minutes ago when the whispered argument woke me up.

Healer Prentiss was holding back a furious Joss, who was trying to push through her hands and get to me.

"Joss, you know that we shouldn't talk to her until the Adept Council does," she implored. "We are not even really sure what happened."

"But don't you think someone should explain to her what happened, so she doesn't have to face the adepts unprepared?" There was anger hidden underneath his voice and something else. Fear.

My ears perked up and I snapped to full awareness. I was prepared to report to the adepts about the dog attack, but I had a feeling that wasn't what he was referring to.

"The point is she lied!" Prentiss sounded miffed.

"Don't forget that Darren and I found her." He gave a pointed look at Prentiss. "I know the condition that she was found in. I was the one that had to heal her wounds while she was unconscious. She had internal bleeding for goodness sake, and after last night I have firsthand knowledge of what she went through. *I know* she didn't lie. And I'm prepared to prove it." He pushed Prentiss to the side and walked to the side of my bed, stopping short when he realized I was awake and had heard everything.

"Hi," I said meekly, unsure of what I was about to hear.

"Hey, little fish," he retorted with a sad grin as he pulled a chair over to my bed and straddled it, leaning his bulky frame upon it.

"I *told* you—"

"Yeah, I know. No more stupid nicknames. I just wanted to be sure that you remembered saying that last night." He paused. "Actually, I wanted to know how much of last night you remember."

"All of it," I intoned sadly. "Though I don't really understand what exactly happened."

Healer Prentiss jumped in. "It's my fault really. I should have given you medicine to numb the pain since you refused the students' help. But I was in such a hurry." Her hands fluttered nervously as if she batted an imaginary fly away. She took a deep breath, apparently steeling herself for what she was about to say. "It seems that when we went to set the bone, the pain triggered some…well, you started convulsing." She stopped speaking and shook her head, bewildered.

"Go on," I prompted her.

"Joss held on and tried pulling the pain from you, but it wasn't enough. Your mind was injured." And with a disapproving glare at Joss, she continued. "He then, without permission or training, tried to heal the pain in your mind."

Joss nodded. "I know, it was stupid of me, but I could see that you were in terrible pain and I did the only thing I could think of. I tried to pull the memories from you, only to be overtaken by them."

I looked at Joss in astonishment, speechless. "I thought I saw you there, in the room with me. How…?"

"I was there, Thalia. I saw it all. I saw that machine they used on you, the one that looked like a giant iron butterfly." He looked grim as he asked, "Was that what it was like for you? Did they put you in it often?"

Feeling ashamed that he witnessed some of my worst memories, all I could do was nod my head. "I'm so sorry Joss. You shouldn't have had to see that." I covered my face with my hands in humiliation. "Those were some of the most degrading moments of my life." My cheeks burned. "There were times I wished for death."

I flinched as his fingers met my skin.

"I'm sorry," I said quickly. "It's a habit."

"No, Thalia, I'm sorry. I should not have touched you. I should know how sensitive you are to being touched after witnessing what you went through. After Darren and I found you, I often stayed awake at night and wondered what happened to you. And now that I know," he paused, as if he couldn't go on.

"It's all right," I tried to console him, because I knew how he felt.

"No, it's not," he was becoming frustrated with himself. "It's almost as if…" He grabbed his head with his hands and stared at me with his intense, blue eyes. I saw my own pain mirrored back at me. "I wish now I didn't know. I wish I could take it all back. That's all I can see now when I look at you. It's torture for me to see you in that much pain, to see what you went through. I can feel how much you distrust me and are scared of us."

He may as well have punched me in the gut. It was a wish I had made a hundred times over. And here I was hoping that Joss would be able to understand me a little better, but as soon as he spoke those words, I felt as if a giant crevasse in the ground opened up and split us apart. He didn't want to know. He didn't care, not really.

I turned my head as if, by blocking the sight of Joss, I could block the pain and maybe erase what he said. The pain was overwhelming. I was being swallowed up and the one person who might have taken it away, who could have helped me through it, now refused the pain and memories.

"And because now there's the other problem."

His words forced my gaze back to him, but he looked away from me unwilling to make eye contact.

"What?" I asked Joss when he didn't respond. I looked to Healer Prentiss and her eyes dropped to the floor. "Please!"

I begged. "Please tell me what has happened. Is Joss in trouble because he read my mind? Tell me what's going on."

"Thalia," he spoke slowly, as if speaking to a child. "I didn't read your mind or memories; it's not one of my gifts." He stopped and looked me dead in the eye. "Whatever happened, I didn't do it. You did. I felt myself go weak and watched helplessly while you ripped away my defenses and in a surge of power I've never felt before, overtook me. I was there because you dragged me there."

~9~

"**We** have a serious problem here." Adept Lorna stated firmly.

We were once again in the Adept Council's meeting room, only this time all of the adepts were in attendance as well as three guards who escorted me from the infirmary. Even now, they stood guard out in the hall, in case I tried to escape.

And in that moment, that's exactly what I felt like doing. You could feel the tension in the air and I found it hard to breathe. I was given a wooden chair because even though the healers had mended and set the bones in my leg, I was still weak. The chair was also much needed support because Joss's words were still echoing in my mind. I hadn't believed him at first, and well, I still didn't believe him.

Nervous, I scratched my healed leg, still feeling the itchy warmth of newly re-knitted muscles. I watched Lorna stand and address the adepts.

She gave the Adept Council Healer Prentiss and Joss's report of what had happened the previous night. I watched as Breah's face paled and then become wary. Her cute pixie face would bob in my direction, and then look away as if she was afraid to make eye contact.

Pax Baton was frowning so hard, I could almost imagine a stormy cloud gathering above his head. Kambel was by far the most excited at the news, and he twitched with excitement, jumping across the table for a spare scrap of parchment, pulling a spare quill and ink set from a hidden pocket in his robe. He immediately started to document this whole affair; after all, this was historic. Cirrus and Lorna were the most calm, with Cirrus being openly curious and thoughtful and Lorna being nothing but cautious.

Lorna continued speaking in a monotone voice. "We offered Thalia shelter and work here because she wasn't a threat, just a child that had, for all intents and purposes, been abused. She was a normal human girl who we deemed safe to have among us. But apparently, through the Septori's experiments, we can say that is no longer true. We don't have any clue to what else the Raven has done to her except that he has succeeded in changing the child."

"She's an abomination, the antithesis of everything that we stand for. I think she was sent as a deliberate spy!" Breah spat out. "Why else do you think she's here?"

"So the experiments worked! Now what? Nothing like this has ever happened before in Calandry or anywhere else in the world," Kambel interrupted. "The Great Council ruled any experiments on Denai or humans to be outlawed. It is considered a serious crime to tamper with either."

"So are we going to hold a child responsible for something done to her without her consent?" Pax Baton intoned with his deep voice. "That would be a crime in and of itself."

Even though Pax looked every bit an assassin or killer, his sense of conviction when it came to right and wrong made me look at him with silent respect. His large frame held an intelligent mind. And though his body language bespoke a quick fighter, he was slow to make any hasty judgments.

"No!" Lorna firmly stated. "And I think I speak for the Council when I say that it would be wrong to punish her for something done against her will." Unanimous nods went around the table, except for Breah. Lorna took a deep breath and looked right at me. "First, we must decide if she is a threat—to us, to Queen Lilyana, to the people of Calandry."

"Well, what is she actually capable of?" Cirrus interjected for the first time. "Mayhap it was a fluke or residual effects that will fade in time."

Five heads turned in my direction waiting for an answer.

My skin itched under their wary gazes. I myself wanted to know the answer. I could barely get my voice to work. "I don't know. I was told that I pulled Joss into my memories." I tried to make myself look as unthreatening as possible and shrunk back into my chair.

"That's not exactly what happened, Thalia." Lorna spoke softly.

"I'll tell you what happened!" Breah spoke up heatedly. "I was the one that interviewed the young man named Joss. What the Raven has done is created something twisted, broken and unholy. He has created a monster!" The way Breah yelled the word monster made me flinch, but only for a moment as she picked up her heated debate with much more fervor. "She ripped the power from a student and then imprisoned him in her memories. He said he could feel his power being siphoned off and that he was weakened, helpless to defend himself without fear of hurting her. We can't trust her; she could steal all of the student's power and then turn against us. Or worse, we know that our power is connected to our physical being. If she hadn't stopped she could have drained all of his powers and killed him. She needs to be locked up, for our own protection!"

Breah was standing to address the room. She was beautiful in her righteous anger, a vision of inspiration. I was almost swayed by her words until I realized she was speaking about me.

"*Breah*!" Pax barked. "You are not allowed to use compulsion in the meeting rooms, we have said this before." I shook my head and all of a sudden Breah didn't look as beautiful and awe inspiring. Suddenly, I realized what her gift was. She had the ability to persuade others—even compel them.

I had to speak up. "I have no recollection of doing it, nor do I know how it was done. I don't even think I could do it again. Lorna, you believe me, right?"

"Thalia, I know that when I read your mind I didn't sense any deceit. But remember, there is a whole section of your mind that is gone." She turned back to the adepts. "I can say this to you: the student Joss will vouch for her and swears that she is harmless and has shown no ill will toward anyone here."

"He barely knows her; we can't take that into account," Pax Baton remarked. "But I think we are missing something important. She may not be the only one out there like her. What if he has done this with more humans?"

Cirrus stood up and looked at Pax. "What are you implying?"

Pax was a born and bred fighter and could see hidden implications that the others could not. "What I'm saying, my dear friend, Cirrus, is what if he is trying a race of humans that was stronger, swifter, more powerful than any single Denai in Calandry. It was reported that she broke through his defenses fairly easily. What if this man is creating an army of humans like her?"

"Then we are looking at war!" Cirrus dropped to his seat, face turning pale. His hands started to shake visibly. "We may have time to prevent it, if we can find him and stop these awful experiments," he spoke slowly. "There may be hope to prevent war."

"What about now? What is to become of her?" Breah kept readjusting her skirt around her feet. "We can't continue to keep her here."

"Of course, you ninny, she has to stay here!" Kambel said, flying from his seat. "Don't you understand? She's the only one of her kind as of this minute that we know of. She's unique; she's irreplaceable and should be studied. If more are created, we can study her and thereby understand their weaknesses and how to stop them."

"*No!*" I yelled.

I had sat patiently long enough, listening to them go back and forth discussing me. Jumping up, I startled the adepts. "I refuse to be scrutinized or studied like some sort of experiment. I would rather live on the street than stay here."

"She mustn't leave. She must be dealt with." Breah paled. "She could endanger all the Denai. She's an abomination, I tell you." I had no idea what she was talking about, but I headed for the door.

"And what do you propose we do?" Pax yelled back. "Kill her?"

He squared off against the small doll-like Breah who pursed her lips in thought and looked directly at Pax. "Why yes. If it comes to that, she's dangerous."

"Stop it! Both of you!" Lorna spoke, her voice echoing with power throughout the room. "We must consider all options."

I made it to the heavy, wooden doors, and pulled on them, but they wouldn't budge. I was locked in. Feeling a moment of alarm, I started to pound and kick the doors, but they were held fast. Turning, I looked for the key hole; there was no lock on the door. The adepts were keeping the doors closed by their power.

"I'm sorry, child," Cirrus said, rising from his seat and placing himself squarely in front of me. "You are an enigma, a puzzle, an unknown, and to the human population that is a terrifying factor. To counteract the rumors that are going to be spread about you--and believe me there will be rumors—it would be best if we understood you better, and that might require careful documentation." He rested his hand gently on my shoulder and turned me to face the others. "Can you imagine if others found out that you somehow acquired or stole powers that you weren't born with, and that you could possibly steal more? It wouldn't be safe for you in Calandry. People may try to hurt you."

"But I didn't steal anything," I shrugged defensively. "Don't forget that I was the victim here."

"But they won't understand that. For your safety, it would be best if you stayed here, under our protection. Maybe we can find a cure or a way to reverse what was done." Adept Cirrus spoke to me like a father calming a frightened child.

"There's one thing I don't understand?" Kambel said nervously, taking off his spectacles and cleaning them before donning them again. "How come the mercury stone didn't recognize her? It is able to distinguish the Denai blood the same way Cassiel does. So does that mean she doesn't carry any of the normal Denai gifts? If that's so, we don't know the range of her abilities or if she is a threat to us."

I felt my heart quicken in dread at the implication. Here it comes, I panicked. The guards, torture, death. My palms were sweaty with perspiration, so I gripped the door handle harder turning it desperately, while shrugging off Cirrus's hand from my shoulder.

"There's an easy way to find out!" Breah stated. She stood up, pulled energy toward her, forming it into a ball of blue fire, and walked determinedly over to my chair, her lips pressed into a thin, straight line. The slight tick of her jaw betrayed the amount of control she was using to keep her emotions in check, but I could read the animosity in her eyes.

I turned to face her, my hands never releasing their hold on the cold door handle. I wanted to cry out in frustration as escape was within my grasp, literally, if I could only open the stupid door. It wasn't even locked and I still couldn't open it. I looked over my shoulder at her ice cold stare and felt that this truly was the end.

Closing my eyes, I prayed for a quick and merciful death, but opened them at the last second. Movement caught my eye.

"Stop!" a clear voice commanded.

I watched the blue fireball stop a hand span away from my face. I sat mesmerized as it danced and fluttered in her open palm. Breah's eyes blazed angrily, she swallowed and slowly closed her fingers and the ball shrank until it was the size of a fly and then disappeared.

The ugly tapestry of the hunter and the horse on the wall began to move. A small, feminine hand pushed it aside, and a beautiful woman with red hair and blue eyes stepped from behind it. Her dress was of the finest blue silk, and a cloak covered her shoulders. It wasn't until I saw the circlet upon her brow that I realized I was in the presence of Queen Lilyana.

Queen Lilyana left the alcove that was obviously her listening room and Commander Meryl followed close behind her. It struck me that I had seen her before when I first came to the school. And that I had seen her leave Lorna's office. She must frequently sit in on the Adept Council's discussions, protected from sight by the tapestry. No wonder Breah would shoot nasty looks at the tapestry when no one was looking. But it didn't explain why the queen was here now.

She stood before me, and I began to fidget, uncomfortable in her presence. "You won't hurt me, will you?" Her voice was neither soft, nor uncertain.

"No, ma'am, I mean, your Highness." I stumbled on the words, still reeling from being in the presence of royalty. She smiled sweetly at my ignorance. "Do you plan on harming anyone here in Haven?"

I shook my head so hard I could hear my teeth rattle.

"I have heard all you have had to say, and I do not take this decision lightly. I really do believe that because of these unfortunate changes in circumstances, we have no other choice but to keep her here. I'm sorry, Thalia." She looked grim, her brow furrowed. "You leave us with no alternative. You must stay here permanently until we release you."

A grin curled her lips. "Or until you graduate from our training program."

~10~

My jaw dropped in disbelief. This was the last thing that I expected. My heart felt like it was trying to escape my chest and the fingernails of my hand maintained a death grip on the door handle so I wouldn't slide onto the floor in a faint of relief.

Glancing at Lorna to be sure I had heard right and that my life wasn't forfeit, I saw a look of satisfaction in her eyes and a hint of mischief. The ever intimidating Adept Pax Baton was nodding his head in agreement, while Breah sniffed in disdain, tracing a stain in the wood of the table with her dainty nail. Her actions shouldn't surprise me, but somehow they did. Maybe it was because she was the youngest member of the Adept Council and, being young, she tended to wear her emotions openly on her sleeve. Or maybe it was because she felt she had to prove herself to them and was wary of anything that would cause problems.

And to her, I think I posed the biggest threat.

I was beginning to feel cautious of Kambel. I wanted to stay as far from him as possible for I had a feeling that if I walked past him, he would poke me with a stick just to see my reaction and response time. And record it. That thought alone made me shudder. Cirrus, I had mixed feelings about, his help in the marketplace showed he was a caring person, but I couldn't find any faults with him, which made him seem too perfect.

"That settles it, you will enroll in the training program and start to learn everything you can from the teachers about your powers and how to use them," Adept Lorna smiled, looking excited about Queen Lilyana's decision.

"You can't be serious, Lorna. That would be unwise; you are going to teach her the secrets of the Denai? What if she runs straight back to the Septori? This could lead to the end of the Denai!" Breah had finished pouting and was up for another round.

"What if you are wrong?" Adept Lorna turned on Breah. "What if she is the answer? What if she is the future? Maybe she can help us understand why we are going extinct."

"We are not going extinct!" Breah shouted. "I happen to come from a long line—"

"Oh shut up, Breah!" Adept Kambel spoke up. The room became still as everyone stared in astonishment at the small adept, whom Thalia could not have imagined raising his voice.

A small twinkling laugh erupted from the Queen, followed by more laughter from Lorna.

Adept Kambel gazed around at the shocked faces of Pax and Breah, and cleared his throat in embarrassment. "I believe Lorna is right. We are going extinct, and if we can't stop the Septori, then they will create more like her. It's best if she helps us as much as she can by understanding her abilities to the fullest. Maybe then we can know what we are up against; as long as she promises to not hurt or endanger any student against their will."

All I could do was shake my head since I was still in shock that Kambel had stood up to Breah. I guess taking a few classes wouldn't hurt, as long as I could control myself and not hurt anyone either.

With the queen's decision made, I was ordered to go and pack my belongings so that I could be moved once again. This time into the student wing of the Citadel, with a warning to never intentionally harm another Denai student.

Lorna nodded to Pax, then took my elbow and led me out the door into the hall. The door opened for her without her even touching it. Proof that she was probably the one holding it closed.

They weren't done discussing me I was sure, and they never even mentioned the attack with the dogs. But in their mind that must be considered a small problem that Commander Meryl could deal with. They were more worried about the fact that there was now a potential for others like me if they didn't find the Raven and stop his experiments.

Queen Lilyana had established the training program at the Citadel because the Denai were slowly disappearing from the world. She was loved by all and had a special place in her heart for the Denai, particularly. This gave the people of Calandry a skewed view of the Denai. They called them the queen's pets. I had heard the slur whispered often enough on the streets.

Lorna had led me toward my rooms but stopped when we were almost there and spoke quietly to me. "Thalia, it would be better if you didn't tell anyone about what happened to you. Try to fit in and don't draw attention to yourself."

"How do you want me to do that?" I asked.

"Pretend to be a Denai."

"You want me to lie? I look nothing like you!" I scoffed loudly. Almost too loud, since Lorna winced and looked around. My head spun at what she wanted me to do. I was unsure about this; I didn't want to deceive anyone. I was already an outcast as it was.

And how was I to fit in? All of the Denai were beautiful, some more than others, but I knew that I fell short in that category. By my looks alone, no one would believe I was a Denai.

"Yes, do what you must, but hide what you are from the others."

"But what am I? How can I pretend to be a Denai, if I'm not? How do you expect me to live this lie and attend classes and not participate? I don't want to hurt anyone any more than you do. In fact, I would take it all back if I could."

"I'm sure you will figure a way to practice without harming anyone." She looked at me slowly, her eyes trying to convey what she couldn't voice.

My head reeled with hidden meanings and implications. "But you heard the rest of the Council. I've been forbidden without their consent."

Adept Lorna's eyes softened and she whispered as if to herself. "Exactly, without their consent. I'm sure there is someone you know that is devoted enough to help you, if you let him. Just don't let the others know. But you need to practice."

"No!"

Lorna's eyes blinked at me in surprise. "What do you mean, no?" Clearly, she hadn't expected me to argue with her.

"Exactly that. No! I refuse to use Joss that way. I will find another alternative." I was beginning to hate myself.

"Fine, do whatever you want. I was only trying to help you," she snapped.

"No, I think you are trying to use me too. And I won't have it." I stormed off, not even caring where I was headed as long as it was away from her, away from everyone. It was too much—the politics, the schemes, the lies.

I wandered for hours until I ended up back at my room. I was actually sad to have to say goodbye to it. And even though I would be transferred to what would be my third room since my stay at the Citadel, I had felt most at home here, with Avina's bright chatter to break up my too-frequent bouts of quiet depression.

I moved to the closet and removed my few belongings and felt a moment of alarm. I realized I didn't know where Berry's gift went after the attack.

My hands flew to my pockets and found them bare. I conjured a picture of it lying in the street being trampled by the horses, and I felt my heart plummet. I slowly closed the closet door, holding my possessions when I noticed something sitting on my pillow. It was the satchel I had thought lost! Oh, Avina! Thank the stars! She must have picked it up.

I heard a quick rap on my door—Forrest announcing his arrival. I deposited the pouch gently into the basket on top of my other belongings, and I paused to scribble a quick note to Avina, explaining that I was being moved into the student wings and not to worry that I hadn't disappeared. I was worried she would return to see a barren room and fear the worst had happened to me.

Maybe it would have been better if I hadn't made it out alive. I quickly pushed those negative thoughts aside.

Grabbing my basket, I carried it out to the hallway and followed Forrest to my new room.

Since my duties had never included housekeeping, I never ventured into the housing wing. Why risk running into Syrani?

I was immediately taken aback by the difference. The servants' halls were simple and utilitarian. Nothing extravagant was needed. The student's wing was opulent. A plush, brightly colored runner lined the hall, adding warmth to the stone floor.

Forrest stopped at an end room and opened the large wooden door into what I first thought was another meeting room because of its vastness, but it was to be mine.

The room had high vaulted ceilings, and a pair of large arched windows filled my room with light. The walls had simple, pale green paisley wallpaper. The room held the largest bed I had ever seen, covered with a down comforter in a soft, pale blue with a sturdy, dark trunk at the foot. A sizeable wooden desk and bookshelf aligned one wall while a fireplace with a plush, blue reading chair was on the other. The window seats were adorned with pale yellow pillows. A small table and chairs were tucked away on one side and a large armoire completed the room.

I walked across the floor, my feet sinking into the beautiful rugs. The windows looked out onto the quiet rolling meadows of the gardens and a horse's field. I could hear running water from the fountain below, and the sound was soothing.

I was frozen in awe and had to look at Forrest to make sure he had taken me to the right room. It wasn't just a room; it was living quarters. Of course, I shook my head in realization, this is where I would live, study, and eat for the next few years. The Adept Council would want to make their students as comfortable as possible. The room wasn't overly extravagant, just large. And since there were so few students, I wouldn't even have to share.

I thanked Forrest again as he left, bobbing his head, and I turned the big key in the lock. I put my belongings in the trunk and headed toward the window seat.

The other students would be heading for a noon meal, but I decided to skip it altogether. It would be awkward with too many questions, and I wasn't ready to face Joss. How would I simply go from serving breakfast to having servants of my own?

Letting everything from the past couple of days sink in, I stared out the window at the countryside and wished to be wholly human again.

~II~

When my growling stomach finally forced me out of my room. I darted to the kitchen to grab some food, thankful that it was still the weekend and classes would resume tomorrow. So the place was deserted, almost. Taking a peek into the kitchen, I saw Donn tending the fires and laying out the bread to rise for tomorrow. Breathing a sigh of relief, I entered and sat at the kitchen table and waited for him to notice me.

"Ahh, so the prodigal has returned." He smiled and pushed a tray of leftover meat and cheese toward me with a loaf of rye bread. Cutting the bread in half, I put a couple slices of ham and cheese between the bread and took a bite. "Sorry, Donn, things have been kind of weird lately," I said, sucking my fingers dry of the sweet ham's juices.

"So I heard. Believe me, Tearsa has been on the rampage since it happened." He turned his back to me and pulled out a cup and pitcher with yellow-pink liquid. "Try this. It's my new recipe. He poured me a cup, and my eyes went huge at the blend of sweet and sour taste. I coughed a little in surprise. Pounding my back with his meat cleaver of a hand, he asked, "Too much?"

"No, it's perfect," I replied to his obvious delight. "Why is Tearsa upset?"

"Well, she's in a quandary. You went from kitchen help to permanent guest overnight. Your status has changed. She is in charge of making sure you have everything you need, but at the same time she resents it."

"I'm still the same ol' Thalia."

"Yeah, but now you'll be making new friends and ordering us around instead; almost like you turned traitor." This was the most that Donn had ever said to me, but one remark did sink in.

"I'm not a traitor!" I took my plate over to the wash bin and started washing it.

"No, but you will be so busy with your new life that you will forget your old friends." He brought over a towel and handed it to me to dry off my dish. "Just don't forget about us."

"Never, Donn. I will be here many nights sneaking food out of your pantry." As I said it, I reached my hand to the bowl of fruit on the table. He grabbed a spoon and playfully whacked the back of my hand.

"I'll be looking forward to it." Donn studied me and frowned. "I'm surprised. Most Denai gifts appear at a much earlier age. You're what, seventeen? You must be a late bloomer, or something." He had no clue how close he was.

"Or something," I mumbled under my breath and waved goodbye.

Leaving the kitchen, I saw the door for Berry's rooms and I remembered her gift. Running back to my new room, I grabbed her gift and delivered it.

"I'm so excited!" She bounced in place with pleasure. "I can't wait to see what colors I can come up with. It's so much cheaper to dye my own material than it is to purchase it. You must introduce me to this Ruzaa."

"I will, I promise you. The next opportunity that we have, we shall go together." I told her a shortened version of everything that has happened in the last couple of days and she sat wide-eyed with disbelief. When it was time for me to go, she ran and gave me a couple of her old outfits to wear now that I wasn't a servant and told me to visit often.

Walking back to my room at the end of the hall, I noticed that my door was opened and slightly ajar. With a hint of trepidation, I peeked into my room and looked around. I saw no one. With a sigh of relief I went to my armoire to hang up the clothes.

When I opened the door, someone dressed in black flew out of the armoire at me, screaming.

~12~

The attacker grabbed me and knocked me to the ground. I yelled, but it was soon squelched as the wind was knocked out of me. I tried to pull free from the weight pressing down on my stomach and struggled to push the attacker off, when I heard giggling.

Looking closer, I saw that it was nothing more than Avina in her kitchen uniform. "I so scared you!" she cackled. "You were white as a ghost." Jumping up she put her hands on her hips triumphantly.

Regaining my composure, I leaped toward my bed and grabbed the nearest pillow and threw it at her head.

"MMMPHFF!" she said as it hit her full force in the face, knocking her braid sideways until it landed on her head in a comical fashion.

With a wild gleam, she raced toward the window sill and grabbed a cushion which started a round of pillow war until we ripped one of the pillows and a spray of down feathers flew around the room. We looked like half-plucked chickens when a loud knock sounded.

Still laughing, I opened the door to see Syrani with blonde hair piled high and a fake smile plastered on her face. Her face pinched with annoyance as soon as she saw me.

"Well, I'm surprised to see you here. I hope the new student isn't going to have you whipped for destroying their room."

"What are you talking about?" I asked, pulling a stray feather out of my hair. Avina ducked behind the door so she could peek through the crack and spy on Syrani.

"Well, I heard that there is a new Denai. I came to introduce myself to him and to offer a private tour. Do you know when he will be back?" Her smile was plastered on her face again.

"Umm, Syrani, I think you're mistaken. The new student that is enrolling isn't a boy." I wondered briefly if this was the tactic she used on Joss. Offering to be the tour guide and latching herself onto him. She was certainly in for a surprise.

"Oh," her smile dimmed a bit. "Well, that's okay. We could always use more girls, as long as they know my rules."

"Your rules?" I asked, puzzled.

Avina was making funny faces, and it was hard to keep a straight face.

Syrani was growing impatient. "Of course, rules." She counted off on her fingers. "Rule number one, stay out of my way and we can be friends. Rule number two, stay away from my boyfriend, Joss. Rule number three...remember rule one." She paused for effect. "I heard rumors that this new Denai is unique, and no one's ever seen anything like them. I mean after all, they were given the largest rooms in the housing wing." She tried to peer around my shoulder to look into the room.

By now, Avina was doing a frumpy impersonation of Syrani ticking off her rules and I couldn't help but giggle.

"I'm very sorry, Syrani, but I don't think the new student is going to be able to abide by your rules."

Her beautiful face snarled in reply. "Why ever not?"

"Because..." I couldn't help it, it was too easy. I plastered the biggest, fake smile on my face and threw my voice into a higher pitch similar to her own. "I'm the new student." Before she could form a retort, I slammed the door in her face.

Picturing her standing on the other side looking at the wooden door made me erupt into a fit of giggles. Avina hooted in laughter. But when we finally calmed down a bit, I thought about what I had just done and a large lump formed in stomach. I had just humiliated my biggest enemy.

~13~

Whoever thought I could slide into the classes without causing a fuss was crazy. Syrani had a head start and had spread some pretty ugly things about me to the other students. I was avoided like the plague. There were some curious stares and a few whispered comments, but no one welcomed me or asked my name.

A training schedule had been sent to my room the night before with a stack of books, and I glanced over it relieved to see that it seemed pretty harmless. I had History of Calandry, Ancient Denai Languages, and a few hours in the arena.

Nothing that shouted, "Hey, you're going to learn to destroy the world." I still didn't see what good it would do to take classes, considering I really didn't believe that I had any significant powers.

Ducking out of my room and locking my door, I rushed to make my way toward the indoor arena, hoping I wasn't late. I wore one of the custom outfits Berry had passed on to me, which consisted of tan pants, a white knee-length wrap-around over-skirt trimmed in blue and purple designs, and a white short-sleeve top with more designs stitched around. It had a leather pouch for books. The outfit felt very light and airy.

I was more comfortable I had been in a while. I felt normal. Well, at least until I approached the three-story high wing-shaped entry doors to the training arena.

This was the first time I dared to approach the doors for fear of being turned away, my charade revealed. We had been told that the doors would never open for anyone who wasn't a Denai. Avina and I had spent many nights trying to guess what was beyond the silver wings. Now I was about to find out and I didn't want to.

Pausing, I stood in front of the silver doors, and deep down, I knew they wouldn't open for me. I knew they would deny me entrance the same way Adept Cirrus's mercury stone denied me.

"Open," I demanded.

Nothing.

"Open, says me," I quipped, playing off of an old child's tale.

Nothing.

The adepts had never told me what to do if the arena denied me entrance. Should I wait to the side of the doors in the shadows and dart in behind another student? Or would the massive doors shut on me mid-passage and crush me? Believe me, the doors could crush a person. They were too large to be moved by sheer force alone.

I was still debating what to do when I noticed there was more to the iron winged doors than I first thought. The detail in the iron wings was masterful, down to each intricately sculpted feather that sprouted from a deep, well-muscled male back.

"Can't get in?" A voice spoke up from behind me, startling me out of my reverie. Turning, I saw Adept Cirrus.

I shook my head no.

"We were wondering if Cassiel would let you in," Adept Cirrus frowned at the winged doors. "Nevertheless, one of us will escort you in, to make sure Cassiel behaves, and doesn't try anything," he smirked.

I was right. The doors would have crushed me.

"I'm glad that I came to check on you. I'll speak with your instructor later." Adept Cirrus walked toward the doors and they immediately opened for him. Staying as close to him as I dared, I scurried after the adept, almost stepping on his heels, making sure to keep one eye on the doors.

They opened only long enough for us to safely pass through and then they closed with a thud once we were inside. Turning, I saw that the front side of the doors was shaped into a thirty foot tall man, arms crossed over his chest with giant wings sprouting from his back. This must be Cassiel. Only the Denai would ever see the true beauty of the doors. Well, except for me.

"Here you are." Cirrus pointed to the arena, and I stumbled into him when I followed his long finger with my eyes.

The arena was an indoor world, magically compressed into a small building. I hadn't noticed upon entering the arena that I was no longer walking on stone, but grass. We had walked right into a realm consisting of every natural element known to man within a few square miles. There were mountains, woods, rivers, plains, and I didn't have a clue as to what any of it was for.

"Just have a seat right over there, and I'm sure you will do wonderfully," Cirrus spoke, and gave me an encouraging slap on the back, which felt almost awkward.

I snorted in rebuttal and gave him an incredulous look.

Cirrus never saw it as he was already departing. The doors opened for him, and then he was gone. Turning back around, I came face to face with Syrani.

Syrani was sitting on a wooden bench, her long legs crossed, surrounded by a bunch of young Denai. Her golden hair, twisted and wrapped upon her head, gave her the appearance of a queen presiding over her court.

"Here she is now," she sniffed as if she smelled something rotten, and moved away from me and sat on the next section of arena seating, her entourage following.

Chewing on my thumb, I waited until the arena began to fill with latecomers. Each of the Denai had a haunting quality about them, and I was the obvious odd one out of the group.

They looked at me with a wary expression and purposely walked passed me to sit in another row. When it was obvious that no one was going to sit next to me, I felt my face heat up.

My eyes started to burn as I struggled to hold back tears. I was stronger than this, I told myself. I could handle a bunch of stupid, petty Denai. I squinted my eyes, pretending to examine my boot. I blinked away any trace of the glittering evidence of my weakness.

A loud thunderclap rolled in, and everyone looked up in expectation. A lone figure appeared out of the woods and literally walked across the flowing river to stand in front of the seated students.

This was my new instructor, I presumed. He was average height with white-blonde hair, and he had the strangest gray eyes. Another clap of thunder rang out and I jumped. The instructor's head turned my way and those strange gray eyes didn't focus on me but looked through me. I squirmed in my seat nervously.

He glanced at me longer than necessary and then another crack of thunder followed and he looked toward the rest of the Denai sitting clustered away from me.

He had a disapproving look on his face as he gave the full force of his odd glare to the other students who started to shift in their seats uncomfortably.

"Well, it seems we have a new student. I am Instructor Weston. What's your name, child?" His voice rumbled like the thunder.

"Thalia," I stated.

"What clan are you from?" he looked at me thoughtfully.

"I'm not sure." I wanted to disappear into the ground.

"No matter. What are your strengths?"

I looked down and shrugged my shoulders in answer, dropping my head down in defeat. I could hear the twitters of laughter echo in the arena.

"Silence!" he yelled as an angry crack of thunder split through the room. Now it was the instructor's turn to turn bright red.

The students immediately quieted, and a few looked duly chastised, while others looked bored.

"Well, let's go on and pick up where we left off last week." He managed to regain control of the class and began a review of basic strengths and weaknesses of various Denai gifts. He spoke of weather, obviously his gift. Controlling earth, controlling water, healing, and mind-speaking were others. Transference, instantly moving from one place to another, Vision seeking- scanning the world outward, and apparently, some of the students could shift forms.

After being called on a few times in class and not being able to answer a single question, the instructor had pity on me and quit calling on me altogether.

A few of the Denai helped demonstrate their gifts when the instructor was teaching. I watched dumbfounded as a small girl went to a tree sapling and made it grow to an adult tree, and a boy controlled the movement of the river. Instructor Weston controlled thunderstorms and seemed to enjoy showing off because every few minutes or so I would hear another crack of thunder.

When he finally dismissed the class, he asked me to stay after. I sat quietly, playing with the hem of my over-skirt trying to not make eye contact with anyone.

"Pathetic, isn't she, came into her powers late. She gives the Denai a bad name." I didn't have to look up to see that it was Syrani and her gaggle of friends laughing on the way out and purposely knocking against me. If only they knew I wasn't even a Denai.

Another crack of thunder and Instructor Weston walked over to me.

"Thalia, I must apologize for singling you out like that. I assumed you had been trained. I have not been given any information regarding your circumstances. I've only been notified that you are different than the others. Can you tell me what training and education you have had?"

"I can read, write and do basic arithmetic, but as to anything else you spoke on today, absolutely nothing."

Professor Westen blanched in surprise. "So no one in your family was Denai? How odd. When did you acquire your gifts? Most Denai achieve them before puberty."

"Well, I can tell you that I only, ah, uh, acquired them recently... as in two days ago?"

He blinked in disbelief.

I blurted out all of the fears and insecurities I felt in a rush of hurried sentences. "I'm in over my head. I'm at a complete disadvantage compared to the others. I don't know what I can and can't do, so how am I supposed to learn here?"

"Do you think you're the only one with a disadvantage to overcome? Look at me, Thalia."

I looked at Instructor Weston, but I found it uncomfortable to stare at his still, gray eyes. I shifted my eyes back to the ground.

"Can you see?" his deep voice rumbled.

"See what?" I asked, looking back to his face in confusion.

"I can't," he answered.

"I don't understand..." And then I did. I looked into Instructor Weston's gray eyes and realized. He was blind.

~14~

"I t happened long ago, when I was a child. I fell from a tree and hit my head," Instructor Weston explained. "When I woke up, everything was dark. My parents found me some time later, but no matter how many healers they took me to, none could restore my sight. I was stricken with grief. I couldn't go on living like an invalid. I felt like I was half a man." Weston smiled crookedly. "Well, half a boy, I should say. I went into the woods and called on the largest thunderstorm possible in an attempt to kill myself. It was then, during the rumble of the thunder that I realized for a split second I could see."

"I don't understand."

"I see through the thunder's vibrations."

"Like a bat?" I asked dumbfounded.

"Very much like a bat. The thunder causes vibrations and, for a second only, I can see the world in black and white. So during the deadliest storm, in the dead of night, when all hope of a normal life was gone, I still chose life."

It explained why the other students never jumped from the thunder, they were used to it. It was why he was never seen in the commons or main hall—he couldn't see beyond the vibrations of the thunder. So he chose a life of solitude within the arena.

Instructor Weston sat thinking for a moment and went to a nearby hollowed tree where he selected a few books from inside before handing them to me. "Here, read these, and hopefully you will catch up on what you need to know."

Reluctantly, I took the books and thanked him for his help. The rest of the day went very similarly to that first class, with students avoiding me. I, of course, embarrassed myself with my obvious lack of knowledge.

I decided to skip lunch again and hide out in my room. Picking up the first book that Weston had given me, I studied it. It appeared to be a child's reading primer, including pictures. I rolled my eyes at the thought of what I could possibly learn from a picture book, but I sat legs-crossed in the window seat and opened the small, red leather bound book.

I was most surprised by the beautiful artwork covering each page. The first page included a tall, beautiful being ethereal in nature surrounded by white light. The caption described the person as being one of the first Denai.

In short, the book told about the coming of Denai to the human plane; how the race of powerful beings was unjustly banished from their ancestral home. Seeking refuge among the humans, hoping they could one day return, they offered their healing services for asylum. The people of Avellgard were wary at first, thinking the Denai gift was nothing more than tricks. Over time, they accepted them and their power as the land and people prospered under the Denai's touch and sickness disappeared. The Denai became the unspoken guardians of Avellgard.

But Avellgard was ruled by a weak-willed king, and it wasn't long before others noticed Avellgard's growing wealth and prosperity and wanted it for themselves. The king asked the Denai to help fight the invading countries, but the Denai refused to take part in the coming human war.

They watched in silence, as war came upon the humans that they had begun to love, followed by years of death, strife, and famine. The country quit flourishing, and the borders of the land were in an ever-changing state. Whole kingdoms were built in a day and destroyed the next.

The Denai were a long-lived race, and the wars made the Denai heartsick as they watched whole generations of friends die by the sword. Another picture depicted a Denai bathed in light crying over the death of a human.

Then a dark day became darker when King Ridgar was crowned. He demanded the Denai power for his own use. When the Denai refused, he began killing their children as punishment. The genocide continued until only the strongest Denai were left.

Then Sinnendor's King, King Brancynal II, with his anti-Denai campaign, began an invasion with the sole purpose of removing the taint of the Denai from rest of the world. The Denai realized their race was coming to an end, so in a final effort, the remaining Denai joined forces and entered the human war knowing that by doing so, they would never be able to return to their ancestral home.

The Denai used their powers to defeat both countries' armies in their tracks, killing Avellgard's King and exiling Sinnedor's King to the Shadow Mountains. This was known as the First Denai War.

The Denai took up an oath to protect their new homeland, with a promise that it would never again be ruled by a king, but always by a Queen. They chose a human girl with a kind heart and made her queen. Since then, the country has always been ruled by a queen and her Denai councilors. The Denai healed the land, gave hope to the people, and rebuilt the country, renaming it Calandry.

I gazed at another picture of a fierce Denai holding a flaming sword, guarding the path to the city, and pointing toward the distant mountains as the King of Sinnendor crawled away in defeat.

As the years passed, the Denai diminished in power and beauty, and the once proud and noble race was on the verge of extinction. They took on human characteristics and traits, and they believed it was their punishment for killing the king and entering the human war.

So they accepted their fate and prayed for redemption as they stood guard over the humans of Calandry.

The final picture showed a Denai holding a human baby girl with curls, and though the baby was cute, it did not capture my attention like the beauty and light that emanated from the Denai.

Closing the book, I let the tears fall for the Denai. My heart ached for the race that was banished here as they tried to live peacefully among the humans, only to be forced into a war to save themselves.

A tear slid down my face and onto the picture of the Denai holding the baby. I wiped it away before it could ruin the ink, but not before the wetness created a faint outline of wings behind the Denai. I stared at it until it faded away.

I had been wrong about the Denai. I'd never understood them until now. I had blacklisted them and thought that they were evil beings only to realize that they were the ones that were the protectors of the human race. I thought about the proud race and how much they sacrificed, trying to live among humans. And it had only led to their downfall. I understood why the Queens of Calandry wanted to protect the race that saved the country. The Denai could have taken control of Avellgard, but instead they gave it back to the people.

The Denai today were nothing but a faint echo of what the Denai had been at one time in all of their glory and beauty. Syrani's earlier statements about bloodlines made sense. It made me wonder what blood ran through my veins and what I was now. For I couldn't possibly be human anymore and I wasn't Denai.

What else did that leave? Something inhuman?

My body shuddered at the thought of the Raven and his experiments. The numerous serums and colored vials of potions he injected me with. I remember screaming for hours at the pain, and feeling as if my insides were turning out.

Maybe Breah was right. Maybe I was a monster.

Sighing in frustration, I closed the book and put it on my shelf, reminding myself to thank the professor for it. I had no sooner closed and latched the window when a huge raven smashed into the glass with a loud thud, making me jump. The bird was huge, at least three times larger than a normal raven. My heart pumped in fear as it kept trying to force itself into the window, pecking, cawing, and scratching at the glass.

Pressing myself against the bookshelf, I watched in horror as it bashed itself until it was a bloody mess, cracking the glass. The bird's eyes looked dead and glazed over. It finally flew away cawing and screeching.

I thanked the stars that I wasn't sitting in the window seat any longer. If that had happened ten seconds earlier, I would have been seriously injured. I knew it had to be coincidence that I was thinking about the Raven and his experiments, and then a few moments later one flew into my window. But coincidence or not, I didn't want to stay in my room. I felt a little spooked sitting here alone.

Jumping up, I grabbed my cloak and headed down the nearest stairwell to freedom. Breathing a sigh of relief as the fresh air hit my face, I made my way toward the stables. Making sure to check the sky for any more crazed birds, as I headed to my sanctuary. Over the past weeks, I had made many trips here to spend time with the horses. The stable master had grown used to my presence and would often hand me a curry comb or a pick on my way in, knowing that I would put both to use as I was not one to sit idle. I smiled in greeting when I saw Stable Master Grese.

"See if you can do anything with that new one?" Master Grese said. "He's not letting anyone near him. We may have to get rid of him."

I nodded in answer. Making my way over to the newcomer, I verbally introduced myself and slowly stuck my hand over the stall near his nostrils. I had learned this was the easiest way to get him used to my scent. The horse was at least 16 hands tall and was so dirty with mud it was impossible to tell his true coat color.

The horse tried to bite my hand and I pulled it back quickly. Nickering and flicking his head, he stamped in impatience.

"Wherever did you find this one?" I called to Master Grese.

"Strangest thing I ever saw. I found him standing outside the main gate as if he was waiting to be let inside. Put up a fight when we tried to approach him, but he wouldn't leave the vicinity of the gate. Only took five of us to rope and bring him in, and we haven't been able to touch him since." Master Grese came over and shook his head. "He's got such spirit. I would hate to break it."

"What are you calling him?" I asked.

"Faraway," he grumbled.

I chuckled at the absurd look on Masters Grese's face.

"Okay, I'll bite. Why are you calling him Faraway?"

Master Grese grinned as he continued. "It's because that's where I want to be, whenever I get near him...very far away!"

I threw my head back and laughed, startling Faraway as he shied away, bumping into the stall. I felt a light touch of amusement skim my mind. The feeling was so foreign, I jumped and looked about.

Not seeing anyone except for Master Grese's retreating figure, I reached into my pocket and pulled out a carromint cookie. It wasn't the same kind that Darren made, but I had Donn the cook experiment with some similar ingredients. Breaking the cookie in half, I stood on tiptoe and slowly lowered my hand over the stall. The warm breath and the whiskers of the horse's muzzle tickled my hand as I froze, fearing to make any sudden movements.

"Shah. Shah," I intoned, trying to calm the horse. To get him used to my voice, I began to tell him of my horrible first day of classes, the whole while feeding him smaller portions of the carromint cookie.

After what felt like eternity, he began to let me stroke him, and I slipped into the stall and rubbed my hands down his flank, feeling the fullness of his muscles. Underneath all of the dirt was a fine specimen of a horse. And I told him so, somehow knowing that all horses are inherently vain.

"You are extremely dirty, and I happen to know for a fact that we have some mares that are very picky when it comes to their stallions. We can't have them meeting you like this now, can we? So you'd better behave, or I'm going to brush the other stallions down and leave you looking a mess," I warned the horse.

I grabbed the brush and began to brush him with the same motions as I'd previously done with my hands. The horse stood absolutely still while I bathed and brushed him down, almost as if he were afraid I really would leave him dirty.

What I thought to be a spotted gray coat actually turned a beautiful solid white. I brushed Faraway until he shone and then tackled his white mane with the curry comb. I spoke in low tones, telling him how handsome he was now that he was clean and how he would be the envy of all the other stallions.

Deciding to test my luck, since he was being so good, I approached his flank and cleaned his hooves. Noticing that he had never been shod, I felt a trickle of trepidation. I had been under the assumption that Faraway was just a runaway horse and had been broken at one time. But here was proof that he was wild, and wild horses could be dangerous.

I glanced over my shoulder to see Faraway turn his head and look at me as if to say, "Me? Wild? Ha!" It was then that I really noticed his eyes. They were a solid blue, which was rare for horses. Not unheard of, just rare.

It was well past dark by the time I had finished, and most of the workers had retired or gone home. The only lantern that had been lit was mine, and Master Grese was nowhere in sight.

Giving Faraway a final pat down and the last of my cookies, I decided to head to the kitchens for some food. Closing the gate to Faraway's stall, I turned just in time to see movement out of the corner of my eye as a cold piece of wire wrapped around my throat.

"HELP!" my mind screamed as the pressure around my neck increased. I had thrown my hand up in surprise as soon as I saw movement and was able to catch my fingers in the garrote. The more I struggled, the more I could feel the wire cut through the flesh of my fingers coating them in blood.

A furious shriek assailed my ears, followed by massive pounding and the breaking of boards. As I was losing the battle to stay conscious, I saw a white being surrounded by light arise and lash out toward my attacker. The pressure on my neck released, and I heard a human cry out in pain as I fell into the hay.

Rolling over, I saw it was Faraway on his hind legs stomping the attacker into the ground in a bloody frenzy, his blue eyes wild, the attacker dead.

"Oh, Faraway!" My heart cried in sorrow, knowing that he was indeed a wild and dangerous beast and would surely be put down.

I felt a bubble of spit, and a coppery taste filled my mouth. My hand went to my throat, knowing that this was the end of my life.

~15~

"I swear this one has nine lives!" It was Healer Prentiss talking to Adept Lorna. "She should be dead!" she exclaimed in disbelief.

"Wha...Wha..." I was trying to speak but couldn't regain control of my simple motor functions. I was obviously still groggy from whatever medicine they had given me. I felt like I was moving slowly through molasses.

"Rest, Thalia! Let us do the talking." Lorna, with her calm demeanor, came and sat on the edge of my bed, but never touched me. "You were attacked in the stable. And we wouldn't have known you were in trouble if that wild horse didn't nearly tear down the stable with his screams. We heard the commotion and rushed out to find a half-crazed horse standing over your body." She looked away from me and out the window.

My hand flinched and I raised one finger toward her. My pathetic attempt to try and get her to continue speaking. She did.

"We actually feared the worst! You have to understand it wasn't a pretty picture. When we saw the dead body, we assumed it was a student and that you were dead too, killed by the wild stallion. Master Grese started crying and blubbering that it was his fault. He'd encouraged you. But the stupid beast wouldn't let anyone come near you until I arrived. Then the crazy horse finally moved away and walked back into his stall.

"It wasn't until closer examination of the other body did we realize it wasn't a Denai student but an assassin sent after you. The bloody garrote was evidence enough." She looked back at me. "We haven't seen anything like this before. Your throat had been slashed and you had lost a lot of blood, but you were still alive, when by all accounts you should have been dead."

Healer Prentiss interrupted by bringing me a cup of herbal tea. "Drink it in slow sips," she commanded. Giving a look to Adept Lorna, she slipped out of the room and left us alone.

Finally I managed a whisper. "Can a Denai control animals?" I asked, taking another sip.

"Some can. We even have a few Denai here that can."

Using the back of my hand to wipe my mouth, I went on to tell her about the raven at my window, using the fewest number of words possible.

Nothing I said fazed her.

"Thalia, I think you should know that Adept Pax and I have come to an agreement that you need to be trained in self-defense. You are still new to your powers, and we don't even know the full extent of them, but he was concerned that you should know how to protect yourself in case this happens again." She stood as if to leave.

"And Thalia, until we catch whoever is behind these attacks, it may very well happen again." She looked frustrated, as if the news bothered her.

"Lorna? What did the attacker look like?" I didn't want to ask the question, but I needed to know if I knew the person. She reached out her long hand and grasped mine.

Closing my eyes I felt a shock, I was in her memories and I was looking at last night through her viewpoint. I could see

Faraway fidgeting in his stall, my body being hefted on a stretcher and carried to the infirmary.

Lorna glanced over to the mangled, bloody form of the stranger in black. Then, leaning down, she grabbed the shoulder and rolled the body over onto his back.

I wanted to close my eyes at the flood of images that was laid out before me, but I couldn't because these were Lorna's memories. I watched as her eyes skimmed his body for damage and any signs of life and then came to rest on his battered face. Revulsion overcame my body as I recognized the attacker as one of the Septori.

It was Crow. The one whose robe I grabbed in the prison and who told me Cammie was dead. I wanted to pull away from the image of the pale, dead face, the gaping mouth opened in a silent scream. A muted whimper came from my throat, and Adept Lorna let go of my hand. The images faded.

"So do you recognize him?" she asked.

Nodding my head, I felt sick to my stomach. "Crow."

"It's as I feared. With the attack in the alley with the dogs, and the assassin in the stables, we can only form one conclusion. That the Septori know you're here and they aren't going to stop until they get what they've come for."

"Which is?" I barely whispered the words. I needed to hear her say it before I could believe it. It wasn't true unless Adept Lorna said it.

"Your death." she spoke firmly without compassion. She didn't sugarcoat it. It was as I feared.

The saucer and cup slid from my fingers to break upon the cold stone floor. The remaining tea splattered against the bedpost and white sheets, but I didn't care. Despair overtook me, and I sat shaking in my bed. All along, hadn't I known this would happen? That my freedom and life were only temporary.

I couldn't hide forever before the Septori caught up to me and finished me off. I think I knew all along, that safe was a foreign word and had never included me.

Her words froze me to the core, and the room began to close in on me. My eyes started to lose focus and I forgot to breathe. Panic started to overtake me when a hand touched me and all of the feelings melted away. In their place, warmth spread over me, leaving no room for terror. Adept Lorna was controlling my emotions.

"I must speak with the Council and with Pax."

She stood to leave but I grabbed her hand in final act of desperation.

"Faraway?" I asked. "They're not going to put him down, are they?"

Adept Lorna gave a solemn smile. "After that crazy beast saved your life, we wouldn't dream of it. He still won't let anyone go near him, and Master Grese is determined that he is to be given to you. So, Thalia, it looks like you've got yourself a horse."

~16~

I spent the next few days in the healer's wing and was kept busy with guests. They distracted me from my fears of the Septori.

Adept Lorna came to check on me often and kept the terror at bay.

Avina entertained me with her lovesick chatter about Niclas. Donn snuck in from time to time bringing me sweetbread, saying how did they expect me to get well on tasteless broth.

Berry visited and brought fresh-cut flowers to brighten up the dreary white, starched room. And Joss brought my homework and read my textbooks to me, even though I could read them myself.

He just grinned and said it was really an excuse to hide out so that way he could avoid the swarm of girls that always seemed to follow him.

But the most surprising guest was Darren.

"Ah, so how is our friend doing today?" he sang as he burst into the ward in a flurry of motion and color. His short blue cloak billowed out behind him as he moved to the side of my bed, grasping Joss in a friendly hug. He slapped his back and leaned down to give me a fatherly peck on my forehead.

"Darren, I'm so glad to see you, but I must apologize for the things I said before you left." I felt heat rise to my cheeks.

"Nonsense, I know why you said them. But it seems to not have deterred Joss at all." He gave Joss a look.

Joss only raised his shoulders in a sheepish manner and offered a crooked grin.

"Are you staying focused on your homework and training?"

"Of course," Joss said defensively.

"So those would be your texts you're studying, I presume," Darren stated while grabbing the book out of Joss's hands and read the title out loud. "Really, Joss, *Remedial Healing?*"

By this time the Assistant Healer was glaring at Darren for being overly loud and making shushing noises. Darren gave her the full force of his vagabond smile, flipping his hair, and I watched as the assistant stopped in her tracks, hand flying to her chest. Joss and I tried to hold back the laughter as Darren awed her into silence with his dashing looks.

"I can't help it if the ladies adore me." Turning back to me, he pulled out a large package wrapped in brown paper and twine. He handed it to me and waited-not so-patiently while I unwrapped it. It was yards of beautiful fabric in shades of blues and greens and rolls of trim with elaborate designs. The final bulky package he handed me was a pair of light doeskin boots that fit.

"Darren, they are gorgeous, but why?" I looked at him curiously.

"What can I say? I'm a sucker for pretty things. Truthfully though, after leaving here I made a couple stops and then went back home to see Melani. After I related our adventures, instead of the adoration I thought I deserved, I got a dressing down. She was appalled that I didn't see you better outfitted before we left. I tried to explain we were in a dangerous situation and were racing to get to Haven."

He made clawing motions with his hands. "The mother lion in her came out and she immediately set to gathering your gifts. I didn't even get to stay one day before she demanded that I bring all of these gifts to you. Saying that any girl who went through what you did deserved to have people that care about her and will look after her."

Darren became really serious and faced me. "Thalia, I know that the Adept Council is looking for your family, and secretly I've been searching too. And even though you don't know Melani and me that well, she agreed—well, no— demanded that I tell you that we would love to be considered as an extension of your family. Also that if you don't find your family or home, that you would always have one with us."

I watched his face closely to see if he was joking, but Darren was serious. Joss sat with his mouth open in shock. Leaning forward, I hugged Darren.

"Darren," I whispered, "It would be an honor to consider you like family."

He regained his composure in record time and quipped, "Well, that is, as long as you don't pick up any of Melani's bad habits and start throwing dishes at me, because I can't afford to stock two sets of dishes in our house only to have them broken each week."

Laughing, I pretended to throw the boots at him, and he ducked in horror. The rest of the afternoon flew by as Joss and Darren stayed past visiting hours and Healer Prentiss, not swayed by Darren's good looks, kicked them both out.

~ 17 ~

The next day I was deemed well enough to rejoin classes. Joss was even in one class with me and made a big show of sitting next to me. There were a few snide comments, but Joss turned on those students and stared them down until they quit talking. It was almost more embarrassing to sit by Joss than to sit by myself. I found it very hard to concentrate with him sitting so close. On numerous occasions, my eyes would drift from the instructor to Joss's strong profile.

A couple of times he caught me staring, and I quickly drew my gaze back toward the instructor, fully aware that the tips of my ears were turning pink in embarrassment. Joss couldn't curtail his knowing grin, and I had to resist stomping on his too-perfect toes. Let's see him smirk with a bruised big toe, I thought to myself.

But having Joss beside me helped my popularity, because soon the students were no longer staring in open hostility but curiosity. I knew what they were probably thinking. Who was this strange girl? Didn't we see her one time working in the kitchen? I wonder if that was a punishment for disobeying the Council? Why doesn't she know anything? What rock did she crawl out from under? Well, maybe not all of those questions.

"Strengthen the mind to strengthen your powers," our instructor quoted. He explained that the more you understood the Denai gifts, the more you could do. I studied harder than any student, and every evening I would return to my room and try to perform the simplest of tasks—lighting a fire, moving an object, farseeing.

And every night it was the same thing. Nothing. In fact I think I was getting worse, not better.

Adept Pax's office held a huge desk and black rug; his chairs were massive to fit his giant frame. His walls were bedecked with many different fighting instruments and weapons. The huge room felt empty until I figured out the real purpose of his office. It was his private training room.

"The Council has decided, Commander, that since there have been numerous attacks on Thalia, she needs to be guarded," Pax spoke.

"It wasn't our fault she was attacked in town!" Commander Meryl stated defensively.

"No, it's no one's fault. At that time we didn't know that she would need to be guarded. And we still aren't sure what the Septori are capable of, or with whom we are really dealing. I mean, are they human? Denai? Mercenaries? We don't really know. Commander Meryl, your guard is the best in the world, but here where the strongest Denai live and train, it is easy to get lax in our duties. Most bandits would either be stupid or extremely desperate to try and attack our towers."

Pressing the tips of his fingers together in thought, he continued. "But it made us realize that we need to be prepared against all forms of threat. Whether it be a Denai threat or human, our soldiers and students alike need to be aware of the danger. Adept Lorna and I have made a decision to start putting students under your care for training." Pax moved away from the desk and started pacing.

"Are you suggesting that we are going to be attacked?" Commander Meryl asked, his face frozen in seriousness. "Do you know something that we don't?"

"No, but look at what we do know; we know there is a madman on the loose that has created a cult following strong enough to make us worry. They are skilled enough to avoid detection and attack one of our students on our campus. It's like they are taunting us. They want something we have, or should I say, someone. We can't foresee the future nor what steps they will take to get her. We can only take precautionary steps to prevent them from achieving their goal!" Pax pounded his fist into the table making a thud loud enough that I jumped in surprise.

Why was I even here for this discussion? This sounded like a conversation that should be between them, not me. But at this point, I felt it wiser to sit quietly and speak as little as possible. I couldn't figure out Adept Pax's reason for me to be in this meeting. And I just prayed that he would forget about me so I could sneak away. But no sooner had that thought crossed my mind, his eyes darted back to me and a smile started to spread across his face.

No chance of that.

Pax grinned. "So, to help us achieve our goal I have devised a training game, to encourage and challenge your soldiers and my students."

Turning back to Commander Meryl, Pax leaned his giant frame against the shelf and folded his arms across his chest. "We are going to simulate an attack on the Citadel. But it will be on a small scale, nothing to worry the queen or the town. Four of your best captains will try to attack our training grounds."

Commander Meryl's eyebrows rose in thought.

"Go on..."

"You will select a group of your best soldiers who will be the attackers. Their goal is to attack, distract and kill the students, while my specially selected assassin will sneak in and eliminate his prime target." Pax moved away from the desk and picked up a book and flipped it open absently before putting it back on the shelf.

"Kill! What do you mean *KILL?*" I squeaked out. I had a feeling I knew where this conversation was going. My palms started to sweat, and I decided I didn't like the idea of being killed one bit.

Commander Meryl stroked his short gray beard in thought. "The idea has great merit. I think it would be something to consider. Thalia's right though. Explain how we are to be killed exactly?"

Adept Pax's eyes turned dark and they glittered dangerously in the candlelight. All emotion left his face, "Like this!"

In a blur of motion, Adept Pax charged both of us and I felt something heavy stab into my chest, knocking the breath from me, as my chair fell backwards and hit the ground. Grunting in pain, I grabbed my chest to see a pool of red blood gush between my fingers.

Pax leapt upon Commander Meryl, bringing him to the ground in one smooth motion. I watched in shock as Pax pulled a knife from his belt and mortally stabbed Commander Meryl in the gut, as blood flowed out and onto the cold tiled floor.

~18~

Pax stood up slowly from his kneeling position over Commander Meryl's body, face deathly white and uniform covered in blood. This was it. My body started to shake and go into shock.

Hearing a slight chuckle, I looked over in surprise to see that it was Commander Meryl. Pax started to laugh as well. Stunned, I watched as their chuckles turned into full-fledged belly laughs. I couldn't believe how a mortally wounded person could laugh that hard. Then I noticed that I wasn't in any pain, other than the slight discomfort of landing on the cold, hard floor. Looking down at my shirt, I saw that I was covered in blood but could find no visible wound.

Upon closer inspection, I saw the remains of a small rubber-like ball that had broken open on impact. Pinching it between my fingers released a red, liquid paint.

Pax walked over, pulled me up, and set to work putting his office aright. Commander Meryl nimbly jumped up and patted Pax on the back.

"That's brilliant, my friend. May I see it?"

Adept Pax handed over what looked to be a real knife, but the blade was made in a soft rubber that, when bent, leaked the red liquid.

"It's a pliable version of a practice knife that has been altered to release paint on contact. We will all be armed with similar weapons like small pellet balls and arrows. Anyone that gets marked with paint is therefore considered killed and is out of the game."

"Absolutely brilliant!" Commander Meryl intoned again. "And when can we expect the training game to begin?" His eyes twinkled at the thought. "You are right, our soldiers have been getting bored and this is just the thing to test them. It gives me a chance to do some internal promotions as well." The Commander sat back in his chair, crossing his legs with a thoughtful grin on his face.

"You have two weeks to prepare and begin the students' training as well as Thalia's. When the fourteen days are up, your captains, along with my chosen Assassin, will begin the attack on the Citadel."

"I see the point of only having a small attack team. You doubt this madman would unleash a full army upon us, when a small group would have more success at sneaking in. But, Pax, my captains are good, but how can four of them attack the whole training facility and it be considered an even fight? Unless you have something up your sleeve?" Commander took one look at Pax's knowing face before slapping his knee in excitement. "You ol' dog, you do, don't you? Who did you find to be the assassin?"

"I have called in a SwordBrother."

Commander Meryl shot out of his chair, his face registering shock. "You know a SwordBrother? How in the world did you get one to agree to come here? That alone will even out the numbers, if not give us an advantage."

I was stunned by the news. Being in the Healer's wing for so long, I had plenty of time to do some reading and had recently just learned of the existence of SwordBrothers. They were the most prestigious and fiercest fighters in the world. Their whole existence centered around honor, battle and sword skills. They were an extremely dedicated Clan who were the personal bodyguards for the kings and queens of old. Only the powerful were important enough to have a SwordBrother for their bodyguard. But during the Denai War, those they swore to protect betrayed them. Now they refuse to swear fealty to anyone—king, queen, or Council member.

Since then, I'd learned, the SwordBrothers had gone into isolation and taken with them their fighting techniques and secrets. Many had tried to find their clan over the years only to disappear and never return. The SwordBrothers had become the stuff of legends and stories—a threat one would give a misbehaving child. "Careful, or a SwordBrother will steal you away in the dark of the night."

My throat constricted in anxiety, and I felt myself wiping my sweaty palms on my legs. The Commander was ecstatic to actually live to see the day where he would not only meet a legendary SwordBrother, but to have him train some of his captains—that was a great honor and privilege.

"Like I said, I had to call in a favor." Adept Pax's eyes became distant as if he had become lost in his memories. With a shake of his head, he turned to us again. "But remember, I want Thalia to be under guard as soon as possible. And her self-defense training starts now. Thalia will be the prime target. For I have also promised the SwordBrother a prize if he kills Thalia. It would do her good to be doubly on guard."

"No!" my mind shouted. "No guards!"

From the shocked looks on Adept Pax and Commander Meryl's faces, I realized I didn't think it, but yelled it. I wasn't emotionally ready to be surrounded by guards; it would be like being in prison again.

"Adept Pax? I know you mean well. But I don't want to live my life under constant guard. What if we never capture the

Septori? Will you guard me forever? Someday I will have to rely on myself." I stood tall and refused to break eye contact.

Under the scrutiny of his dark eyes I could feel myself shrink in size, but I clenched my teeth in determination.

"Well then, you'd better hurry and learn to defend yourself with either a weapon or your power." Turning back to his desk, he dismissed me and began to debate defensive plans for the Citadel.

Stopping myself at the doorway, I turned around and addressed them both in the most determined voice I could muster.

"Adept Pax… Commander, I won't participate in your training game or agree to be the bait for the assassin unless we change one thing."

"What's that, my child?" Adept Pax looked confused.

Pulling on my ruined shirt and holding it away from my body in disgust, I made a disgusted face. "The color of this awful paint. Blood red is impossible to get out." And with that I left the office with the echoes of their combined laughter following me down the halls.

~ 19 ~

nder Adept Pax Baton's orders I started learning self-defense and combat training. I reported each afternoon to the training field and waited for my instructor to arrive. I was apprehensive the first day as I waited, sitting on the fence to see which soldier was assigned to train me and beat me into a pulp.

When Garit's smiling face arrived, I breathed a short sigh of relief. Short, because he may not have beat me to a bloody pulp, but it didn't mean that he was going to take it easy on me. He had two weeks to get us ready for the attack.

And I was the target.

I tried to imagine what that would be like as we began the day's training.

"Thalia, where are you?" I barely ducked in time as Garit's practice blade flew over my shoulder where my head had just been.

Scuffling out of the way, my feet kicking up dirt, I moved around to Garit's weak side. It didn't matter; he was right, my mind had been somewhere else. He feinted a lunge at my face, swept out his leg, and kicked my feet out from under me.

Staring at the clear blue sky, I longed for the day when I could be back inside doing dishes, instead of being submitted to a daily beating.

"Your mind was somewhere else and you lost focus." Garit stretched out his hand and pulled me up from the ground.

I quit dusting off my pants because it wouldn't matter. I would be seeing the ground again very soon.

"I'm sorry. I'll try harder," I said weakly.

"Come, sit." He motioned to two barrels, and I sat on one, waiting for him to take the other.

"For you to regain your focus, we first need to address what it is that has you so worked up and scared."

"I'm not..." I began.

"You are!" he interrupted.

I didn't like being vulnerable and having to share anything personal, especially to a young man. Even though I didn't want to admit it, he was right.

"I don't want to be the target." I focused on the distant mountains and the shape of the cloud passing over them, so I wouldn't have to make eye contact. Briefly I gave him a simplified version of my life story. And I had to give him credit, because he didn't even blink an eye. It was nice to not have an overly dramatic reaction from someone for once.

"I feel as if I'm a scared rabbit just waiting for the hunter to take me out. The thought that I'm going to be hunted down and killed terrifies me. Even if it is just a training game, my heart quickens and my palms go sweaty and I freeze up at the thought. I'm back in the cell all over again, and I don't think I can do it."

"Bull!" Garit said vehemently.

I turned my head and gaped at him in surprise.

"The only person that can make you be a victim again is yourself. There is no cage, Thalia. It's only in your mind." Garit rapped his fingers against my temple roughly.

Looking into his face, I saw he meant every word. His red blonde hair seemed even redder in the sunlight, and the small scar on his chin stood out on his tan skin. He tossed me my practice blade. I caught it with ease.

"Thalia, if you don't want to be the prey anymore, then you can only do one thing. Become the hunter."

Our lessons changed. Instead of learning defensive moves, Garit taught me to go on the offensive and to use every dirty trick he knew. Attack the eyes, or kick to the groin, jab into the solar plexus to give yourself time to run away. My size and speed would lend to swift attacks and evasive maneuvering.

I couldn't overpower any attacker with strength, but if I could keep out of their reach and attack them from a distance, I would have a chance at survival.

We worked every day on hand-to-hand combat and evasive fighting. Then we went over knife techniques, because if I let someone get close enough to me to get caught, I would need a knife.

But I was most surprised on my third day of practice when I went out to the training field and Garit wasn't in the training ring. I spotted him in the far field next to a fenced-in pasture where the horses were grazing. I glanced at the pasture to see if I could see Faraway. Yep, he was prancing around the field in happiness, grateful to run, his beautiful mane that I brushed every day shining in the setting sun. I smiled at Faraway's youthful antics, and then climbed the fence to reach Garit.

Garit had a silly grin on his face, and I saw that he had constructed a large man out of hay, feed bags, and old clothes. Looking closely at the dummy, I noticed a beard painted on the face in a very bad imitation of Commander Meryl.

"I got the clothes from Berry. When I told her what they were for, she was excited to help me with my project, even going so far as to add buttons and decorations to the uniform."

"What is it?"

"Well, it's a human target!" Garit pulled out a beautiful dark wood bow and a leather quiver full of arrows. The bow wasn't the same size as the ones the archers used; it was much smaller, fit to my height and arm length.

Picking it up, I let the wood pass through my fingers feeling the coolness of it. The string vibrated my soul when I touched it. It felt right.

"Since this is serious, I didn't want to start you off hitting at a pile of hay. We needed something man-sized, so you can get used to aiming at a small target. Of course, they have them at the training yard, but I thought you would feel more comfortable training away from everyone's prying eyes."

That was exactly what I needed. I had been feeling very self-conscious in my lack of ability of Denai power. I was beginning to wonder if maybe Joss and Prentiss had been mistaken in their assessment of what had happened in the healing ward.

We started the session fifteen paces away from the Commander dummy, and Garit walked me through how to string the bow, nock an arrow, sight a target, and release. My first shot hit the dirt and stopped eight feet from the target.

Faint laughter tickled my mind, and I looked at Garit. He was grinning from ear to ear at my pathetic attempt.

"It's okay. Try again. You don't have the arm strength yet, but you will."

Nocking another arrow, I sighted down the shaft at the target aimed for the large round stomach. Pulling the bowstring and arrow back, I was about to release when I heard *HIGHER* brush against my conscious.

Making the adjustment, I released the bowstring and watched the arrow fly true. It hit the stomach of the target dead on, only to bounce off and land pathetically in the grass.

I raised an eyebrow to Garit and threatened, "Not a word, not *one* word or I'll use you as the dummy."

He wisely held his tongue.

Frustrated, I stormed away from the dummy to an even farther distance and fitted the arrow on the notch, pulling the bowstring back as far as I could with the intention of sending it flying as hard as I could without even aiming.

Patience, the voice came again.

Breathe slowly.

I did what I was told.

Aim higher.

I made what I thought to be an adequate adjustment.

Breathe out, it commanded.

Feel your heartbeat?

I listened to the sound of my heart, and it seemed to slow.

Release between beats.

I did, and I watched in amazement as the arrow flew straight into the chest of the dummy. Garit was walking toward the dummy and fell back into the grass in shock as he saw the shaft buried inches deep into the heart of the target.

"Whoa, Thalia, I didn't think you were serious about making me the target, but well done!"

I couldn't help but smirk at him laid out on the ground. He hadn't expected me to make it that far.

"Thanks, but I couldn't have done it without your last minute directions."

"Thalia, what are you talking about? I haven't said a word since you threatened me." Garit's brows furrowed in confusion.

Looking around the empty field I felt the hairs rise on the back of my neck, until the sound of a soft nicker drew my attention to Faraway, who, sometime during the lesson, had come over to the fence and stood watching.

Staring at his intense blue eyes, I let a million possibilities fly through my head, until I felt the same familiar touch on my mind.

Finished? Can we get cookies?

"Garit? Did you hear that?" Stopping, I watched as he cocked his head to the side to listen.

"You mean the students arriving for their lessons?"

He was right. I could hear the chatter of the students arriving at the practice ring across the field.

The students were lazy and unambitious in their practices. Most believed they were invincible and didn't need any hand-to-hand skills to disarm a soldier. They came each day because they were ordered to, and no matter how hard Commander Meryl drilled them, they lacked motivation. Even the youngest Denai among them was able defend themselves with powers, and I thought the guards were too scared to press and train them. Because who wanted to be on the wrong side of an angry Denai?

Since I had yet to display any more Denai traits, I preferred to train alone.

"Which reminds me," Garit yelled over his shoulder. "I need to get over there. Thalia, will you promise to keep practicing? You need to start building up your arm muscles."

He picked up his extra bow and set of arrows from the grass and slung them over his broad shoulder, giving me a brotherly pat on the head as he passed.

I watched him join the other soldiers in the training of the Denai and felt a pang of envy.

Joss's blonde head stood out among the students even from a distance; he was one of the only ones that took the practice seriously and refused to cheat.

Last night, I'd heard the guards grumbling about how they played dirty. Some students used wind to knock sand in their eyes, or trip them during practice, but they didn't have solid proof. Joss was all work and no play when it came to training. He obviously had previous training in sword fighting.

I watched as he tested the weight of the sword in his hands and adjusted his grip before stepping into the painted circle on the ground with his partner, one of the captains. He was skilled and kept pace with the Captain, as they each took a turn being on the offensive.

Joss never tried anything too dangerous or bold, and instead tried to wait until his opponent became too tired. They were tied, one win each and were about to start the third round, when a thought flitted into my mind.

Hungry.

The feeling of hunger reached my belly and I quickly jerked my head back to my horse, remembering my earlier concerns. Walking over to Faraway carrying my bow, I set it by the fence as I let my fingers rub his muzzle. He nudged my shirt sniffing around for a treat.

"Am I going nuts?"

You have nuts? I like nuts. You should bring me some.

"Not if I have to admit myself back into the infirmary for head trauma, because now I am definitely hearing things."

Of course you're hearing things. You're hearing me. Faraway sounded a bit miffed.

It was my horse. I was hearing my horse speak in my mind.

Climbing the wooden fence, I sat facing him, so I could be eye level. It also put me in a great position to scratch behind his ears which he loved.

"Faraway? How come I can hear you?"

Because I'm your horse, he stated, as if that explained everything. Trying to rephrase my question I asked instead, "But why?"

He looked at me and nudged me in the shoulder. *Because I'm yours. Your mind is open to me; we can share thoughts and feelings.*

"I don't understand." I was new to the whole world of sharing thoughts and speaking mind to mind. Not many Denai could.

Some could speak mind to mind, some could share feelings, while others could take over your whole mind and force control of a person's body. The thought of anyone having that much power gave me goosebumps.

I'm a guardian. You called me, and I answered the call. Faraway looked into my eyes and all of a sudden pictures, thoughts and feelings flashed in my head of the night of the attack.

I saw it all from Faraway's viewpoint from the stall. I looked so small in Faraway's mind and he thought of me as the-Small-One-Who-Brought-Good-Cookies. I could see myself walking away in the dark of the stable as Crow moved out of the shadows. Looking at the attack from this angle made me want to scream at myself to watch out. Faraway's body stiffened as the attacker lunged for the attack, but he was frozen, unable to act. I could feel his desire to attack and his body quivered with excitement and nervousness. But there was a moment of hesitation, as if he were waiting for a signal or command.

I heard my own voice pierce the darkness in his mind. *HELP!*

Yes! His body hummed with an instant possessiveness. My call was what he had been waiting for. I could feel the adrenaline rush into his body as he kicked the stall door open. The anger he felt at seeing the blood run from my neck was directed toward the man behind me. I could feel his rage. I felt sick to my stomach as Faraway rose onto his hind quarters to attack the back of Crow's skull with his front hooves.

"Stop! No more, please. I don't want to see the rest," I pleaded.

The images faded from my mind, and I placed a shaking hand over my heart to try and calm the feelings of adrenaline and power that vibrated through my body. Feelings, I knew, that belonged to Faraway and not to me.

That is my duty as a guardian to answer the call. You called me; I'm yours.

He tended to speak in very clipped tones and there was a haughty undertone to the way he spoke.

So we could share thoughts, feelings, emotions and even memories. But it still didn't answer the question of how was I able to call a guardian. I never heard of anyone else at the Citadel ever speak of Guardians, and I wasn't Denai. I was unnatural.

You are wrong. You are perfect.

"No, I'm not. I'm twisted. It's because the Septori used immoral experiments and in a fluke stole another's power. What I can do is not natural. You don't understand what has happened to me."

I had been picking at splinters on the fence and one pricked my finger. Letting the blood well into a drop, I held up my finger to Faraway.

"Can you tell me what blood I have in my veins? I can imitate the Denai but that's it. I'm a fraud, a fake."

I let Faraway see some of my memories of what had happened to me.

"You see, I don't deserve you. I'm not whole, I'm not pure." All the pain I had been trying to hold back over the last couple of days flowed from my body.

Nonsense, if you weren't a pure person, you wouldn't have been able to summon me.

"But I have no other abilities. I can't control the weather, light a fire, move earth, nothing!"

Hhhmmphh, overrated, he snorted. *You're the only one in a thousand years that has been able to summon a guardian.*

"What?" The idea seemed preposterous to me.

You don't have to speak out loud. If you think your thoughts and direct them at me, I can hear them. As long as you're not blocking me.

"I'm sorry. I didn't..." I cut myself off as I realized I was talking out loud again. Scrunching up my face, I concentrated on Faraway and thought the words. *...mean to.*

Faraway blew air out his nostrils in an obvious attempt at a laugh. I felt his amusement fill my body as he sent me an image of my face scrunched up in concentration.

I started sputtering to cover the obvious snorting noises that exploded from my mouth at the ridiculous image I saw of myself. Settling down, I wiped the wet tears of laughter out of the corners of my eyes.

It felt so good to laugh. I looked out across the field to the Denai students who were practicing on disarming guards, or working on sword drills, and for once I didn't feel jealous. I felt whole.

The setting sun over the horizon drew my attention away, as a breeze brought my hair across to tickle my face. The open plain called to me. It spoke of freedom and new beginnings, of hope, second chances, and new friendships. A smile pulled at my mouth.

Run?

Yes! Grabbing his mane I swung onto his bare back and let him lead me to the gate that I kicked open with my foot.

Once the gate closed, we ran. The wind blowing in my hair, I shifted my weight and hunched closer to Faraway. When he opened his mind to me, I saw the world through his eyes. I felt then and there that we were one.

He was right. I was his and he was mine.

~20~

Faraway helped me the next few days with my archery skills, and every free moment I had, I practiced. Through his eyes, I could study my stance and posture and see what I was doing wrong. Soon after, I was hitting the target every time and from greater and greater distances.

Garit still came to train me and was amazed at my speedy progress and natural skill. I had decided to not tell anyone about bonding with my guardian Faraway. It was nice to have a secret of my own, and I wasn't yet ready to share him.

Knowing full well that I would have to tell the adepts about him sooner or later was depressing enough. If Faraway was right and there hadn't been anyone that could summon a guardian since the Denai wars, then that would make me different, unique, and obviously a candidate to be studied. I was willing to put off that torture for as long as possible.

Faraway had encouraged me to try shooting from horseback, softer I tried a few practice shots with him standing still, we tried with him walking.

I was becoming so in tune with his stride that the motion rarely bothered me. He taught me how to hold on with my leg muscles and how to direct him. We were beginning to anticipate each other's actions. For once, something was coming naturally to me.

Faraway was trotting and I had nocked my last arrow when I heard a voice yell, "What is it you think you're doing?"

Releasing the tension in my bow and pointing the arrow at the ground, I turned Faraway around toward the speaker. I had recognized the voice of Joss but I was still surprised to see him there.

Maybe it was because I had been avoiding him for the last week, eating in my rooms, ducking out of class early, coming in late. I was a failure at a lot of things and I was punishing myself by denying myself a friendship with Joss.

I kept telling myself I was an embarrassment to the Denai and until I could become stronger, better, then I wasn't going to embarrass Joss by my existence.

It was pathetic, demeaning and also unfair to Joss, but he practically glowed with power and perfection, and I felt like a dim candle next to him.

"I'm practicing. What does it look like I'm doing?"

"It looks like you're about to get yourself killed." His tan face had gone pale, and I felt a small shadow of guilt. "You aren't even holding on. That horse could throw you any minute."

I felt Faraway's amusement at being called "that horse." I had yet to explain to Joss that Faraway was special and not some crazed horse. "He won't harm me, remember? He saved my life."

Joss strode over and grabbed Faraway's reins in an effort to still an already perfectly behaved horse. He gave the horse a cautious look as if he was sure he would bite his hand any minute.

"Joss, what are you doing here? Shouldn't you be preparing for the training game that begins tonight?"

Just mentioning it made my mouth go sour with fright. It had been announced during lunch that the two weeks were up as of midnight tonight.

I still didn't understand how this training program was fair and, from what I could tell, only Adept Pax, Commander Meryl and I knew that the fake assassin was a SwordBrother.

"I wanted to let you know that I petitioned the Adept Council to stop the game." His eyes glanced up from Faraway and pleaded with mine.

"What? Why?"

"I told them to choose someone else to be the target."

"What? Joss, how could you? You had no right." I could feel my anger rise, but I was also confused. It's what I secretly wanted, wasn't it, not to be bait?

"I don't think it's fair after what you have been through."

"I agreed to this, I did. No one made me do it." My fingers dug into Faraway's mane and I felt him send calming emotions to me.

Taking a deep breath, I went on, "I won't let myself be made a victim again, and right now this is exactly what I need—a chance to be able to fight back against the unknown and defend myself. How will I ever be able to go out into the world again and feel safe and secure? The only one I can rely on for protection is myself. I need to do this." And right then, hearing the words from my own mouth, I realized I did need this. Looking Joss straight in the eye, I jutted my chin out.

"It doesn't have to be," he said quietly, looking up at me with his intense blue eyes. "I would protect you if you would let me." His jaw clenched and unclenched in hidden emotion. "It seems like whenever I'm around, you withdraw from me and try to build a wall between us."

He was right; I had tried to accomplish this without his knowledge and without hurting him, but I had failed. Without speaking, he pulled the reins and led Faraway over to the fence and looped them around the post.

Joss reached up and placed his hands on my waist, and I let him help me down from Faraway. His hands burned with heat through my shirt as he let them linger lightly on my waist. I moved away uncomfortably.

Now that I was off of my perch and looking up to Joss, my head barely reaching his shoulders, I felt more vulnerable. Wishing that I still had the advantage of height, I tried to make myself appear taller by standing up as straight as I could and putting my hands on my hips.

"I'm sorry, Joss. But you must understand I'm still missing a lot of my memories. I don't know who I am. How can I let someone else get to know me, if I don't even know myself?"

"I don't care about who you were in the past; I care about who you are right now, in the present." His voice was rising in frustration. "I don't even think you're giving our friendship a chance. And that's all I'm asking for is friendship. If anything else develops, so be it."

Joss turned his back to me and leaned both arms on the top rail of the fence. He stared out over the mountains in the distance. "But you have to admit, it's a fair request, and I have been really patient."

I stared down at the top of my scuffed boot in resignation, kicking at a stubborn pebble that refused to come loose from its home in the ground.

"Joss, I can't make any promises to the future, especially if I don't know I can keep them, but I can promise you friendship." I looked at him warily as he turned his blond head to me with his crooked grin.

"That's all I ask for, a chance to be your friend." Standing up he reached for me and pulled me into an embrace, his chin resting lightly on my head.

I selfishly let the comfort of his hug wash away all of my insecurities. Tears started to come to my eyes when I realized the last time I had been hugged was by Mara. Taking in one last deep breath of his earthy scent, I pulled away. I couldn't help but notice his look of disappointment.

Turning away, I ran my fingers through Faraway's mane. "So what was their decision?" I asked, almost dreading the thought of them changing their mind after I had gone through so much preparation.

"What?" Joss looked a little puzzled, as he was deep in his thoughts.

"The Adept Council?"

Regaining his composure, his eyes darkened. Climbing the fence he swung his long legs over and jumped down. He made eye contact as he spat out the words.

"Don't worry. You're still the target." And with that he left, his tall head walking proudly toward the training grounds.

~21~

With only hours to spare before midnight, I ran around the training grounds gathering the supplies I thought I would need. I wasn't about to go on with my daily routine when I felt as if there were a crimson target painted on my chest.

Earlier we had each been given specific instructions for the game. When the bell tower rang out its twelfth time at midnight, the training game would begin.

The game could only take place within the training grounds. Leaving the premises would result in disqualification. If a student got hit with a paint pack, they would need to report to the main hall. There, they would be inspected to make sure it was a legal hit. Guards hit with paint were to report back to the barracks.

Whoever could take out the most attackers would win a purse of gold. Anyone caught cheating and trying to wash off dye would be punished. The adepts would also be patrolling the grounds and halls to make sure that the game stayed fair. Healer Prentiss would be ready in the ward in case any students or soldiers got too carried away. We were allowed to outfit ourselves with various paint-filled weapons, similar to those we'd use in training.

Upon my request, the paint had been changed from blood red to blue for the SwordBrother, yellow for student. Soldiers were assigned pale green. I couldn't help but chuckle at the change, which was to make sure that the game stayed fair, and there wouldn't be a mutiny among the Denai.

Avina had gone to the market for me to pick up some special-ordered items. In the course of preparation, I had spent almost all of the money that Adept Cirrus had given me. But it was worth it if I learned anything from this.

Handing me the sack of supplies, Avina asked me what I planned to do. I told her she would have to wait and see.

I watched her leave and gently latched the door before I opened the sack and began to work. Inside were arrows, paints, clothes and a large jar of a special blend of Ruzaa's perfume. I broke the tips of the arrows off and padded them with balls filled with paint.

Then, with a wooden clothespin on my nose, I transferred Ruzaa's perfume into smaller clay vials with a rubber stopper. Being careful not to jostle them too much. I put them in a thick leather pouch on my hip.

Garit agreed to furnish me with a small grappling hook and grinned at my initiative. I wound the rope around my slim waist and used the hook to loop around the rope, holding it there. It wouldn't hold much more than my own body weight, but that's all I needed. I couldn't afford to get a bigger one because I needed to carry my arrows and bow over my back.

I pulled my hair into a ponytail and rubbed the black grease paint all over my face, which made it itch. I stared at myself and noted the changes in my face since I first arrived at the Citadel. I had gained weight in my face and body. Before the grease paint, I'd noticed a healthy glow instead of the pasty white my skin had been. My eyes were still huge and had softened with happiness and health, but tonight they looked dark with determination.

I shut my window and wrapped a piece of very fine thread around the window latch. The string would break if someone tried to enter my room through the window. Donning my cloak, I let myself out of my room and knelt down to pour a fine powder of dust around my door. It was so fine that only by getting down to the floor with my cheek pressed to the marble could I see it.

I took the quickest exit to outside, knowing that midnight would be fast upon me.

As soon as I got to the stables, I opened Faraway's stall and attached the new set of reins I had specially made for him. They no longer had a bit, but went only around his muzzle and ears.

Faraway didn't need a bit anymore. He was my guardian, and he had expressed his displeasure at them. Horse Master Grese had stared at me, dumbfounded, when I had it commissioned. That's where the rest of my gold had gone. Leading Faraway at a slow walk, I took him out to the pasture and let him loose.

If he were not penned up in the stall, then he would be an extra set of eyes watching out for me. From this pasture, he had an excellent view of the training grounds and would be my eyes and ears.

Quickly, I slipped into the shadows and watched the guards patrol around the keep's grounds. If I were the SwordBrother, I thought to myself, I would probably already be on the grounds in hiding. Just because the game didn't start until midnight didn't mean that he couldn't already be here. And I was about to do the same thing.

Hide.

Waiting, I leaned my head against the outer wall of the stable and tried to steady my nerves as I silently inventoried everything I had on me.

It's clear. Go now.

The signal from Faraway. I slid along the building, staying in shadows until I slipped into the stable. Climbing up the ladder into the loft, I moved through the hay until I came to a small window. I had gotten the idea from Jury and Pim. I was impressed by their resourcefulness. I pushed the loft door open and crouched in the window sill. It wasn't very far to the roof, so I swung the hook and rope and pulled myself to the very top. Carefully, using my bow, I closed the door.

Since the stable was a fairly large building in the shape of an L and two stories high, it gave me enough of a vantage point to see the layout of the yard. Carefully moving to the far-facing roof, I laid down in the shadows facing the keep. I pulled my cloak over my body and rested my head on my hands to wait. It was an hour until the bell would toll, and I could hear the guards talking excitedly amongst themselves.

"This is going to be so easy. Who would be stupid enough to take on a whole training facility of Denai and the Citadel's guards? This game will be over in an hour," a gruff voice commented.

"And that purse of gold will be mine," another challenged.

"Ha, not if I have any say in it."

"What does it matter about a purse of gold when there are promotions at stake? We have the chance to prove ourselves and make captains." A few grumbled agreements followed. I heard someone spit into the bushes, and then the men moved away.

Trying to wiggle my toes to keep them from falling asleep, I decided to count how many lighted windows I could see in the dorm rooms. There were a lot of lights on when the bell rang out twelve times. A cheer of excitement rang out among the guards and they began patrolling at a frenzied pace.

I had scouted out this spot days ago. I knew for a fact that you couldn't see onto the roof unless you were in a far field outside of the grounds.

The stable backed right up to the edge of the grounds, so in order for anyone to see me they would have to be out of bounds or get a ladder. After about an hour and no commotion, many of the students that were celebrating or out hunting decided to go to bed.

It was almost two in the morning when I heard the first scream, followed by a second. The sound sent chills down my back it was so real. But then I heard some cursing, name calling, and laughter.

"He's over here. Get him!" a male voice called.

"Hey, you are dead; you can't call out for help. That's not fair," a loud female voice chided.

A unit of guards hurried over to where three students, cloaks covered in blue dye, were emerging from the greenhouse. They were too far away to distinguish faces.

"Where did he go?" a guard yelled. I could see a female student glare at her fallen blue- splattered comrade and shake her head stubbornly.

"Sorry, can't talk. We're dead and must report inside. It wouldn't be fair to tell you." She pulled her comrade by his cloak and he started walking, grumbling and complaining.

Her third companion was chuckling at their misfortune and just shrugged at the guards and followed behind. The guards took off running in the direction they came from, as the three students headed inside.

It wasn't long before more yelling, shouts, screams and laughing were heard, as student after student was taken out.

"He's in the Citadel! Go...go...go!" yelled a captain. A line of guards rushed inside, only to come back out covered in blue paint, cursing and swearing.

One short man threw his sword on the ground and kicked the dirt. They made their way back toward the barracks in humiliation. I could hear the jeering as they went inside and waited. Soon, five more guards joined them with bright blue spots on their back.

"He's a sneaky turd, isn't he!" one of the first killed, yelled at the newcomer. "He shot us one by one when we came in the front. Couldn't even see where it came from."

I watched as more lights came on, students waking up during the commotion. My hands itched for action, but the last place I wanted to be right now was in the middle of that madhouse.

The one advantage I had was that I knew that he was eventually going to come after me, and I wasn't going to be an easy target and wait quietly in my room. The next hour was similar to the first with more screams and laughter. My skin crawled in nervousness as I realized he was going for the students first. Students, who in all reality, really were the biggest threat over the guards.

Now the guards weren't treating this like a normal attack, because they knew that no one was actually going to get hurt. They were counting on ambushing the assailants with stealth.

Soon I saw Adept Pax and Lorna walk out of the main hall across the courtyard and head toward the barracks and Captain Meryl. A mere twenty feet from my hiding spot.

Captain Meryl wiped his sweaty bald head and asked, "How's it going inside?"

"Unfortunately, good and bad," Adept Pax remarked. His dark skin looked even darker under the moonlight. "The SwordBrother is very good and is teaching many of our uptight students a lesson; you need more than just Denai power to defeat an opponent."

Adept Lorna frowned, her body stiff. "Too bad, it's somewhat humiliating to the students and to our training. It shows how unprepared we really were."

"Ah, come now, Lorna," Adept Pax patted her shoulder reassuringly. "How often in their life will they really be fighting against a SwordBrother? We agreed that this would be a good lesson for them. We believe Captains Rugen and Barstol have already been taken out by Joss."

"Not to mention a few of the younger more eager students created elaborate traps with nets. Despite all of their effort, they only managed to catch their fellow students."

In my head, I calculated how many attackers were left. There were a total of five people that we would have to contend with; four of Commander Meryl's Captains and one crazy SwordBrother. If Joss took out two, then that meant that there were three left?

"What about the SwordBrother?" Commander Meryl asked, his face gleaming with wild anticipation.

Adept Lorna threw her head back and laughed. "That one walked right in the front door."

"WHAT! Impossible! How…the three students?"

"He walked in wearing a cloak splattered with his own blue paint. He followed the first two students he killed, right into the main hall. He's also taken the highest number of students and guards out. He is one to be reckoned with."

Commander Meryl clapped his hands in delight and laughed out loud. "Aha, that is one cocky son of a SwordBrother. I wouldn't have expected that." After wiping the tears from his eyes his face became serious. "Any word on Thalia?"

"No one has seen or heard from her since this afternoon," Lorna said turning toward the courtyard, a worried look on her face.

"She was last seen running around the keep," Adept Pax replied, eyes darting to and fro looking for movement in the shadows.

Commander Meryl brought his voice down to a whisper. "She wasn't planning on running away, was she?"

Adept Pax snorted in reply. "No, I think she was getting ready to hunker down and wait out the SwordBrother. She had been practicing all week for this. I don't think she would run from this chance. I truly believe she would rise to the task."

Movement. By the south tower.

I quit spying on the adepts down below and turned my eyes to where Faraway saw something. Sure enough, there was either one the captains or the SwordBrother lying flat on the ground and crawling along the side of the wall in the shadows.

Moving to my knees, I blew heat back into my fingertips and flexed the muscles. Pulling out my bow, I notched my padded, paint-filled arrow and took aim. Following all of my training, I aimed and released, watching it fly through the air to come down on top of the sneaking assassin.

A loud "OOMMPHH" coming from the person in shadow declared it to be a true shot, as well as the splash of yellow that slowly moved from the ground into the form of a standing person. But it also gave away my position as the adepts and Commander Meryl's gaze immediately flew to the top of the stable where I kneeled. Slinging the bow over my shoulder, I gave a spry little wave to them as I ducked down and slid to the low end of the roof using my hook to climb down.

I could hear them laughing as Adept Pax said, "Definitely has risen to the occasion."

Mentally I counted down. Three left.

Wait! Faraway commanded, I froze and tried to slow my beating heart and breath.

On your left, he's coming around the armory. It's a captain. He's going to try and surprise you. He's fifty feet, forty-five feet, forty feet. NOW.

Nocking another padded arrow, I quickly followed my bow around the corner and shot the captain. He was very close and tried to dodge my arrow, but I was faster and grazed his shoulder. He let out a grunt in pain.

Rats, I thought, a shoulder graze wouldn't be considered a killing wound, and the captain knew it. He ducked into a doorway to wait me out. Slowly reaching into my leather hip pouch, I pulled forth one of Ruzaa's concoctions that I had transferred into a vial.

I peeked just enough around the corner to aim and threw the vial as hard as I could at the ground. It broke open and a heady potion spilled out, a sleeping potion.

I ducked back around the corner and pulled out a black cloth mask that covered my nose and the bottom half of my face, waiting until I heard a soft thud.

Holding my breath I dashed around the corner with the painted knife in hand. Feeling awful at what I was about to do, I almost backed out, but decided to run the fake knife across his stomach, so there wouldn't be any chance of accidental injury. The scent of the sleep inducing potion was making my eyes burn. I needed to move away quickly.

Two left.

GO! GET GOING! RUN TO THE RIGHT!

I ran and followed his directions past the garden and courtyard. Stopping when he told me to and moving when it was clear, I reached the locked wood chute that led down into the kitchen.

I pulled out the keys that I had borrowed from Donn that morning and conveniently forgotten to return. Grabbing the cold iron lock between my fingers, I quickly looked over my shoulder to make sure no one was near and prayed that no one had filled the chute a day early.

My nerves made me drop the key twice before I heard the quiet click of the lock. I was in luck, the wood chute was low enough on wood for me to squeeze through. But the darkness inside intimidated me. I almost decided to turn around and go in the front door of the main hall, but that would be suicide. And the training game over.

Taking a deep breath, I gently placed each foot into the chute and waited until the logs quit moving before I applied more weight. Once I was fully inside, I pulled the outside doors closed, encasing myself in pitch black nothingness. Taking a second to calm my nerves, I made my way down the wood chute inches at a time, stopping every so often to listen for sounds.

By the time I reached the bottom and the floor began to level out, my hands were full of splinters. I could see a faint glow coming from the kitchen fire under the chute doors.

Pressing my eye to the crack, I waited to see if anyone was in the kitchen. The fire was dim and the kitchen deserted.

Here was the final test. I had asked Avina to sneak into the kitchen and unlock the wood chute door after dinner.

Pressing my splintered hands to the door I gently pushed against the heavy door and felt it give.

But then it met resistance. Was I locked in? Did Avina not get it unlocked? Glancing up the chute the way I had come, I doubted I would be able to make it up without anyone hearing me. Before I started to panic, I pressed my eye to the bottom crack and noticed something was leaning against the door.

Once my eyes adjusted to the light, I saw that it was a mop and bucket. The mop handle was leaning against the door. The ground was about three feet from the bottom of the chute, and if I swung open the door, I would knock over the mop handle and the bucket of water. Weighing my options, I decided to chance it.

I pushed against the door with one hand. The mop started to slide sideways.

When the door was opened far enough, I darted my free hand under the door and caught the broom as it fell to the floor. The water in the bucket sloshed precariously back and forth making a small puddle on the floor. Sweat formed along my brow as I stepped out of the chute, closed the door, and moved the mop handle back.

Moving silently through the kitchen, I peeked into the dining hall. I was surprised at how many students were gathered there covered in green and blue dye. Almost the whole student body was there. I couldn't see Joss anywhere, so that gave me hope.

There were long tables set up like a buffet, with fruits, rolls, desserts, drinkable chocolate and spiced cider. My stomach growled in desire, and I envied the casual students laughing and eating.

Adept Cirrus and Adept Kambel were monitoring the students coming in and both looked to be in good spirits, taking the whole training game in fun compared to Adept Lorna and Pax.

Syrani was furious, sitting on a table, legs crossed with evidence of a green paint pack still plastered to her head and smeared along her chin. A group of younger students listened in awe, fawning over her.

"I so would have had him," she sniffed, taking a handkerchief from a young love-struck boy and dabbing at her face. It only seemed to make the green paint smear more. "I had followed one of them into the library and watched as he snuck into the archives. Just as I was about to send the whole shelf of books on top of him, one of them somehow got behind me and hit me in the face. He must have cheated; I can see no other possible explanation."

A chorus of agreements followed her statement. She looked like a queen addressing her subjects.

Looking at the fresh paint smearing her face I knew that I had little time, because both of my targets were at that moment in the library. Not about to take them both on at once, I took the servant staircase toward my room.

I stopped a few feet from my door and knelt, pressing my cheek to the cold marble floor. The dust hadn't been disturbed; no one had entered my room...yet.

Slipping into the room across the hall from mine, I closed the door with a quiet click. I glanced around the empty room to check for any signs of intruders. This room wasn't occupied, but it was a complete mirror of my own room, except that it was empty.

Seeing that the armoire was open and empty, and after doing a quick check under the bed, I moved back to the door and kneeled in front of the keyhole to spy on my own room. I pulled another sleeping potion from my pouch and waited, with the intention of throwing the vial at whoever tried to enter, while I hid behind a locked door until they fell asleep.

All of the excitement filled me with adrenaline, and I realized I was no longer afraid. I licked my lips in anticipation as a thought hit me.

I enjoyed being the predator instead of the prey.

My fingers itched with the eagerness to act, and I felt a bubble of -pride filling my body. Reflecting on my earlier conquest, I did a quick tally; I had taken down two captains, and Joss had taken down two. Which left the one SwordBrother.

I felt a trickle of fear and confusion as I did the math again. There was only supposed to be one left, but replaying Syrani's conversation again in my head, that she followed one and was attacked by another, that left two. Something wasn't adding up.

It was then I felt the light breeze brushing the hair on the back of my neck, and I froze. Turning toward the window, a black outline of a man's form was stepping slowly down from the window sill.

Mentally, I cursed at myself for not checking and locking the window. The figure pulled out the fake knife and advanced toward me with purpose. Quick as I could, I threw the vial at him and rolled away from the door, trying to put as much distance as I could between the man and myself.

He expertly darted out his hand and caught the jar in midair, bringing it down and pocketing it. Without wasting any more time, he lunged at me.

Shocked that he caught it, I couldn't do much more than grab my own dyed knife in hope that I could stab him first. I evaded the first lunge by jumping backward with the knife, but I was cornered. And foolishly, I had moved away from my only exit.

I dashed for the window he had entered and felt the slash of the knife strike my arm. Realizing that it would count as a hit, I quit running.

"Darn it," I said, turning toward him and grabbing my arm where he slashed it. "That will definitely count. I'm dead and you win!" I held out my hand to him in a congratulatory handshake, when I realized my palm was covered in red paint, not green. It took a moment to realize it wasn't paint, but blood.

Feeling my breath catch in my throat, I looked up at the person to whom I was extending my hand.

He was short, unshaven, and had greasy dark hair. I didn't recognize him, but his smile held pure evil as he chuckled at me.

"You're absolutely right," he said in a sinister voice. "You are dead."

I stood frozen to one spot, fear radiating off of me in waves that I was projecting to my horse.

The man moved toward me swinging his knife. I couldn't move.

Faraway physically took control over my mind and body and shoved me out of the way of the downward thrust of the knife. The knife sliced at my cloak, but I regained control of my body and senses and moved into action. *Thank you for saving me—twice.*

I leapt to the far side of a table, using it as a barricade between us as I tried to maneuver myself toward the door, but he just kept coming. I glanced to the window which led to a forty foot drop that I knew I couldn't survive.

Grabbing the last sleep scent jar I had, I threw it at him as hard as I could. The killer ducked and it crashed into the far wall, too far away to do any good.

That was it, I was out of options.

In a last-ditch effort, I shoved the table as hard as I could into his stomach. He grunted and doubled over in pain. I used the moment to sprint toward the door and grip the door handle. It was still locked.

I was just able to open the door when my attacker yanked me back into the room by my hair, tossing me across the floor. I slid until my back crashed into the armoire, then my skull cracked against it as well.

Stars filled my vision and pain screamed through my head as I watched him close the door.

I'd been so close! Just a few more seconds and I could have escaped. Now my body was throbbing, I couldn't focus and darkness filled my vision. It didn't last long, as the blackness morphed into the form of the man looming over me with his bloodstained knife.

"Please!" I begged. "You don't have to kill me."

"Yes, I do. Raven is afraid you'll regain your memories and reveal us." He kneeled in front of me.

My hands flew out in defense, hitting him to keep him as far away as possible.

"You are a costly loose end. You need to be disposed of."

The moon chose that moment to go behind a cloud, and we lost all light.

Grabbing the dirty hand that held the knife I tried to pull it from his grasp, but he was stronger than me. Unwilling to lose the battle, I kicked, scratched, and finally bit his arm until the taste of blood flowed into my mouth.

He punched me in the jaw and I went slack with dizziness. With a wicked grin of triumph, he raised the knife to slice my throat.

I prayed God would make it quick and painless and closed my eyes.

A soft thud and a grunt were all I heard as I opened them to see the man drop the knife inches from my neck and fall onto my body. Blood trickled from his mouth.

Crying out in fear, I struggled with the weight of his body and tried to push him off of me. His blood flowed onto me, and he was still breathing, rasping in my ear.

Soft sobs escaped me, as I was helpless to move his dying form. The sound of footsteps drew near, and the body was rolled off of me onto the floor. I didn't care if I lived or died, or if the other person in the room meant me harm. Curling up in a fetal position I watched the man fade. All thoughts of being brave abandoned me as I watched my attacker struggle for life.

"We will keep coming," he rasped out. "Until she's dead. There are more of us. There are always more, willing to die for the Raven and his ideas." He began to cough and spit blood.

Wherever he was wounded, he wouldn't last long.

"We are like the sands on a shore, numerous beyond measure and everywhere. Eventually we will have her and she will die."

The other stranger in the room leaned over the body and grabbed the head, evidently tired of his threats. , Though he blocked my view, the thought hit me that this must be the deadly SwordBrother.

The sound of the neck snapping brought me back to awareness and hysteria at all at once.

"NO. NO. NO. NO. NO. NO!" I heard myself say. A faint pressure was building in my head, the signs of another headache coming on.

"Shhh, Thalia, shhhh. It's all right. You're safe," the SwordBrother kindly intoned.

Turning toward me, he used his body to block the sight of the dead assassin. He raised his gloved hand and stroked my hair from my forehead in a gentle and reassuring manner.

"Who are you?" I whispered into the dark.

"I'm a SwordBrother."

I wasn't in the mood for games. "No. What's your name?"

He leaned back on his heels, bringing his face into the moonlight.

"But you already know it," he spoke softly. The moonlight illuminated the strong jaw, the long black hair and dark, stormy eyes of Kael.

~22~

y heart fluttered in excitement and apprehension at seeing him. "What are you doing here? Are you following me?" I asked defensively.

Kael pulled back his hand, his face becoming stone, hiding all of his emotions. "I'm here because I was asked to be here by Pax Baton as a favor, to test the Citadel's defenses." His eyes looked into mine, and he rocked back onto the balls of his feet, hands resting on his knees.

"But you showed up in the marketplace and saved me, and now here. How did you know I was in trouble if you weren't following me?" I blurted out angrily.

He snorted. "You must think pretty highly of yourself, if you believe you're important enough to have a SwordBrother protecting you."

I gave Kael a startled look.

Leaning in close to me, his breath whispering against my ear, he spoke very slowly. "Believe me, you're not."

My blood boiled at his words. He drove me to insanity with his apparent disregard for me. How can a person save your life in one breath and act like he can't stand you the next?

"If I'm not important, maybe you should have left me to die," I snarled at him, showing him my teeth and displeasure.

"Believe me, I've thought about it."

Jumping to his feet, he walked over to the dead assassin and began to rummage through his pockets, pulling out a garrote, a small piece of paper that looked to be a sketch of the

Citadel, throwing knives, a small clear vial of fluid, which Kael sniffed and announced as poison, and another piece of paper with ancient symbols drawn on it.

Obviously the attacker was one of the vile Septori, but he had told us nothing of where he came from. Kael found the side pouch and pulled out my clay pot and put it on the floor without opening it, giving me a look.

"Why don't you smell that one?" I asked, wishing full well he would, so that he would fall asleep. It would serve him right for the way he treated me.

He raised an eyebrow at me. "No, thank you, I've seen what this can do."

The hair on my arms stood on end. That was all the proof I needed. He'd just given himself away.

"You can deny it all you want, but how do you even know what is in that jar if you weren't following me?" I gradually slid up the armoire with my hands pressed against the wood. "I didn't even pick up those items, Avina did. And I transferred them to those clay bottles myself, alone, in my room."

Kael stopped rummaging in the pack and slowly stood facing me, his face unreadable. "You forget that this whole thing is a test, for which I am paid, mind you, to kill you. I would be lax in my duties if I didn't stake out my target before I attacked." He took a step toward me, and the way his voice changed and became deeper made me want to bolt for the door, which I did. I grabbed the handle only to be stopped at the last minute as his full weight slammed against mine, the door trapping me and his arms holding the door closed. His body was pressed close, so I couldn't escape under his arms.

I turned and studied his profile, which was more rugged and dangerous than Joss's good looks. Where Joss made me feel safe and secure, Kael made me feel like I was on a cliff about to fall off into a mass of rolling waves. He played with my emotions, and I hated it.

"Open the door!" I demanded, looking at him straight in the eye. "Get away from me!"

His eyes darkened with hidden meaning. "I can't."

In frustration he hung his head down, his dark hair covering his face. "You don't understand. I can't let you go. It's you."

I'd had enough of his hidden meanings and mind games! I tried to push him away but his fingertips grabbed my upper arms, digging in hard.

"It's all you and I hate you for it." He pushed me back into the door and my already bruised head hit the door again. I winced in pain. I saw bright lights and, blinking hard, I glanced at him. He was grimacing at what he'd done. His eyes started to lose focus.

"Kael," I said in a very calm voice, as I tried my best to talk reason into him. "Kael, listen to me. I have no idea what you are talking about."

"Don't you see? I have to kill you; it may be my only chance."

He sounded mad. Not angry mad, insane mad. Which only made my temper rise.

"Kael, you are hurting me." I reached into my pocket, hoping he wouldn't notice, as I could see that his mind was somewhere else. I gripped the dye knife hard in a final act of desperation, and I went limp.

He would either have to drop me or catch me. He chose to catch me. As he pulled me closer, I stabbed him with the dye knife.

His eyes went wide as the contact of the yellow dye on his shirt spread. He dropped me and winced as I hit the floor. I moved away as he stared at the spot, touching it with his hand and pulling it away covered with yellow.

His face became hard again, and his eyes regained their focus. He looked at me, his jaw set in anger, hate emanating from his stance.

"You see, this is entirely your fault," he spat out.

"I didn't do anything to you!" I screamed, letting the anger flow. "I wish I had never met you. Never in my life have I met someone as uncaring as you, except for the Raven and the Septori. And since this training game is over, I never, ever want to see your face again."

Pulling open the door, I stormed out and marched toward the main hall. Holding back tears, I dropped the stupid knife on the ground. How could this happen? How could someone who has saved my life three times care for me one minute and the next, loathe and hate me?

And why did I care? Would it matter so much if he did like me?

Did I want him to like me?

Stopping in the middle of the hall I pressed my head to the cold stone wall and let the tears flow, letting all of the hurt and anger pour out.

When I finally felt composed, I realized I didn't want to be in the main hall, surrounded by people. Changing directions I decided to head outside. I would let Kael address the Adept Council and tell them he had lost to me.

Once I reached the courtyard, I made a beeline for Faraway, and stopped in the shadows of a column as I saw Adepts Pax and Lorna, Commander Meryl and his troops rush inside.

They have been notified of the dead assassin upstairs. Faraway spoke.

"How?"

Kael is in the main hall and spoke with Adept Pax. Pax then mindspoke to Adept Lorna.

"How do you know this?"

I knew that the Adept Council members and some of the students were strong enough to speak to each other using their minds, but I wondered how Faraway knew that.

Because I like to listen in on their conversations when they're not shielding, he said smugly.

I rolled my eyes. Of course my horse would like to listen in on gossip.

When I finally made it to the pasture I ran to Faraway and hugged him. He nuzzled my shoulder affectionately.

I could also enter their minds and speak to them if I wanted to.

Lifting my head from his mane, I said out loud, "Why didn't you earlier, when I was attacked?"

Because the SwordBrother was already on his way.

"What? Kael? How?"

But Faraway gave me one of his enigmatic looks and took a bite of grass, ignoring me. After no more information came forth, I sighed in frustration and leaned against his shoulder. I lightly ran my hands along his breast and over a light tattoo-like emblem that had mysteriously appeared.

It appeared shortly after the first attack when Faraway saved me. I originally thought that Master Grese had branded him without my knowledge, but after an awkward confrontation he denied it. The mark was actually quite beautiful; two beautiful connecting whorls in an S which was transected by a simple wavy line.

It felt right and only enhanced Faraway's beauty. He wore it like a badge of honor or a medal.

"What did you do to me, when I was frozen with fright?" I asked him. "I felt you take over my body and force me to move."

I had to, Faraway replied. *I'm your Guardian. Your mind was frozen in fear and your body wouldn't move. We are linked through our bond. I'm sorry. I shouldn't have done that without your permission. But I'm still learning my boundaries.*

All this did was create more questions about what kind of bond we had and this whole guardian thing. I was going to have to spill my secret and talk to one of the adepts and soon.

"So at least you have more power than me?" I actually felt a little disappointed at that thought. I hadn't shown signs of power since Faraway saved me.

I have power because you chose me as your Guardian, Faraway encouraged, lifting my spirits. *I have power because of you.*

Someone called my name.

They are looking for you. They are worried, Faraway reflected calmly.

"I don't want to go in," I said. "I refuse to look at or talk to Kael ever again." My response caused an exasperated snort from Faraway who pushed me in the back with his muzzle, forcing me to walk forward or get knocked on my butt.

"Watch it, Horse!" I joked. Leaving my hand on his shoulder we walked back to the stables. It was interesting; now that we were bonded, I couldn't get enough of touching him. Faraway didn't mind. He loved it, but touching him seemed to calm me on many different levels. It was like a drug, and it was addicting. The connection was a power source that could rejuvenate and calm me at the same time.

The closer we got to the stables, the more chaotic it became. Guards and soldiers, who were moments ago laughing and teasing each other, now searched the grounds, faces serious and deadly.

The Denai students were mingling about in small groups, whispering nervously. I put Faraway in his stall and gave him fresh water and hay, delaying the inevitable as long as possible. When there was nothing else to do but go inside, I stepped out. All five of the adepts descended on me, surrounding me like an armed guard and ushering me inside the Citadel.

I watched as the iron doors shut and were locked. I knew it was to keep anyone from getting in.

But in that moment, it felt more like they were keeping me from getting out.

~28~

I was beginning to hate the chair.

I sat in the same hard chair in the Adept Council room again. I shouldn't be surprised. I had been tempted to ask to stop by my room and get a pillow to sit on, but one glance at their faces and I knew to not even ask.

They kept the meeting short, asking me to recap my steps the previous day and explain what happened when I got to the spare room. I gave them a condensed version of everything, though I left out Kael's erratic behavior, not really understanding why I chose to.

Since it was almost dawn, I was dismissed to go to my room. Adept Lorna said I would have a guard assigned, and I should get some rest. I made a motion to argue and she cut me off with a look that said: *don't you dare.*

Sighing in defeat, I left the meeting room. As soon as I stepped through the door, I came face to face with a worried Joss.

His handsome face looked ragged and tired but lit up when he saw me. He pulled me into a bear hug. "I'm so glad you're okay," he murmured into my hair. When he reluctantly let go of me, he still held onto my hand.

Too tired to pull it out of his grasp, I let him lead me back to my room. I gave him my key. His sure hands inserted it and unlocked the door.

Lighting a lamp, he did a thorough search of my room, under the bed, in the armoire, and behind the curtains. His actions made me smile as I pulled off my boots, and washed what was left of the grease paint from my face. Most of it had rubbed off in the fight, and I was too tired to go to the baths or care.

Crawling into my large bed, I collapsed into my pillows and felt Joss pull a blanket over me, stopping mid motion to pull a flyaway piece of straw from my hair. He reached for my injured arm, and I started to jerk it away when he caught it and pulled it into his lap. I watched him close his eyes in concentration. Warmth spread through my arm as the cut slowly healed and turned a faint pink. Rejuvenating energy flowed into me followed by a calm and content feeling. My eyes started to droop.

"Thank you, Joss," I mumbled sleepily.

"I wish I could do more," he grumbled. Going over to the couch, he stretched his large frame out upon it, trying to get comfortable.

Sitting up in alarm, I cried out, "What do you think you are doing?"

"Taking a nap. What does it look like?" he retorted.

"You can't stay here! It's not proper."

Joss just gave me a stubborn look. "I really don't care about what's proper. You have been attacked twice in the last two weeks. For goodness' sake, this is the Citadel! It's supposed to be the safest place in the city."

"Obviously not."

"I don't care how many rules it breaks, or how many guards you get, or even if I get expelled. I'm not letting you out of my sight. So get some sleep. I'm not going anywhere."

Giving him an icy stare wasn't making him change his mind. He walked over to my sparsely stocked bookshelf, picked up a book, went back to the couch and began to read it—completely ignoring me.

I huffed and gave in, plopping down on my pillows. After I made a childish show of trying to get comfortable again, punching my pillows to show my displeasure at him staying, sleep finally overtook me and I dreamed.

This time I was back in the prison and it was burning. Fire surrounded me, the beams in the ceiling were burning, and the tunnel came crashing down behind me. Flames licked at my feet and I could smell burning flesh. I gagged as the stench filled my nostrils. The smoke made it difficult to see and breathe. I tried to move down the hallway, but a ring of fire raged in front and behind me.

Through the flames and smoke, I could see Kael standing there watching me. I started to reach out to him for help, when I remembered what he had said earlier about wishing he had let me die. I dropped my hands limply to my side, my eyes burning with tears, refusing to ask for help. The flames burned brighter and the smoke made it a deep breath impossible.

Choking, I fell to my knees, my fingers digging in the dirt as I tried to breathe in the cleaner air that was lower to the ground. But every breath burned fire down my lungs, as I felt myself suffocating from smoke inhalation. The flames licked at my skin, making it burn and pucker.

I could see Kael, angry, standing over my listless form, his mouth forming words I couldn't hear. Kneeling down, he yelled out again but I was deaf to them.

Refusing help, I closed my mind from him. He wanted to let me die, so I was giving him his wish; I would let myself die in this dream world.

As my world faded away, I felt him grab my shoulders hard and force me to look into his eyes. Barely able to stay conscious, I forced myself to meet his angry gaze, and I heard him clear as day shout into my mind. "WAKE UP!"

I awoke, gasping for breath, coughing. A hand pounded my back and someone spoke my name.

"Thalia, it's okay. You're all right. Just breathe." Joss's words calmed me.

Looking around my room in confusion, I started to cough and spit up black stuff into a handkerchief. Pushing him away, I threw off the covers and tried to reach the window, stumbling weakly as if the room were still filled with smoke.

I threw open the windows and leaned out, coughing, to let in the fresh air. It was now midmorning and the sun was shining. Joss brought me over a glass of water. I drank all of it. After I had settled down, I collapsed on the couch and asked him. "What happened?"

"I've never seen anything like it," Joss explained. "I was asleep when a loud sound woke me up. I went to check on you, and you had stopped breathing. I could feel power in the room, and I couldn't get you to wake up. I tried to look into your mind, but it was blocked."

I told Joss about my dream. Not feeling comfortable revealing that I was dreamt about Kael, I conveniently left him out again. I was doing that a lot lately. Joss looked worried as I described the burning cell and how I felt I was dying of asphyxiation when I suddenly awoke.

"Thalia, you were attacked by a Denai in your sleep," he said.

"How can you know for sure?" I asked.

"Because...Thalia, look at your wrists."

Sure enough, small burn marks appeared along my wrists and arms.

"And," he paused. "I can still smell smoke."

~24~

"That's it! I'm out of here."

I scrambled off the couch, ran to my armoire and started throwing clothes into a bag. Joss came over and tried taking the items of clothes out and putting them back into the closet.

"Thalia, what are you doing? You can't leave."

Joss tried to grab a shirt out of my hands. We both tugged on it until I surrendered it to him with a glare.

"Oh, yeah? Watch me."

I grabbed a pair of socks and threw them in my bag. He reached in to pull out more clothes and pulled out one of my undergarments. Face turning beet red, he sputtered and dropped the garment on the floor as if it had bitten him.

"Thalia, you'll be even more unprotected in the city than in the Citadel." Excellent. Instead of the unpacking approach, he would try to reason with me.

"Hasn't worked so far," I argued. "You were even in the same room with me, and I was still attacked. He's here, Joss. The Raven is close. Even if he's in the city right now, he could still reach into my mind."

"That's because you haven't been fully trained. If you stayed and learned how to use your powers, you could shield yourself from these attacks better."

"While I'm sleeping?" Somehow that didn't seem possible.

"Once you're trained, using your power can become as natural as breathing. But if you leave now, you leave yourself open to more attacks."

"I can't fight the same way you can! I can't do anything the same way you can." Despair raised the pitch of my voice with each word.

"Truthfully, Thalia, I'm at a loss when it comes to what you are capable of. I know what my limits are. But you are different, the rules are different."

Turning from him, I let out a sigh and threw my whole bag back into the closet, shutting it with a slam.

"Joss, I have no idea what I'm capable of either. The only thing I've been able to do is subconscious, like pulling you into my memories, and being able to speak with Faraway."

"Who?" Joss raised one eyebrow at me and folded his arms across his chest while leaning against the armoire. The pose showed off his muscles and his tall stature. My eyes went wide and I lost my train of thought for a second until I felt a faint familiar brushing of my mind.

Stop staring and continue with what you were going to say.

"I...I...what?"

You were about to tell him how you are bonded with a very intelligent horse, who is charming, quick-witted, handsome, can run like the wind...and...

"Who's as vain as a prince?" I interrupted his thoughts. "Now leave me alone, before he thinks I'm completely nuts."

Don't worry, he doesn't think you're nuts...He knows it. Faraway left my mind with a hint of laughter, or the snorting sound that would pass for a horse's laughter. . I stared, focused, at a far spot in the wall the whole while I was having a silent conversation with my horse. When I was finished, I looked back to Joss.

He stood up from where he'd been leaning against the armoire and stared at me in confusion.

Biting my lip, I explained, "Faraway, my horse. I have a connection with him and we can speak to each other." Now that the cat was out of the bag, I waited in trepidation for Joss to make fun of me.

"Well, that's great!" He clapped his hands together excitedly, moving to the middle of my room. "That just proves that you have great potential and you still have a lot to learn."

Spinning around to look at me again, he placed his hands on his hips. "Not everyone can speak with animals, and usually only those that make it to the Journeyman or Adept levels can." He started pacing the room. "So you see, you have to stay and finish training. If you can make it to Adept, you would be strong enough to fight off anyone who comes after you."

"Joss, I highly doubt that." Walking over to the couch, I plopped down on it and rested my arm and chin across the back. It was calming to watch Joss move around the room. "For instance, it's been proven by Adept Cirrus's Mercury ball, er, stone thing or whatever that I'm not Denai. And so far all I've been able to do is suck, literally. As in suck your power or energy from you and use it against you, which also could explain why I don't have much control over my ability. I don't actually have any Denai blood in my veins. Admit it, what I did isn't normal. I'm a freak. I'm beginning to wonder if I can call myself human anymore."

His stopped pacing mid-stride and froze at my words.

Placing my hands over my mouth, I wanted to kick myself for bringing up my lack of Denai blood and how I got my powers. I remembered how he had acted when we first found out I had powers. He was fine with me being a normal human being, and he would have been fine with me being a Denai.

I could see that something about it bothered him—put him on edge. I think it was the unknown and the possibility of changed bloodlines that bothered him the most. Not the fact that I had access to powers, but what was done to me to give me those powers—the method itself—is what bothered his code of ethics.

I decided the best course of action was to change the subject. "All right, Joss, we have an assembly, and I really need to get a bath and dressed, so you need to make yourself scarce."

I stood up, grabbed his arm and physically pushed him toward my door. "By the way, what was it that woke you up a few minutes ago?" I asked, my curiosity finally getting the better of me.

Joss put his hands up and grabbed the doorframe, stopping my forward momentum. Dipping his head low, he actually started to look a little red in the face. "Well, now that you mention it, it was a knock on the door. Since I didn't want to open it and get caught in your room, I went to wake you instead."

Feeling the blood rush from my face, I motioned for Joss to get behind the door as I placed my hand on the doorknob and prayed that whoever had knocked earlier had given up and left.

Opening the door slowly and peeking outside, I saw that I had no such luck. For who should be leaning against the far wall looking furious but Kael? Meeting his cold eyes, I jumped back into my room with a small squeak and slammed the door. Of all the people who could come to my door! I let out a furious scream between clenched teeth, trying to stifle my anger.

"Who is it?" Joss whispered. I looked at his anxious expression and almost laughed.

"It's the SwordBrother." At the mention of Kael, his face became hard.

Grabbing my towels and soap, I steeled myself to face him again. I opened my door, ignoring Kael altogether, and walked toward the baths, hoping he wouldn't follow me. That left Joss inside my rooms to wait it out until the coast was clear.

Kael moved away from the wall and tailed me all the way to the baths, his footsteps silent as the night. Only his shadow on the wall revealed his presence behind me. Quickening my pace, I reached for the handle of the door to the women's bath and turned, giving him a pointed, challenging look.

I shot him a smug glance and proceeded to close the door in his face. His hand shot out and kept the door from shutting completely, and with a slight shove he pushed around it and stepped into the women's bathing rooms. Glancing around the interior sitting room, he went and picked out a vacant private suite. He checked behind every column and curtain before allowing me to enter.

The baths had become one of my favorite luxuries since becoming a student. The servants' bathing chambers had soaking tubs. The student baths were much more complex, with different levels of comfort and bathing suites. Some suites were closed off and completely private. A sign on the door marked if it was occupied. The larger suites consisted of beautiful benches, columns, and a heated marble soaking tub.

I generally preferred these smaller private rooms and would often fall asleep in them, but today, out of spite, I walked past him and entered the adjoined co-ed bathing pools instead. Besides, they were big enough to swim in, and I needed the distraction for a moment.

The co-ed pools were in an open solarium with frosted glass. Large exotic plants and trees separated each of the pools to give privacy. They were all connected so the water ran from one basin to the other and felt very much like a flowing river. You could actually swim from one to the next around a curve.

I chose to walk the length of the solarium and to pick out my favorite swimming spot. It tended to be the most secluded and least used. Even though I enjoyed frustrating Kael, I knew enough not to swim right in the middle of a crowd. Nearby splashing indicated there were others using the bathing pools.

I had found that I loved swimming. Today I chose it for two reasons: trying to secure something with so much foliage and so many bends and twists and turns would make Kael uncomfortable, and there was a back exit.

So far I hadn't spoken a word to him, but I knew without even asking that the adepts must have assigned him as my bodyguard. That rankled, because right now, I couldn't even stand to be near him.

I swam a few laps, making sure he was busy on the other side of the pools, then quickly bathed, changed as fast as I could, and slipped out the back door. Walking on tiptoe, I rounded the corner and walked right into Kael's broad chest. I jumped in surprise.

"What are you doing?" I demanded, trying to regain my composure.

Kael raised an eyebrow at me.

"Well, I would think that was obvious." he scowled. "I'm keeping you safe. I've been given an assignment. I'm your new guard."

"Thanks, but no! You can tell the Adept Council that I politely declined your services." I moved down the hall with no particular destination in mind, as long as it was far away from him as possible.

"So you think of sneaking out the back door of the baths as your way of politely declining? If that's the case, then I think your manners could use some improving."

"Maybe it's what you deserve."

"Or maybe it's that you would prefer someone else as your bodyguard altogether; someone like Joss? Who is probably still hiding in your room, by the way."

The inflection of his words hinted at some other meaning and froze me in my tracks.

Turning on him in a blaze of fury, I struck out my hand toward his cheek in anger and he deftly caught it midair. Pulling on my captured wrist I spat out the words, "It is none of your business who I invite into my room. And yes, anyone would be preferable to you."

"Too bad, you've got me."

"Then I will speak with the Adept Council myself."

Kael had still not let go of my wrist and it was starting to hurt. I could see his jaw set in anger and I was feeling a faint pounding in my head, which happened whenever he was near me. Looking at his hand, I saw that he kept a short leather bracer on his right arm and not the left.

He caught me staring at it and dropped my hand suddenly.

Trying to rub the feeling back into my wrist, I noticed I would have some bruising. When Kael noticed what he had done to my arm, his blue eyes turned down in shame.

"You're right, you need to find someone else—anyone else—and fast."

He walked away from me, but then stopped and waited for me to follow. "It's time for the assembly. We need to get going."

He was right. Knowing we would both be heading in the same direction anyway, I followed. I was trying to make my hair decent by running my fingers through it and pulling out the knots. I had left in such a hurry from the baths that I spared no time for my hair. I quickly twirled it into a bun and was trying to get it to stay without any pins, when Kael knelt and pulled out of his boot a very slender silver knife in its sheath. Spinning me around, he grabbed my hair. I was scared that he had gone crazy and was going to cut it all off in punishment.

Instead, he deftly inserted it into the bun. I gave my head a test shake, and it held tight. I gazed at him puzzled.

"The women in my clan often wear weapons in their hair for protection. It isn't the right size for you, but it will do until we find you something else."

I was left speechless and confused.

The main hall was packed for the Assembly. Spotting Avina and Berry, I waved and tried to make my way through the tables to where they sat. My foot hit something suddenly. Feeling myself fall forward, I felt a jerk as a hand steadied me. Turning toward my antagonist, I wasn't surprised at all to see Syrani. She'd tripped me.

"There is no way you could have won last night without cheating. And I'm going to prove it. I was one of the last students to be hit, and I'm going to appeal the contest results." She smiled smugly.

Kael released my arm and turned toward Syrani. She smiled in delight when she saw how handsome Kael was. She brightened as he leaned in and whispered in her ear. Her smile quickly disappeared, and her face turned white when Kael moved away, looking every inch the deadly SwordBrother.

Feeling a moment of smugness, I hurried over and sat on the bench by Berry and Avina, greeting both of them with kisses and hugs, reassuring them both that I was good.

"Oh, Thalia, I did what you asked and unlocked the wood chute door. But when I came in this morning I noticed that someone had put a mop and bucket there. Please tell me that wasn't there earlier?"

"Everything's fine, Avina. You did great!"

Sitting back, I held each of their hands in mine. For once in my life, I felt happy and content, which was odd considering how I had almost been murdered last night.

Joss came in and made his way over to me. Avina moved over to make room for Joss, but before Joss could sit, Kael's large form occupied the spot.

I rolled my eyes at Joss over Kael's head, and he grinned and sat behind me, giving me a quick shoulder squeeze. Kael glared at Joss's hand until he dropped it back into his lap.

Faraway, I called to my horse. Instantly an image of him in his stall came to my mind.

Yes?

"Remind me that the next time Kael and I are near you, that you will kick him for me."

He sent an image of Kael face down in a mud puddle back at me. I chuckled, until I saw Kael looking at me. Feeling somewhat chagrined, I waited patiently until the assembly began.

Each of the Adept Council members spoke in turn, congratulating various students and guards for their prowess and abilities. Joss was recognized for his kills. I was announced as the winner of the game, since I had taken out two attackers and was able to kill the SwordBrother. Looking sideways at Kael I felt a blush run up my cheek, and I decided that my feet were more interesting. I felt guilty in the way I had won, considering Kael had just saved my life and I killed him to save mine.

Today Kael did seem more sane, but not by much.

Commander Meryl arose and awarded his soldiers and captains with prizes and medals. Garit was given top marks for taking out the second greatest number of students. I whistled in encouragement when his name was called.

When Commander Meryl talked about Kael, the room became quiet and still. He described the SwordBrother's cunning and courage, how he disguised himself as a student and walked in the front door. When the Commander counted out how many of the students and guards were taken out by him alone, the room was so quiet you could have heard a pin drop. Kael alone had taken out seventy percent of the guard and student population. The sheer implications behind the numbers woke up the students and the guards. The mood of the room shifted to apprehension.

Commander Meryl became deadly serious when he made his final address. "Students, faculty, guards, one man alone decimated over half of our numbers. This tells us that we have become apathetic to the notion of being attacked. Yes, we have lived in peaceful times for over a century, but that does not leave us any excuse for what happened."

Adept Pax and Lorna stood up next to the Commander at the podium.

Pax spoke up first. "Last night, during our training session, a genuine attempt was made on one of our student's lives, and it was the SwordBrother who intervened." A shuffle in the crowd followed as necks strained to turn and look at me.

Heat flushed the back of my neck and I tried to make myself invisible or sink into the floor.

"But we will never again be caught unaware. You must understand this is highly unusual--unheard of actually—but SwordBrother Kael has agreed to help train you. You will give him your respect. This is indeed a great honor."

Exited whispering and more glances my way made me squirm in my seat. Adept Lorna stepped forward, a grim expression on her face.

"We have talked about canceling the Founding Celebration this year in lieu of what has happened." The whispers turned into gasps and pleading. "But," she paused dramatically, "we feel that we will be better prepared and will continue with the celebration. The Founding Celebration will take place next month as planned." Shouts and applause drowned out anything else she might have said.

I saw her make eye contact with me and nod toward the side door. When we were dismissed, I made my way out the side door and met with her.

"I see by your expression that you have something you wish to say about your guard," she grinned at me.

"Please, what did I do to deserve this?" Waving my hands dramatically I continued. "I will do anything you ask, but I beg of you to give me a different guard."

Her brows creased with worry. "What's wrong? Did something happen? I thought you would be happy to have the best, considering he already saved your life. I thought you would be grateful."

Now feeling guilty and terrible, I let out a long sigh. "No, it's just we don't really get along well."

Adept Lorna laughed, "Oh, nonsense, it's just the SwordBrother ways. Remember, there aren't many of them. If you want to learn more about him, maybe you should visit the library and do some research."

Nodding my head in agreement, I felt like a child trying to merely appease their parent. I quickly filled her in on how I was attacked in my sleep, and her frown became deeper. I told her about Joss and she didn't blink an eye.

"We need you to catch up on your defensive training as soon as possible. And I will have to discuss this with the Council." Her hand went to her hips. "Now remember," she went on, "you are to go nowhere without Kael, unless he is busy instructing, then you are to either have Captain Garit or Joss with you at all times. Any questions?"

I opened my mouth for a rebuttal, but she cut me off.

"Good, now get going."

The next couple of days settled into a different routine: classes, combat training, meals and sleep. I worked hard from sunup to sundown.

In the mornings, I would report to Garit who put me to work running laps around the compound and practicing hand-to-hand combat. Even though it wasn't required, I still enjoyed working out with Garit, and his jovial attitude was a relief from the stern, almost resentful attitude of Kael. Then I would attend morning classes in the arena, always careful to follow another student through the doors. If I was late or if I was early, Instructor Weston was usually waiting by the doors for me.

Today, I was so frustrated in my inability to do this simple task, that I wanted to rip the doors off of the arena, march in there, and destroy something. Of course, Kael had already worn my patience thin, and I was at my wit's end.

I walked straight up to through the great winged doors before I realized that Cassiel had opened for me. And a Denai hadn't accompanied me.

Turning to the great steel man, I whispered a quick thank you before taking my seat along the bench. Instructor Weston announced his arrival with his regular clap of thunder, and I was proud that I didn't jump. That pride didn't last long when he told us to pair up for training.

Looking up, I saw Syrani smirking at me. "Are you ready, rat?"

Taking a quick glance around, I noticed everyone had already picked a partner. I had a gut feeling that Syrani had orchestrated our pairing on purpose. We were supposed to test each other's limits. So I knew that this was going to get ugly.

"Let's see what you've got," Syrani smiled serenely at me. That was all the warning I was given. The ground shifted beneath my feet as giant pillars of stone shot out of the ground, knocking me backwards.

I gasped in surprise as I rolled out of the way of the falling pillar of stone. She was gifted in earth-moving; somehow that wasn't what I had expected.

Her tinkling laugh filled the air in challenge, "Come on, lil' Thalia! Show your teeth!"

I couldn't do anything but run, so she caused a giant hole to erupt around my feet. The earth I stood on crumbled and fell away into nothingness, and I backpedaled to keep my feet on solid ground. But I kept sliding with the earth toward the hole.

Screaming, I reached out and caught a tree root and held on as my feet dangled over nothingness.

"Come on, Thalia! Show me how strong you are; Show me what impressed the adepts so much they thought you worthy to train among us."

Did no one see what was going on? Was no one going to help me?

More laughter rang in my ears, and my anger started to build. Reaching hand over hand, I pulled my own body weight out of the hole using the tree root, and I stood back and glared at Syrani in challenge.

"Stop it," I yelled.

"Make me," she yelled back, and as fast as the hole in the earth appeared it disappeared and was solid earth again. Syrani walked across the earth and came to stand in front of me. She raised one polished finger and tipped my chin back so I could look into her eyes.

"That is, if you can."

Anger boiled over and I pushed her finger away from my face. I stood up straighter and did the only thing I could think of to fight back. I punched her.

Syrani shrieked in pain and backed away from me, wiping her nose to reveal a small trickle of blood.

I smiled crookedly at her.

"I don't care what the SwordBrother threatens to do to me," she spat out between gritted teeth, breathing in rage. "You are dead."

The ground shifted again, became finer, softer and I started to sink into the earth as it hungrily pulled at my boots.

Quicksand!

This was not how I thought I would die. It couldn't be, could it? The sand was to my knees, and I turned and tried to struggle toward the edge of the sandpit.

"Come on. Do something!" someone shouted.

Then another voice picked up. "Fight her back."

I glanced up through sand-filled eyes and saw that everyone else had stopped what they were doing to watch Syrani and me battle. What surprised me the most was that they were cheering for me.

The sand pulled harder and faster; it was up to my chest. Desperately, I swam through the sand, trying to find some sort of foot purchase or hand hold. A clap of thunder alerted me to the presence of Instructor Weston, and I breathed a sigh of relief, knowing he would make Syrani stop.

I stopped struggling and waited for help. As the pull of the quicksand continued, I searched the crowd and saw Weston standing fifteen paces away; immobile. He didn't move a muscle to help me; his gray eyes were riveted on me.

When the sand reached my neck; I knew no one was going to help me. No one cared enough to help, and that infuriated me. My breathing became ragged and I had trouble focusing. The sand started to fill my mouth and I could only scream with rage.

I was not going to be made a victim again. I had one final breath of air, and then I was under the sand. It was cool, dark, and slightly moist against my body that felt too warm, too hot.

Pain wreaked havoc on my body. Searing light burned through my body into my soul. If I could have screamed, I would have. I heard a loud crack and felt as if a piece of me had broken in two. Something was wrong; it didn't feel right. I wasn't surrounded by light but by darkness.

Power like no other surged through my body, my fingers and bones aching with the electric current. I burned with anger. I wanted someone to pay for hurting me.

I could see with my subconscious; I could see through the sand and see the worry among the Denai students. I didn't care, I wanted them to hurt.

I saw the light that surrounded Syrani, and I pulled at it—her power, her life—and squeezed. I could see her panic and start to cough as she tried to catch her breath.

THALIA. This isn't the way, Faraway's voiced echoed clearly in my mind, calming me. You must not steal power from others or destroy them. It's not right.

"Then how?"

You know how.

And I did.

Looking down at myself with my inner vision, I saw that my own inner light was not a bright, glowing white like the other Denai, but full of darkness and shadows.

The Denai power isn't free. It has a cost, physically, every time they use it. And for whatever twisted reason, I was now able to steal another's life energy and use it without depleting my own strength. No, not just able to—I wanted to.

Something was wrong with me, something within me hungered for power that was not my own, and it terrified me.

Faraway's words made me see what I was doing, and I released Syrani's power, released her life. Instead, I reached for my own inner twisted darkness. It crackled; it jumped and flew to me willingly.

And the ground around my feet became solid and rose upwards. I started to rise from the sand like a phoenix rising from its own ashes, reborn with more power, strength, and anger. Turning on Syrani, I saw her expression of worry and disbelief, and I turned her own strength upon her: earth.

Syrani began to sink into mud, faster than she was able to control it. She moved ground aside, trying to keep up, but I swatted her measly attempts to distract me aside. She sank rapidly up to her neck. I walked over to the ground around her and made it harden and crack, trapping her beneath the surface; all but her head.

She struggled, mud dotting her pretty face, and she screamed in anger, "Get me out of here!"

I felt her attempt to move the earth around her, but I nullified it with my own force of will.

"Game?" a Denai student yelled, asking if Syrani conceded the win to me.

Looking up, I had forgotten we were still being judged.

"Game!" she called heatedly, refusing to make eye contact.

My anger which had been so evident before dissipated almost instantly. Was that all it took to stop the practice? Had I been so focused on being paired with Syrani that I missed the rules of the game?

My skin went cold, and the full effects of what I had done physically taking a toll on my body. I felt weak, faint, and sick.

Weston dismissed us. A few stopped to help Syrani out of the ground, dusting her off, while others clapped me on the back and congratulated me.

Once freed, Syrani stormed out of the arena, leaving a trail of dust behind her. A few hoots and hollers followed. The knowledge that I wasn't the only one who didn't like Syrani would have made me smile if I weren't feeling so sick.

A rumble of low thunder alerted me to Weston's presence. Turning on him in anger I asked him, "Why didn't you stop her? I could have died!"

"Would you have?" Weston spoke critically. "What makes you so certain you would have died?"

"I...just know."

"But you didn't."

"No, I didn't."

"Because..." he asked, waiting for me to finish.

"Because I stopped her. Instructor Weston, you don't understand, I was dying. I was in pain."

"And then you fought back, you won, because you were put through the fire, felt its burn, and overcame. You're stronger now, I can feel it. Or are you going to deny that it was really Syrani in danger, not you? It was you who tried to kill Syrani."

The coldness started to spread further throughout my body as dread crept across my skin. He knew.

"I felt what happened beneath the earth. I was monitoring your life energy, and not once were you ever in danger of dying. After all, this is a special arena."

"I don't understand."

"The arena won't let you die."

"Does everyone know about this?" This was absurd, I thought.

"Only the Denai students who have graduated through our program know. I could feel the power surround you and I have never in my life felt such strength, such power. You actually used Syrani's gifts against her; which went around the safety measures set in place by the arena."

I collapsed to my knees in the dirt and shook my head, my dark hair falling forward to cover my face. "I'm sorry, I'm so sorry. I didn't mean to."

"I've never seen a Denai do what you did; use someone else's strength instead of their own. I was about to intervene, when you stopped and used your own. Thalia, how can a Denai do this?"

"They can't." I looked up and around the beautiful arena in longing, knowing that I may be giving everything up by my next sentence. "No Denai can," I whispered.

"Then how?"

"I'm not a Denai."

I let the words sink in. Hearing them spoken aloud made the truth seem more real.

"I don't understand," Weston frowned. "Cassiel opened for you today. I watched him. I just assumed it was because you were too new into your gifts that the doors wouldn't open."

"I don't know why either. Maybe you should ask him." Pushing up from the ground, I turned and headed out of the arena. My stomach rolled from the physical exhaustion I felt, and the anxiety I had at the possibility of the doors not opening for me again.

Cassiel didn't keep me waiting as he opened for me, and I bowed my head in thanks and walked through into the hallway, knowing that Kael would be waiting to silently escort me to my next class.

He was, but instead of heading to my classes, I returned to my room, collapsed on my bed and slept through the night until morning.

~25~

It wasn't long before everyone had heard what I had done. My newfound confidence brought a spring to my step as I made my way over to Joss for our lessons with Kael. I had been hiding behind Joss's presence ever since Kael had been assigned as my bodyguard. I made sure that I was with Joss or Garit as much as possible, trying to prove to Kael that he was unneeded and unwanted. Joss also enjoyed all of the extra time I was spending with him.

Kael ignored me most days as he ran us through combat training. I studied Kael whenever he wasn't looking at me, and I looked for any hint of the madness I saw earlier. His eyes, though stormy, were sane, but I kept my guard up either way.

Kael trained us to fight with a variety of weapons including long sword, short sword, staff, knives, and even an axe. Each change in weapon made me feel gangly and uncoordinated, but I stubbornly worked through the routines and practices. And with Faraway's whispered hints, at least I wasn't the worst student.

When a mace was dropped at my feet and I looked up into the smug face of Kael, I'd finally had enough. He was enjoying watching me struggle through these exercises.

"Kael, are you insane? I can't see myself ever having to use half of these weapons in battle. Shouldn't we be specializing on just one weapon instead of ten?"

"Who are you to question me or my sanity?" His voice became louder as he stalked me, drawing the attention of the other students. His tall body blocked the sun as I peered up into his angry eyes.

He spat between clenched teeth. "I'm a SwordBrother with a lifetime of knowledge and experience. I live, breathe and eat fighting and battle. This is what I was trained for. You, Thalia, are nothing, a nobody, a mere pip of a girl who doesn't know anything about surviving in the real world."

"I do too!" I clenched my fists to my side and spat out at him. "And you know it."

Joss came up behind me and put his hands reassuringly on either side of my shoulders, standing firm with me against Kael's anger.

Kael glared at him. "Back off, Denai! I won't hurt her. This is between teacher and student. Don't interfere."

I glanced at Joss and gave a slight nod, indicating that I would be all right.

Joss reluctantly stepped away.

Kael shook his head at me. "Do you even know what you will be up against?" Dropping his voice to a bare whisper meant for only our ears, he continued. "Did you ever expect to find yourself in a prison, tortured? Or attacked by dogs, and being hunted by the Septori?"

"You forgot to mention being attacked by an angry SwordBrother."

Kael's eyes narrowed in fury, but he didn't deny it. "Well, did you? How could you possibly know what you are up against? What I'm teaching you right now, despite your complaints, could one day save your life."

His angry words made my breath catch and I duly listened to his chastisement, my lungs burning for air. My heart hurt from his accusations, but at the same time my injured soul cried out for action against him.

Kael began to move away from me and turned at the last minute toward me in rage. "And don't you ever question a SwordBrother again!"

A few of Syrani's cronies who had stopped practicing to watch the spectacle we were creating, clapped and hollered in encouragement to the SwordBrother.

My cheeks flamed and my eyes stung with unshed tears. I quickly blinked them away. A glance at Joss showed that he was furious at Kael, possibly about to challenge him when I strode away. Practice was over, and I kept walking straight to my room, motioning for a guard to follow me.

I refused to allow Kael to treat me like this. So I skipped the following couple of days of practice and instead opted for private lessons with Garit once again. I was still training—just with someone else.

Faraway acted as my eyes and ears on the practice field.

You know he's mad.

"I don't care."

For every practice you're not there, the cloud around him gets darker. And he takes it out on the other students, making them practice harder and longer. He has even begun challenging students to combat. He's been ruthless to Joss.

I had no idea what Faraway meant by a cloud, but I was happy to finally be free of the headache that was Kael—and also the one that seemed to follow me whenever I was in his presence. Lately I'd been able to lessen it by mind over matter, so I barely even notice it anymore. But I felt a small victory in having won over Kael.

The victory was short-lived, as after the fifth day of skipped practice, a knock came to my door. I was surprised—

but at the same time not—to see that it was Kael. His enraged posture and demeanor spoke volumes.

Faraway was right, I could actually see a slight darkness around him.

"You will report for practice tomorrow," he stated slowly, calmly. A faint flexing of his jaw was the only hint I had that he was keeping his temper in check.

"No, I won't. I'm still practicing, just not with you."

Kael's body went still. Something I had seen him do right before he attacked, with deadly accuracy. I was worried. "And you think you can learn more from this person than from me?"

"Probably not, but at least I don't hate this person like I do you." There, I'd thrown down the gauntlet. Let him know what it felt like to be hated. I had hoped to anger him, ruffle his feathers, but all he did was smile and turn his head to me.

"Good. You should hate me. Nonetheless, you will report for practice tomorrow, and the next day, and the next, or I will go to the Adept Council and tell them I withdraw my promise to train all of the students and guards. After all, I know for a fact that your queen, Commander Meryl, and the adepts are very excited that I'm here. It would all be your fault."

He was right. I knew the adepts were pleased to have a SwordBrother here and would blame me if he left. I think they were hoping he would choose to be Queen Lilyana's guard. He really was well-liked among the students and the staff, even if he was a bit abrupt.

I was the only one, as far as I could tell, that he actually detested.

Even Syrani had gotten on his good side after she stopped picking on me. And I was really surprised that he had not yet told the adepts I was ditching practice. I had thought the knock on the door would have been them, and I would have hated to get expelled.

Deep down, I had known it was too good to last.

He'd gotten me and by the knowing smirk on his face, he knew it.

"Fine," I said.

"Fine what?" he asked with a grin.

"Fine, I'll be at practice. So don't go give your notice to the Council. Even though I wish you would disappear, it wouldn't be fair to the others."

"That's good to hear. I'm glad you came to your senses." Kael chuckled.

"Don't be. Just because I agree to let you train me does not mean I have to like it. I will actually hate every minute of it. I would rather have my teeth pulled."

Again he chuckled. *So annoying.* I'm not sure why it bothered me to see the SwordBrother laugh, but I was more surprised to see that the darkness surrounding him lighten and then disappear. I was too confused to make sense of it and my iffy powers.

"Thalia, I already said: You should hate me. It's safer." And before I could come up with a quick-witted response, he was gone.

~26~

alking up to Adept Kambel's door I knocked and waited, listening to the sounds of expletives and things crashing over. After a few more bumps and crashes, the door opened. I saw Adept Kambel, wild, gray hair splayed everywhere, and he was squinting more than usual.

"Ah, good, good. You're here. Now you can help me." Taking a step back to open the door wider, he crashed into a pile of books and almost slipped on a loose piece of paper that had floated to the ground.

"My glasses seem to have been stolen," Adept Kambel said, patting himself down as if searching for the hidden item on his body. "I took a nap in my chair and put them on my desk, but when I woke up they were gone."

Stepping into his office, I had to wonder if this is what his office usually looked like. There were telescopes at every available window, star maps, astrological calendars and many other machines, some I'd never even heard of. You could tell that Kambel's hobby was stargazing, which seemed kind of fitting for him. His rooms still held the rows upon rows of books that you would think a historic nut would need, and his clothes still sported their usual ink stains. Kambel's fingers stroked his gray beard in worry.

I searched around his napping couch and got on my hands and knees to look under it. Working out in a circle from the couch, I felt along the floor and under every table and desk. It wasn't until I heard a twittering noise that I looked up and saw movement along a curtain. A *monkey* nimbly crawling along the curtain rod!

"Adept Kambel? Do you have a monkey?" I know it seemed really silly, but this was the first I'd heard of any kind of pet being kept at the Citadel.

"Ah yes, that would be Atticus—a gift from Adept Breah. Nasty little bugger, loves playing tricks on me, but I can't get rid of him because it would offend poor Breah."

As if he heard his name being said, Atticus swung down from the curtain and crawled up Kambel's leg to perch on his shoulder. The little monkey grabbed hold of one of his large ears for support, and his long brown tail wrapped around Kambel's neck and face resting under his nose. It gave the impression that Kambel had a bushy mustache.

"Ah...the worst part is...ah..." he kept starting and stopping and finally sneezed, then said, "is that I'm allergic to him."

Atticus opened his mouth wide and blew a raspberry with his mouth as Adept Kambel flailed his arms until he jumped off.

"So I take it," I couldn't stop laughing, "that your glasses didn't just walk off. They were literally stolen by a monkey."

He looked at me in all seriousness. "Why, of course, they were. You really didn't think I could misplace my glasses while I was sleeping did you? That overlarge, good-for-nothing squirrel stole them." After I was able to get the chuckles out, I pulled out a chair and started to feel along the top of his bookshelves. When I had checked out two of them and had moved on to the third, I noticed the title of a book that caught my attention. *The King's SwordBrothers*. Picking the book off the shelf, I flipped a couple pages before I asked if I could borrow it for reading.

"Ouch! You can borrow anything you want if you can find my glasses," he yelled, rubbing his head where he bumped it on the desk. A moment later, good luck won. The glasses had been left on top of the very last bookshelf in his study. Stepping down from the chair, I handed the silver spectacles to him and he donned them to look at the book I was borrowing.

"Ah, an interesting read, if I do say so myself. There is some of the SwordBrother's oral history, from their old clans." He looked at me with some interest. "What makes you want to read that?"

"Extra credit. I figure I need all the help I can get with my studies," I lied.

Walking over to me, he gave me back the book. "Well then, I think the answers you are looking for are in that book. But beware; they may not be the ones you truly want." Walking to his chair, Adept Kambel sat down, his eyes merry. "So, other than a book on SwordBrothers, what brought you to my door this evening?" He studied me as if trying to see inside of my head.

"Yes, I do have a question." I'd been so distracted by all of the fuss with the monkey and excited about finding a book about SwordBrothers that I almost forgot the real reason I came. I was too scared to ask any of my teachers during class in case I was made fun of. Licking my lips nervously, I rushed through my question with absolute zero finesse. "Um, yeah, well, have you ever heard of a Guardian?"

At the mention of a Guardian, Adept Kambel's face blanked. "No, I haven't heard of a Guardian. But I'm making a trip to the ruins next month."

"Ruins?"

"Ah, yes, the ruins are all that is left of the Castle Avellgard after the Denai War. The Denai rebuilt the city of

Haven in a new location, miles from the old castle, in hopes of leaving the darkness and taint of the old monarchs behind. Avellgard's extensive libraries still survive deep underneath the castle ruins. I'm always hoping to find a new tunnel with books and artifacts to study."

"You think there may be something there?"

"Maybe. There are many secret tunnels under there where the Denai hid during the war. I'll see what I can find. How's that sound?" He looked exited at the thought of excavating and digging through piles of books.

I was a little disappointed that I would have to wait.

"Sounds great! Can't wait to hear what you find." I plastered a fake smile over my disappointment and closed the door behind me.

~27~

I showed up for practice the next day but made sure I walked in three minutes late. Kael just growled at me to pick up a weapon and start warming up. The next few days were the same. On the days we actually used power in the arena, which were few, I would be physically exhausted by the time I reached practice with Kael. I wasn't sure if it was because I was new to using power, or if it was because it took longer for me to recover than everyone else. But either way, today was not a good day. I was beat and in no mood for sparring, though I couldn't tell anyone why.

I excelled at archery. Joss no longer worried about me getting hurt and was oftentimes the one cheering me on the loudest during our shooting competitions. Kael always looked dissatisfied with my results, or angry. Well, he always looked angry when he was around me. Sword fighting wasn't my strength, and he took great pleasure in pointing it out.

"Watch your footwork!" he yelled. "Too slow."

Breathing heavily, I dodged Garit's downward swing and spun to my right, bringing my practice sword up to strike his side. But Kael was right; I was slow. Garit anticipated my move and easily blocked my swing with the flat of his blade.

"You're not concentrating!" Kael yelled.

"I am too," I grunted back as I went on the defensive and did all I could to keep Garit's sure swings away from me. I was constantly moving around the ring, trying to stay away from the edges. But I was just dancing to Garit's tune, and he already knew all of my maneuvers. He disarmed me in the next two moves. I watched in dread as my practice sword hit the dirt, sending a little dust cloud into the air.

Kael's shadow crowded my view as he stood over me. "Not good enough. Garit, Thalia, again!"

"I can't," I said.

"You can and you will," he ordered, kicking my sword over to me.

Garit moved to the middle of the ring and waited for me.

"No, I won't." Grabbing the wooden sword in anger, I flung it across the yard and walked away. Silence filled the training yard in my wake.

Watch out.

Faraway spoke and I saw through his eyes at the last minute Kael move behind me for an attack. Turning quickly and kneeling, I swept my leg out behind me to try and knock him off of his feet. Kael jumped over my leg swipe easily, landing on one leg and sending a sideswipe kick my way.

Jumping back, I retreated again.

"See! You won't engage in combat," he taunted. "You keep running from it." He threw a fake jab at my head, and I ducked and circled him again, backing away. Kael's lip went up in a knowing smirk. He was right; even now I was letting him lead me back toward the training arena. He made a motion, and Garit tossed a practice sword to both of us.

"Come on, Thalia. Fight back," he argued. "You will never overcome anything if you keep letting yourself be the victim."

"I don't let myself be the victim," I retorted.

"Yes, you do. During the training exercise, you fought from a distance. A bow and arrow can only help you so far.

You would never have survived the exercise, if it weren't for me." Rushing me, Kael swung.

I blocked and moved away.

"You would still be a prisoner if it weren't for me."

Moving around to block my retreat, Kael tried to egg me on into fighting. "You're weak!" he spat. "Pathetic. This is a world where only the strong survive, Thalia. And you will never survive if you can't engage in combat."

My arms felt like jelly as I tried to continue fighting him, but he was both stronger and faster than me. The truth of his words sank into my soul like an anchor, and my body felt like it was encased in lead.

Kael changed the grip on his practice sword, a signal that he was about to do a dangerous finishing move. "You have to learn to rely on yourself."

The world seemed to slow down, as I waited, counting the seconds off in my head, my sword at the ready. Knowing Kael, this would be a feint for the head and then a stab for the heart, and he would expect me to block it. Tensing, feet planted squarely, I waited in anticipation.

Rushing me, he brought his sword up. At the same time, I brought mine up one-handed, chest height, blade parallel with the ground, glinting in the sun. When he pulled back to stab for the chest, I made eye contact with him.

I could see the puzzlement in his eyes as he moved to thrust the blade forward the same time I let go of mine.

Smiling, I watched his eyes widen as my sword fell to the ground, and the momentum of his powerful thrust brought the sword toward my chest. I closed my eyes and waited for the thrust of the sword followed by the waves of pain I expected to come.

Instead, I opened them to see Kael, eyes wide and staring at me, breathing heavily as drips of sweat beaded across his brow.

Glancing down, I saw he held the pointed practice blade mere millimeters from my heart. It took a lot of skill and concentration as a fighter to be able to pull the strike that close to the target. I smirked, unable to help taunting him. "I can't be made a victim if I'm not afraid to die." Pulling power slowly toward me, I concentrated it on the sword and made the blade shatter into a dozen pieces, using power to shield Kael and me from any damage. Kael looked at the wooden handle remaining in his hand and grinned.

"Very good, Thalia."

Nodding my head, I turned and walked away, beginning to shake. Using that much concentrated power after a few hours in the Denai arena made me weak, and I knew I would have to sit.

"Wait!"

I kept my position as Kael ran up to me. Placing his hand on my shoulder he leaned into me and whispered. "Don't you ever do that again. If it were anyone other than me, they wouldn't have been able to stop that. It was suicide."

Clenching my jaw, I glared at him and used power to send a jolt into his hand, causing him to retract it. "Don't ever call me weak again." Now knowing that I was going to faint, I hurried around a corner and leaned against a wall as stars filled my vision. I had not pulled that power from another source, and now I was paying for it.

~28~

y dream started out peacefully. I was running in a field with Joss. We were kicking off our shoes and splashing water at each other in the lake. Joss picked me up and playfully threw me over his shoulder. I kicked and hit his back as he dropped me into the lake. Gasping for breath, I emerged sputtering water and splashing him. He scooped me out and carried me to the shore. Looking deep into my eyes, he leaned in for what would be our first kiss.

I closed my eyes, too, tilting my head to meet his in a slow, tender kiss. The kiss deepened, becoming passionate. Grabbing his hair, I pulled him closer to me so the kiss wouldn't end. When we reluctantly parted, I looked deep into Joss' eyes—only they weren't green but stormy blue. My hands weren't clutching Joss's blond hair.

They were buried in Kael's dark hair.

Jerking awake, I sat up in bed and pressed a hand to my heart to try and calm the frantic beating. How did I end up back in my own bed? The last thing I remembered was passing out behind the stable. Luckily I was still in my day clothes, but it bothered me that someone must have carried me to my room and put me in my bed.

I shivered, stepped out of my bed and went over to throw another log on the fire. Whoever it was at least started a fire, but it had already started to die down. Grabbing a blanket from the bed, I curled up on my sofa and stared into the fire. It had to be close to two in the morning. A slight knock on my door drew my attention, and I opened it, somehow knowing that it would be Kael.

He stood outside the door. Just being near him made my heart flutter apprehensively. It must be because of the dream. I involuntarily shivered at the thought of kissing him.

"I can hear that you're up. Is everything all right?" he asked. His eyes showed a hint of worry, and then I saw it disappear behind an unreadable face.

"No, it is not all right. How did I get here?" I answered angrily.

"I found you passed out behind the stable and even though you are a nuisance and a pain in my side, you didn't deserve to be left there. Though I probably should have left you after the stunt you pulled this afternoon."

"But why to my room, why didn't you take me to the Healer's wing?"

His eyes narrowed at the mention of healers. "I hate healers, so I bypassed the main hallways, went up the back stairway and brought you here." His mouth twitched. "I thought you would be grateful."

I studied him thoughtfully; maybe I wasn't being fair to him. "Why are you here?" I asked, tilting my head to the side.

"I'm here because I was asked to be your guard." His answer was clipped. His body language portrayed his lie.

I was disgusted by the betrayal, after everything we had been through; the least he could do was tell me the truth. "You're lying. There is another reason you're here, and you won't tell me. Is it because of the Septori? Do you know something that you aren't telling anyone else?"

I could almost hear the frustration in Kael as he ground his teeth. His silence was the answer I needed.

"Fine, you know what? I'm tired of covering for you. I'm going to the adepts to tell them that you were in the prison with me—that you have been here under false pretenses. I must have been mad to try and cover for you." I threw the blanket off of my shoulders and headed for the door.

"What makes you think I haven't already told them? I'm not stupid, they would have found out eventually. I don't need a brat like you to lie for me."

I turned and pointed my finger at the door, "If you are not going to tell me the truth, then leave. Joss can guard me."

Kael rolled his eyes.

"What's your problem?" I shot out, dropping my hand to my side.

"He's my problem," he replied, moving out of the doorway to stand close to me, his towering frame made me feel small in comparison.

"I don't understand. He hasn't been anything but nice and supportive of me." Squaring my shoulders, I tried as hard as I could to make myself seem intimidating.

"If you let this go on much longer, you will end up getting hurt. You should stop hiding behind the Golden Boy." Kael said, flexing his knuckles.

"Is that a threat?" My eyes widened at his hands. "Are you threatening me if I don't quit seeing Joss?"

"No, I'm telling you, he's not the one for you. So, in the end, you are going to get hurt," Kael spoke, his voice going dangerously quiet.

"You don't know that. In fact, you don't know anything about me. And what could you possibly know about love? The only emotions I've ever seen from you are resentment, disgust or intense hate. Never love, never happiness." I was getting worked up again.

Kael leaned in dangerously close to me, whispering, "Is that it, then? Are you saying you're in love with him?" Just being this close to Kael made my heart race, either from intense fear or excitement; it was too hard to tell.

"If I were, I definitely wouldn't be telling you," I countered, my voice dropped to a murmur.

His eyes darkened. "You're wrong about me." He leaned into my doorframe and stretched his arm to the top of the door as he looked down into my eyes. I felt trapped by those eyes, those stormy eyes that flashed from different shades of blue depending on his mood.

He brought his face precariously close to mine and I froze as his breath tickled my neck. He whispered softly into my hair. "I am capable of feeling more than resentment and hate. But when I'm around you, that's all I feel."

Frustrated, I shoved him hard in his chest. He backed away, and I closed the door on him and locked it.

I heard him chuckle and wish me pleasant dreams through the door.

I had decided I wasn't going to go out the front door. I had my fill of Kael and his mood swings. Today was supposed to be a fun-filled day spent with Joss, and I didn't want a tag-a-long. He would try and spoil my outing with Joss. Especially if he knew I was planning on spending the whole day with him alone.

I wasn't about to take Kael's warning.

I opened the window and leaned out to look at the ground twenty feet below. My mouth went dry at the prospect of slipping and falling to death. Biting my cheek, I grabbed the rope I had kept in my room after the training game, tied it to the bedpost, and threw the ends over the window sill.

Glancing warily at the door, I waited to see if it would burst open with an angry Kael.

It didn't. I hadn't figured it out, but it seemed like the SwordBrother always knew where I was, and had made a habit of following me. Did he never sleep?

Well, he wouldn't bother me today. Today I had decided I was going to get away from him and his disapproving looks.

Sitting on the window ledge, I took a deep breath and swung down. Hand over hand; I lowered myself, using my feet to brace against the wall, refusing to look down. Finally, my feet touched the earth and I let myself breathe in success.

A hand touched my shoulder. "And where do you think you are going?"

"EEEEK!" I screamed jumping back and knocking into Kael. "How did you—where did you—?" I couldn't find the words to describe my frustration.

Kael just smiled at me and pointed toward the gate, "I think Golden Boy is waiting for you."

My mouth kept dropping open in embarrassment. I couldn't believe he caught me sneaking away from him. No wonder royalty wanted SwordBrothers as guards. They were harder to get rid of than a wart. I turned my back on him, flipping my braid over my shoulder and stormed over to where I was supposed to meet Joss.

Joss was waiting by the gate but he wasn't alone. My heart sank when I saw Syrani and another boy I knew as Cooper with her. I had been under the impression that we were spending the day together alone. Obviously, I was wrong.

"Hey, there you are! Are you ready?" Joss's face lit up when he saw me.

Syrani's darkened.

"Uh, yes," I stammered and wiped my sweaty and rope-burned hands on my pants. Syrani's eyes followed my hands and she made a look of disgust. I looked down and saw that I had gotten dirt on my pants. I was instantly aware of how I looked in comparison to her.

Joss reached for my hand and pulled me toward the gates. "So what would you like to see first? The jugglers, acrobats, or the musicians?"

"Um, maybe..." I tried to give an opinion.

"The shops," Syrani interrupted. "We need to see the shops."

I turned my head to look over my shoulder and she smiled innocently at me.

Cooper spoke up. "I'm slotted to compete in an hour and you want to go shopping, Syrani?"

She batted her eyes at Cooper. "It will only take a moment. Besides, you want us to look our best don't you?" Cooper nodded his head blankly at Syrani. I had a feeling that he would have agreed no matter what she had said.

"Then it's settled." She released Cooper's arm and latched onto mine. I tried to pull away from her, but her grip was like stone. Joss released me and slowed down to walk with Cooper, while Syrani led the way through the town toward a particular store.

I cast Syrani a side glance wondering what she was up to. I knew she hated me, but I couldn't figure out what brought on her sudden charade of friendship. Her grip lessened the closer we got to the shop and once I saw the dressmaker's sign on the door, I froze.

"It will be fine. Come on." Syrani pulled me into the shop.

Joss and Cooper shifted uncomfortably on the doorstep. "If you don't mind, we'll wait for you girls out here," Cooper called out.

Joss looked at me and sheepishly nodded his head at me. I was stuck. No one was going to save me from this embarrassing and confusing mess that I had gotten myself into.

Syrani bustled around the shop pointing at dresses and skirts, while the owner of the store took her selections and put them aside. Never once did she make any effort to make small talk, or explain what she was doing.

"Now, take these and try them on." She hurled the clothes on me and pointed to the back room impatiently. I passed by the shop owner who seemed flustered by Syrani's orders, she moved out of the way and pointed toward a small side door.

I entered the small room, threw the dresses on the floor, and stomped. How dare she command me to try on clothes that I didn't even want? I thought we were stopping here so she could buy dresses, not me.

I heard the door creak open behind me and I turned to snarl at Syrani to get out, when hands grabbed me roughly from behind. I tried to scream, but someone punched me hard in the face. I felt dizzy and instantly wanted to vomit.

Another door opened, and I was dragged out the back of the dress shop into the alley. My head started to clear, and I opened my mouth to yell when my eyes landed on Scar Lip.

My body froze.

I was incapacitated as my worst fear had come back to haunt me.

A cold knife touched my throat and Scar Lip threatened me, "Scream and they die. Use any of those powers on me and they die. Fight us and they die." I looked past Scar Lip to see two hooded figures holding Pim and Jury hostage. The kids were bruised, tied up, and gagged. "Do you understand?"

I swallowed and felt my throat brush against the blade of his knife. There was much shuffling as the kidnappers pulled Jury and Pim toward themselves and arranged their long blue robes to hide the children. Hidden from plain sight, they looked like any ordinary traveler visiting for the celebration. Scar Lip bound my wrists and grabbed a third robe to cover me. It wasn't until he led me into the street that I saw the reasons behind the blue robes.

There was a dancing troupe that was late coming to the city, and their caravan filled the streets. The entire troupe wore same blue robes. Scar Lip and the henchmen pulled us in line with the caravan. No one paid us any attention as we walked down the street. I was able to glance out the side of my eye to see Joss and Cooper still lounging outside of the dress shop, oblivious to what was going on around them.

Why hadn't Syrani told them I was missing? She must have heard the commotion that was going on in the backroom. Or was she in on the kidnapping?

Thoughts flew through my head as I tried to put together what was happening. Nothing made sense.

I tried to mindspeak Faraway but the distance was too great, I couldn't reach him. What I needed was a distraction and a plan. The caravan stopped as another parade made their way down the street. It was the queen and her guard, heading toward the castle.

The guards moved through the streets ordering everyone to move aside and let Queen Lilyana pass. I could almost see

Captain Meryl at the head and the red hair of Queen Lilyana behind him.

Scar Lip looked at the queen and whispered under his breath, "So close. We are so close. Next time, Queen Lilyana, it will be different."

All heads were turning to watch the queen pass. This was my distraction. My muscles tensed with anticipation, knowing that this may be my only chance for help.

Scar Lip felt me tense and pressed the knife deeper into my back. "Don't even try it!" He growled into my ear and slammed my head against the stone building to prove his point.

I cried out from the pain and no one noticed, or almost no one noticed. An old woman couldn't seem to take her eyes off of Scar Lip.

"Get moving!" He hissed to his companions. "We are supposed to meet Raven's carriage around the next bend."

The Raven! He was here—in the city!

"What about the other one? Weren't we supposed to bring both of them?" asked the Septori who had Jury under his cloak.

"I'm not waiting around for that one." Scar Lip hissed. "Besides it was this one that Raven specifically wanted back, the one that worked. He doesn't care about cast-offs or failed experiments. He wants this one so he can duplicate her results. Now get moving, before I tear you to pieces and leave you for what's left of Raven's demon dogs."

The Septori, obviously scared, closed his mouth and shuffled faster toward the road. Scar Lip mentioned Raven's demon dogs, or what was left of them. It was obvious then, who controlled the beasts.

The crowd started to dissipate as the queen and her guard turned down the first street. I looked after them longingly, knowing that I would have to find another way to get Pim, Jury and myself out of this mess.

The two Septori and Scar Lip pulled us into another alley and I could see an enclosed carriage. I knew, if I got into that carriage, it was over. I started to struggle with Scar Lip, and he grabbed the back of my hood and a handful of hair and pulled hard. Tears formed in my eyes but I didn't stop.

"Kill the girl!" Scar lip ordered. "She's fighting me." The Septori looked up at Scar Lip and grabbed at the bundle under his robe. I could hear Jury start to cry.

"NO! Please, no." I screamed and instantly went limp, showing Scar Lip that I would behave. He looked at me before motioning one of them to open the door. I saw a dark carriage with velvet padded seats, something that only someone rich could afford. Scar Lip reached inside the carriage and pulled out a vial of green liquid.

"Drink this, and I will let them go." He spoke to me and his foul breath made me gag.

"You promise? Do you promise me that if I drink this, you will not harm Pim and Jury?" I looked at the kids who clung to each other as tears ran down their faces. I raised the vial slowly to my mouth.

"Yes," Scar Lip answered and held up his hand as if making an oath. "I promise I will not hurt them. You should be familiar with the contents of that vial; it's what we gave your kidnappers when we first acquired you from your village."

The vial froze on my lips. This was the first news I had heard about concerning my family. If that was true and drinking the drug would erase my memories again, then I had to at least reconsider. My hand shook as I asked, "What village was that?"

"Doesn't matter, does it? You will never remember them, an unfortunate side effect of this particular drug. I brought it just for you. Now drink!" He raised his hand and motioned toward Jury.

I felt a silent tear slide down my cheek and tasted the first bitter taste of serum as it touched my tongue.

A scream racked the alley as an old woman with wild eyes, charged into me knocking the vial from my lips. I watched as it crashed to the ground and broke.

"What the..." Scar Lip broke off mid-sentence as the screaming banshee of a woman turned on him and started scratching at his eyes with her nails.

I spat out as much of the serum as I could and looked up as poor old Ruzaa attacked Scar Lip. "I remember you...you evil VERMIN! You will pay for what you did to me!"

The Septori stood dumfounded and released their hold on Jury and Pim. I looked up in horror as Scar Lip took his knife and turned it on Ruzaa.

Anger overtook me; and I felt my blood boil as I reached for power, not caring who or what got hurt as long as the Septori paid for their sins. Jury and Pim ducked under the cover of the carriage as I held out my hands and pulled not on my own energy, but the Septori's.

I saw Ruzaa fall to the ground, her body still, and more hatred poured out of me. The ground started to shake, and the wind picked up as I tried to lift the carriage and protect the children under it. I was breaking it apart, little by little, but what I had swallowed of the serum was already starting to dull my senses.

I didn't have much time left.

Scar Lip turned toward me, bloody knife in hand and fell backward onto the ground. He had no leverage over me now, the children were safely behind me and my enemy lay unprotected before me. The Septori tried to run but were struggling to move as I drew their energy away.

A loud metal scream could be heard as I ripped apart the carriage in the air and brought it down with a loud crash onto Scar Lip and the two Septori. A mass of wood, wheels and iron sat in the alley, all that was left of the noble carriage. Under it were their three bodies.

I fell to my knees, exhausted, and crawled toward Ruzaa. I touched her warm body and rolled her over.

"Oh, please no, not Ruzaa!" Tears fell freely as I touched the old weaver's face. Her eyes slowly opened and she smiled at me, blood trickling down her chin. "I got 'im back. I did. I got 'im. He won't hurt nobody anymore."

"You mean Scar Lip?"

Ruzaa coughed and more blood trickled out her mouth. "He was one of them that hurt me years ago. I will never forget that face, but I didn't see the other one. He's a tricky one that one."

"Ruzaa, tell me what to do? I've never healed anyone before, please help me. Just tell me what to do?" Jury and Pim crawled over by me and were hugging each other.

"Don't know how to heal, it's not my gift. Never much worried about it before now." She laughed and her familiar bark of a laugh was weak.

"Please! Someone help us!" I screamed down the alley toward the roads, and someone heard. I could hear voices and people shouting. "Just hold on Ruzaa, please hold on. Someone will come; we will get you to a healer." I grasped her hand in both mine, and I could feel her squeeze them slightly.

I looked at my hands and tried to mimic what Joss and the other healers had done, but all I kept picturing in my mind was what I had done a few minutes ago, and in the arena. All I had ever done with my gift was steal power and destroy. What if I accidentally destroyed Ruzaa instead of healing her? I let my own fear hold me back.

Her breathing became more ragged and people rushed to aid us. All of them reached toward her, trying to help staunch the flow of blood from her wounds, but there were too many.

"Someone run and get a healer," a large man yelled.

Ruzaa looked at me. Her eyes were turning glassy, her face pale. "No one will hurt no more...I did it." Her hand became slack in mine, and I let the people in the alley pull Ruzaa from me and carry her away. I knew it was too late.

She had drawn her last breath.

Two pairs of hands reached around my waist and hugged me. I didn't need to look down to know that it was Pim and Jury. I put my arms around them and cried. We didn't know who was comforting whom, but we knew we needed each other at that moment.

I felt a familiar pull on my spirit, and somehow I knew Kael was near. He came running down the alley, out of breath and pale. He looked upon the mess of carriage parts and stared. Thankfully, he was apparently the only one that noticed the blood pooling underneath the wreckage.

I didn't care that he had come to rescue me; I was angry and sad, and hurting.

"Where were you?" I cried out loud, letting my frustration out on him. "You who are supposed to protect me, failed. When I needed you most, you weren't here! And look! Ruzaa's dead, and it's all your fault!"

Kael stopped and stared at me, bewildered. Clearly he wasn't expecting my outburst, but I had just taken three lives, and I wasn't prepared for the emotional havoc it was causing on me. I should never have had to face Scar Lip alone. If only he had killed him when he had the chance, instead of letting him escape then this would never have happened. I wouldn't be a murderer.

I knew it was unfair to blame him, though. After all, this is why Queen Lilyana and the Adept Council wanted me to be trained in self-defense. It was what Kael had been preparing me for—to attack, to fight back, to be able to save myself.

And I had done it, but at what cost?

Ruzaa's life.

Jury and Pim buried their faces in my hip, and I turned them away and started walking with them toward the Citadel. Kael reached forward and tried to touch my arm.

I snarled at him, "Don't touch me. You weren't here when I needed you!"

Kael's hand dropped quickly to his side and he held his breath as if he were in pain, I could tell I had deeply wounded his pride. "You're right. I should have been here."

"But you weren't, and it's obvious I don't need you to protect me anymore."

"Thalia let me explain..." Kael reached for me again.

"Leave me alone!" I slammed Kael with a flash of power. The blast lifted Kael off of the ground and sent him spinning through the air to hit the wall. I grimaced as I heard the smack of his body against the stone wall.

Kael's reflexes were those of a fighter. He dropped and nimbly landed in a crouch, ready to spring back into action. Slowly standing to his feet, he circled me, keeping his distance. It was like two wolves sizing each other up, and I had two cubs I was ready to protect.

Kael's jaw twitched in anger and his blue eyes stared into my own. I wasn't expecting to hear a pained voice reply, "If that is your wish. You will never see me again." Kael turned and was gone.

Breathing a sigh of mixed relief and remorse, I felt a sudden chill of apprehension. What had I done?

~29~

The next morning a very disgruntled Tearsa awakened me. "Wake up!" she hissed, shaking my shoulder roughly.

Groggily, I tried to open my sleep-encrusted eyes. "I already sent Forrest to wake you earlier, but you wouldn't answer any of his knocks," she went on, grumbling, but I only caught bits and pieces as I tried to make sense of my muddied memories from last night. Ruzaa had died and I had killed three people. My chest felt like it was going to explode.

The curtains on the window were thrown open, and the blinding light pouring into my room made me throw the blanket back over my head to block it. My armoire opened and the impolite sound of shoes and other objects being thrown around the room made me want to burrow deeper in my covers and hide from the formidable Tearsa. She was obviously on a rampage, because she had to personally wake me up.

I groaned because there was no justice in the world. The Adepts had questioned the shop owner, Joss, and Cooper, and they couldn't find any deceit in them, even Syrani. Apparently she had nothing to do with the kidnapping and the Septori had been following me for days, and found a lucky moment to grab me. The truth was, Syrani was only being nice to me to get near Joss, but of course she didn't want to be seen in public next to someone covered in dirt, so the stop was purely to dress me. How typical, how very much like Syrani.

What worried me the most was that I hadn't even had a chance to speak to Joss, to tell him I was fine. I had been sequestered in my room after the battle and given very little time to adjust or mourn for Ruzaa. It was not what I had wanted.

Nothing happened the way I wanted it to.

"No one had a key, so I had to drop everything I was doing to come and help you. The Council Session starts in fifteen minutes, and here I am playing maid to you." Her words finally started to filter through the down comforter into my foggy brain, and I sat up in a panic.

"Finally, you realize the importance of the situation," she harrumphed.

Jumping out of bed, I put on the clothes she had laid out, barely giving them a glance. I tried to run a tangled comb through my disheveled curls from the night before. Using some water, I was able to pull them back and secure the curls with a blue ribbon.

I had forgotten that the queen had called an emergency session and the Adept Council had asked me to be there for the proceedings.

"Now remember," Tearsa said, as she looked me over, giving me a nod of satisfaction. "You have been asked to sit in, not participate. There is a viewing section to the side where you can watch and listen from. You hear me?" She placed her hand on her hip and began waving her finger at me. "You are not to speak unless spoken to." Her fingers waved dramatically.

Looking at Tearsa, it was hard to hold back tears. She reminded me of Ruzaa. I had made it back to the Citadel last night, and Tearsa had taken one look at Pim and Jury and immediately given them baths, food, and put them to bed. Yes, she was a rough and tough mistress, but she did it for the right reasons. Running to Tearsa I gave her a quick hug, which surprised her and made her blubber in admonishment at me. Shooing me away with her apron, she yelled at me to get going or I was going to be late.

Running down the halls, I was almost to the Council Hall when someone grabbed my shirt and pulled me into a small alcove. Warm strong arms embraced me, and I started to fight before I looked up into the concerned green eyes of Joss. I was once again struck by how handsome he was, and I felt weak in the knees. His hand went to my face and he cupped my cheek before leaning down and pressing his lips to mine. At first I was startled, then I struggled, and then I melted. It was soft, warm, gentle.

Before I could respond to the kiss, he pulled back enough to whisper softly into my ear. "I had wanted to do that yesterday before…" he trailed off, unable to finish the sentence without bringing up the horrible events.

"I know," I whispered lamely. I didn't want him to speak of it either. I buried my forehead in his chest to find comfort and let him hold me close as I tried to battle with the emotions that began to overtake me.

"I can't tell you how worried I was when we couldn't find you. That was when I realized how stupid I had been. I know I had said I wanted to be your friend, but Thalia, I lied. I'm not happy with being just your friend."

I pulled back and opened my mouth to speak, but he pressed his warm hand over my lips and hushed me.

"Don't say anything. I know you. You will try and deny what we have, but the feelings I have won't go away Thalia. So it's better if you don't say anything at all right now. I want to talk to you tonight. Will you meet me after the Council Session by the arena?"

I nodded numbly.

Joss gave me a quick kiss on my forehead before pushing me back into the hall and toward the meeting hall. I stopped a few paces in front of the Council Hall doors so I could catch my breath before entering. The guards at the door watched me silently, and opened the double doors so I could go in.

"You almost didn't make it," the guard on the right winked at me. "Another minute and you would have been late."

My cheeks burned, and I tried to put all thoughts of our kiss from my mind. It was hard, but once I remembered the importance of the Council Session, I was able to settle the harried beating of my heart. But just barely.

Entering the main Council chamber I was astounded at the vastness of it. The room was a giant circle with raised boxed seating for each of the twelve clan leaders, guilds and adepts; each section clearly marked by banners. The viewing section was a small boxed area closest to the entry doors. The round room created equality among the clan leaders, because there was no obvious head of the table. In the middle of the room, on the floor, was a small dais for the speakers. The room echoed easily because of the high vaulted ceilings.

Sliding into the viewing section, I sat among a few of the older Denai students. A few had quills and parchment, obviously prepared to take notes of the proceedings. I turned to Tydus, an older Denai with small spectacles and brown hair, and asked him if he had been to one of these before.

"Of course, I'm the council recorder. You?"

"Uh, first time."

Tydus frowned. He obviously took his studies very seriously.

Queen Lilyana came forward to address all of the clan leaders and adepts.

"We are here today because of an incident that can no longer be ignored." She paused for effect. "And that is the persecution of our people, Denai and Human alike. Someone has been kidnapping the people of Calandry and performing heinous experiments on them. This will not be allowed and will not be tolerated. We don't have all of the facts yet, but we have found the remains of an abandoned prison, where these crimes have taken place."

I sat up straighter; this was the first I had heard of them finding the prison.

"We could not find the ones who are doing this, the ones known as the Septori, because we were looking for them in our land. It seems that they are not locals but come from Sinnendor."

Silence befell the room, and then loud rumblings were heard as everyone began to talk at once.

"Impossible!"

"How can that be?"

"How do they get past Sinnendor's elite?"

"Is Sinnendor behind this?"

The queen raised her hand, and the room fell silent again. "We don't know how much King Tieren knows, for the Septori were hiding underground right along the river that borders both of our lands. But there were numerous paths that led straight into Sinnendor territory from the Septori's hideout. We cannot lay blame without proof, and right now we have none. I will not risk another war without more proof."

Heads bobbed up and down in understanding. A few murmured disagreement, and I was careful to watch those boxes closely. I couldn't help but notice that throughout the whole proceedings there were two clan sections that remained empty. Tydus had already mentioned that one was for the

Skyfell clan, their clan leader's wife was ailing, and their leader refused to leave her side, so he sent his deepest regrets about his absence.

Leaning over to Tydus, I asked him about the other empty box.

"Oh, that's for the Valdyrstal Clan. They've never acknowledged the actual delegation of the Council and have yet to ever make an appearance for a Council Session. Supposedly, their clan leader, Bearen Valdyrstal, is extremely against any Council business and progress. He is supposedly even anti Denai."

Something about the name made my pulse start to race. "But why do they continue to keep a spot for him on the Council then?"

"Well, they are one of the larger clans, and because of that and by clan right, they are allowed to have a vote. By his absence, his vote is automatically cast as a negative."

"Where is this clan from?" I could feel something deep inside start to stir.

"Their lands cover the parts of the Shadow Mountains and the Ioden Valley that borders the northern edge of Sinnendor."

There was definitely something, a memory, a flicker of snow, of mountains. Turning away from me, Tydus ended the conversation as he quickly scribbled notes on his parchment to catch up with what he had missed during his explanation.

Leaning back as well, I tried to adjust my weight in my chair to find another comfortable position, but no luck. The chairs were meant to be uncomfortable and to keep people awake during these proceedings. But I was now desperate to find out what I could about the Valdyrstal clan. I couldn't sit still.

After two more hours had passed, Adept Pax stepped forward to address the missing children. Before he could go on, the Council Hall doors opened, and one of the most fearsome looking men I have ever seen strode through the doors. Large, muscular, outfitted with dark furs and brown leathers, he looked like he was ready to war with the cold. On his back was a very large battle axe. His long, dark beard covered a hawk-like nose. The retinue of men that came behind him was similarly dressed in furs of all shades and kinds. A few wore wolf and bear pelts, and I could see one man wearing the red furs of a fox.

Their battle gear and leather armor looked out of place amongst the formal robes each of the Councilmen wore. The leader strode into the room, showing no fear and stood before the Adept Council, not saying a word. His gait and demeanor looked familiar to me, but I couldn't place where I'd seen him.

"Bearen Valdyrstal." Adept Pax stood up and addressed the giant of a man. The council erupted into titters of frenzied whisperings. "We are honored that you have decided to join us for the Council Session, albeit a bit late."

A few snickers were heard from Bearen's men.

"You do realize that weapons are forbidden in Council Hall? And if you had been here earlier, you would have had time to change into your formal robes," Adept Pax stated stiffly.

Bearen showed his teeth then, in what could only be considered a pass at a smile. Something I could tell didn't come very easily to him. "Come now, friends," he said in a slight accent, holding his hands out in an imploring gesture to the Council. "I am here now, and you must excuse my lateness and forgive me for my attire because we just rode in. We thought it..." he paused for a second, "prudent to come right away rather than miss more of the proceedings because of our lack of grooming."

A barked laugh came from one of the men standing behind Bearen. The leader spun and gave him a dangerous look. The laughter stopped, and Bearen turned back to the adepts and the Council and waited patiently.

Adept Cirrus leaned over and spoke to Adept Pax. "Very well," Cirrus went on. "You may take your seats. But be forewarned for next time that you will come in appropriate attire and be on time."

Bearen then did an amazing feat. He bent his large form into a deep and mocking bow. My eyes widened in awe at the disdain he showed to the Council members.

Walking past me to his seat, his men following close behind. Bearen caught me staring at him. Stopping abruptly, his lip lifted in an obvious attempt at another smile, but came out a sneer, before heading into his assigned box seats. My palms started to sweat as I felt his continued stare long after I looked away.

"It seems to me," Adept Kambel said and stood up, looking over his notes, "that someone has been stolen or kidnapped or ran away from every large Clan, except for..." Dropping his parchment, Kambel stooped down to pick it back up. In the process, he knocked his glasses askew. Stubbornly placing them back on his nose, he looked at his parchment one last time before going on. "Except for Valdyrstal." He looked pointedly at Bearen, who was leaning back in his chair at that moment with his large boots stretched out before him and resting on a chair in front.

"Would you care to respond?" Adept Cirrus asked.

Bearen slowly stood up, lifted one foot off of the chair and turned to address the council. His deep voice rumbled in the room. "Aye, we have only lost one child, my daughter, but unlike you, we have actually found her." Turning his hawk-like nose and deep blue eyes toward me, he said, "Hello, Thalia."

Those words dragged out into eternity, searing into my memory.

~30~

My hands started to shake, and I grabbed the banister in front of me to steady myself in case I should faint. I stared at the man across from me who seemed familiar, yet at the same time, was a stranger. The family resemblance in our hair and eyes was undeniable.

But the joy that I thought would surround me at finding my family had turned into trepidation.

All of the adepts stood up at once and began talking. Tydus reached over a hand and slapped me on the back, making a joke about pretending to not know the strongest clan in Calandry and then being the clan leader's daughter. My eyes never left Bearen, who grinned at me in triumph as he walked down into the center of the room.

"Brothers!" his deep voice rang out. "I have been looking for Thalia for months, and had only recently heard rumors that my daughter had shown up in Haven. I came to the Citadel not to participate in this year's Council Session, but to retrieve my daughter." Pointing a finger at me, he beckoned. "Come, daughter, we shall return home." Moving toward the exit, all of Bearen's men stood up in formation behind him.

Pax Baton's voice roared after him, "Stop! What do you think you are doing, taking one of our students and leaving?" Pax leapt from his box and strode toward Bearen and his men.

Bearen Valdyrstal turned on him in a flash and placed one large hand on Pax's chest as a small knife appeared in his other. "Don't come any nearer," Bearen spat. "You know my viewpoint on Denai and your training program. How dare you take my daughter and bring her here into this filth!" Turning, Bearen spat onto the ground. "Now she must return home and be cleansed. She doesn't belong here with your kind; she belongs with us, her family."

The word family brought my head up in surprise. Maybe I had brothers and sisters, a mother. The urge to follow Bearen to find my family became overbearingly strong.

Adept Pax lifted his hands in an unthreatening manner. "Forgive us. We did not know that she was your daughter. There are quite a few things that have happened in the last months with your daughter that you should be made aware of."

All of the Denai in the room could take out my father if they wanted too, but Bearen kept the knife far enough away from Adept Pax to not warrant an attack. I saw that despite his anger, he did possess wisdom.

"Aye, I will be informed. But this is a family matter. She's underage, and she must come home with me." Pushing Adept Pax and sheathing his knife, he looked to me. "Let's go, Thalia." He turned, offering me his large hand.

Pausing, I stood frozen amongst all the clamor and commotion, taking in my father standing before me. I tried to bring to life any memories at all; and I couldn't. His eyes darkened at my hesitancy.

"You either come now, or don't come home at all. Ever."

That did it. Spurred into action, I stepped down out of my seat and made my way over to Bearen and his men. At that moment, Bearen reminded me of Kael. The clansmen formed a protective ring around me, and I followed the fur-covered back of my father out of the council room. Pausing in the hallway, I turned toward my room to get my things.

"Leave 'em. Anything you have has now been tainted by them," he growled. We walked into the courtyard and made our way to the stable, where a herd of the largest, sturdiest horses I had ever seen stood. These must be the Valdyrstal's horses.

Making my way over to Faraway's stall, I grabbed his bridle and reins and began to saddle him. One of the clansmen followed me and was about to make a remark, when I cut him off.

"I will not leave without my horse," I gritted out, showing my teeth the way I had seen Bearen do. The clansmen grinned and laughed out loud. "It seems our vixen still has her temper," he chuckled, and moved away.

Where are we going? Faraway asked.

"Home, I think."

Saddling Faraway, I followed in line behind Bearen, and once again the clansmen formed a protective circle around me. Whether it was for my own protection or to keep me from running away, I wasn't really sure. By this time, quite a crowd had gathered. The assembly was dismissed, and the word had spread throughout the keep. Students kept pouring out of the hallways and peering out windows.

"HO!" Someone yelled and the horses started moving.

"Wait!" a familiar voice interjected. "What's going on?"

Turning in my saddle I saw Joss running out of the main hall at a sprint toward me. Joss was stopped short by the clansmen wearing fox fur, who quickly pulled a sword and pointed it at his throat. Joss's throat bobbed nervously as the sword rested calmly against his Adam's apple. The caravan of horses stopped.

"Where are you taking her?" he asked bravely.

"None of your business. This here is clan business and you are not clan," Fox Fur retorted.

Joss's eyes sought mine for an answer.

"Home," I answered softly, feeling a catch in my throat at the thought of leaving him.

"But you are home." Joss stated, refusing to blink and break eye contact. "You belong here."

"No, I don't. Not really." I broke eye contact first as I looked down at my shoe and then back up. "Joss, I don't remember anything up until a few months ago. I need to find out who I am and where I come from." A stir followed my answer as the crowd parted, and Syrani stepped forward and grabbed Joss's arm possessively.

"Joss," she purred. "Let the sewer rat go home with the smelly dogs, and then it can be just the two of us again."

Whether it was her verbal attack on the Valdyrstal clan, or me I wasn't sure, but Fox Fur spurred his horse forward and knocked Syrani down into the mud, spewing a few unknown curses at her in his native tongue.

It startled me to know that I understood what Fox Fur had said to Syrani, and it wasn't pretty. Trying to hide my grin behind a straight face, I looked into Joss's handsome one and rode Faraway over to him, amazed that the clan members let me through. I could see Bearen astride his horse ready to be on the move.

"I'm sorry, Joss. I have to go," I spoke quietly.

"Will you come back?"

Looking over my shoulder at Bearen's stiff posture, his body language spoke volumes, speaking what he would never voice aloud.

"I don't know. Maybe someone needs to come back for council meetings, but I can't make any promises."

Joss took another step forward to try and reach up to touch me, but Fox Fur moved protectively to my side, and Joss backed up, giving him a look of pure hatred.

"Thalia, we need to go!" Bearen called out.

Nodding my head to him in understanding, I turned back to Joss.

"Please tell Avina and Berry that I'm sorry I didn't get to say goodbye, and tell Garit I will keep practicing everything he taught me."

"What about me?" he asked. "What would you have liked to say to me?" He gazed at me intently.

"Joss, you saved me, and you are one of the most important people in my life right now. I will never forget you."

"It sounds like you're saying a permanent goodbye." He looked angry and hurt at the same time.

Fox Fur move forward again and grabbed Faraway's reins to get him turned in the right direction so we could get going, but Faraway violently jerked his head in protest and almost unsaddled Fox Fur from his horse.

Bearen had waited all he cared to, and started the horses toward the Citadel's gate. Faraway could do nothing but follow as he was trapped in the middle of the pack. Glancing over my shoulder, I saw Joss standing there looking after me, and I waved good-bye.

It was not how I imagined leaving.

I desperately wanted to turn around and run back and tell him how I really felt. But I didn't. I couldn't. My heart felt heavy as we passed through the gates, turned onto a side road, and headed toward the Shadow Mountains, toward home.

Toward answers.

The End of Book 1

Chanda Hahn takes her experience as a children's pastor, children's librarian and bookseller to write compelling and popular fiction for teens. She was born in Seattle, WA, grew up in Nebraska, and currently resides in Portland, Oregon, with her husband and their twins; Aiden and Ashley.

Visit Chanda Hahn's website to learn more about her other forthcoming books.

www.chandahahn.com

Also by Chanda Hahn

The Iron Butterfly Series
The Steele Wolf
The Silver Siren

Unfortunate Fairy Tale Series
UnEnchanted
Fairest
Fable

Special Thanks

I want to say a special thanks to everyone who took part in the process of helping me with the Iron Butterfly, whether you were a reader, editor, encourager, or critic. Thanks to Philip Hahn, Steve Hahn, Jane Hawkey, Alison Brace and Richlie Fikes. I have the best team ever.

7|15

Printed in Great Britain
by Amazon.co.uk, Ltd.,
Marston Gate.